*Poppy's
Pin-Ups*

Poppy's Pin-Ups

Aishling Morgan

Published by Xcite Books Ltd – 2011

Print ISBN 9781908086068

Printed and bound in the UK

Cover design by Madamadari

Dedicated to Squadron Leader R. G. E. P. Freeman whose many anecdotes made this novel possible

Glossary

The RAF of WW2 employed a rich slang, much of which has entered the common language and needs no explanation, but some terms may be unfamiliar, along with the many abbreviations and acronyms which would then have been in day to day use. When doing my research, I was struck by how similar RAF slang was to that of my own schooldays, such as the term "bumph", which was applied to the extensive trivia every child had to learn before gaining social acceptance by passing a "bumph test". Other, non-military, terms, such as "invert" and "totting" have simply fallen out of general use over the years.

A/CDRE – Air Commodore, RAF rank equivalent to an army Brigadier.

Ack Emma/Pip Emma – AM and PM respectively.

Ackers – Egyptian piastres, worth one hundred to the Egyptian pound. According to the song *The Soldier's Lament* a Cairo prostitute could be had for ten piastres.

Airships – as in "their Airships", senior RAF officers who float serene above it all, oblivious to the mayhem caused by their decisions.

Black – a bad performance or by extension a punishment, as in "up for a black".

Bluebird – WAAF

Bumph – originally lavatory paper, but quickly extended to include any sort of paperwork.

Buses – bombers, of any sort.

Desk Jockey – somebody who flies a desk, i.e. has never been in the air, or more usually has never been on a combat mission.

Gallibaya – long, loose Egyptian shirt typically worn by men.

Gen – information of any sort.

George – the automatic pilot on a Lancaster

Invert – a popular, relatively polite term for homosexuality in the early 20th century, especially for lesbians.

Night fighter – a plane designed or adapted to operate in darkness, by extension a prostitute.

KV – "on the look out", from "Qui vive?", meaning "Who goes there?", first abbreviated to QV and then to KV. Anything which would attract official disapproval is done "on the KV".

Recce – reconnaissance, a word borrowed from French during the Napoleonic wars.

Shaky do – a dangerous mission.

Sjambok – a particularly vicious whip characteristic of Africa and traditionally made from plaited rhinoceros or hippopotamus hide, but sometimes from the stretched and dried penis of the same animals.

Snowdrops – RAF police, who wear white caps.

Totting – sorting through waste, or anything that isn't

obviously somebody else's property in order to find things that can be sold on.

Wing Co – Wing Commander, RAF rank above Squadron Leader but below Group Captain, equivalent to a Lieutenant Colonel in the army.

Chapter One

'YOU CAN KEEP YOUR stockings on,' Henry Truscott offered.

Poppy responded with a glare that suggested she was far from impressed by his generosity. Nevertheless she had stood up and was quite clearly going to go through with it, surrendering both her girdle and her knickers. That would leave her all but stark naked, with her neatly proportioned young body exposed to his gaze, and to those of their friends. The poker game had not gone well for her, a run of bad luck compounded by a risky betting strategy leaving her first penniless, then without her smart grey-blue WAAF uniform. Even then she had refused to back down, but her shoes, slip and brassiere had soon followed her uniform into the growing pile on Henry's lap, to leave her in nothing but her cap and stockings, with her high, round breasts naked for inspection. Still she had continued to play, handling her cards awkwardly with one arm held across her chest to protect her modesty, and still her luck had failed to turn. Henry, who remained in full uniform, now owned her remaining clothes.

Her face showed pink with embarrassment even through the smoke-laden air, and grew pinker still as she unfastened one suspender clip after another. Henry watched, not troubling to hide his pleasure at her discomfort and only with difficulty resisting the temptation to adjust his rapidly swelling cock. "Ginger" Green, his navigator, was staring open-mouthed, but no more so than Poppy's fellow WAAF, Sarah "Hills" Hennigan, whose face was almost as pink as her friend's. Only Gorski remained placid, sipping his arrack and watching Poppy sidelong as she turned her attention to the fastenings of her girdle.

One of the catches stuck and she gave what might have been a soft curse or a gentle sob as she tugged it loose. Henry swallowed as her girdle fell away, revealing the soft contours of her midriff, her hips spreading from her trim waist, her belly a low bulge neatly pinched where the central button showed just above the waistband of her full, navy blue knickers. His cock was now rock hard, and he was very glad indeed that he had managed to get her stripped down without having to surrender any of his own clothes, especially his trousers. With her stockings now loose and nothing but her knickers to cover her modesty, Poppy hesitated. Her eyes met Henry's in a pleading glance, while her mouth had come slightly open, with her lower lip trembling visibly.

'By all means turn around, if it makes it easier for you,' Henry suggested.

Poppy's mouth went tight and the expression in her eyes changed back to the furious glare she had worn when she had begun what amounted to a slow striptease, but she did as he had suggested, turning around with an angry toss of the honey-coloured curls spilling from around her cap. Now faced with the swell of her bottom in nothing but the skin-tight navy blue knickers, Henry found himself swallowing once more, and as she pushed her thumbs into her waistband he took a hasty gulp of his arrack.

Absolute silence had fallen on the room as Poppy began to push down her knickers, even Gorski had his full attention on her and her friend was no less rapt than the men. She did it slowly, intriguingly slowly, Henry felt, making him wonder just how reluctant she really was as the taut waistband of her knickers moved down to expose the twin dimples to either side of the base of her spine, the gradual swell of her cheeks, the neat pink V at the top of her slit, and more, inch after tempting inch of pale, resilient flesh, smooth as cream and unmarked save for a few tiny freckles.

'Right off,' he ordered, no longer able to restrain himself when she hesitated with the knickers slightly more than halfway down over her glorious rear cheeks.

'I know,' she answered, her voice sharp and high but breaking to a clear sob as she pushed her knickers right down with a single, angry motion.

For one perfect instant she was bent over just far enough for the dim glow of the oil lamps to illuminate the crease between her bottom cheeks, showing off the sweetly puckered mouth of her anus and the plump swell of her sex, both densely thatched with golden hair only a shade or so darker than on her head. Then she had straightened up, to shake her knickers down her legs with a brief, petulant wriggle before kicking them off one toe and into her hand. She turned and held the discarded knickers out to Henry, showing off the thick curls of her lower belly and mound for an instant before she had covered herself with a hand. Her eyes were burning into his, full of rage and humiliation, but the condition of her sex when she had bent to remove her knickers and the strongly feminine scent in the air suggested that those were not her only emotions. He decided to risk having his face slapped.

'Put your hands on your head,' he instructed, 'and then turn around, very slowly.'

'You are an absolute beast, Henry Truscott!' she snapped, but her hands had already gone up to rest on the smart grey-blue cap which was all that remained of her once immaculate uniform.

Henry nodded in acknowledgement, then lifted a finger to indicate that she should turn around. Poppy obeyed, stood naked in the soft, golden light, her face scarlet with embarrassment but her chin lifted in defiance as she displayed her body, or perhaps sheer pride. She was magnificent, her flesh soft and rounded but remarkably firm, so that it seemed a miracle that her breasts and more especially the cheeks of her bottom could hold their shape against gravity. Her stocking-clad legs were impressively long, especially as she was relatively petite, and as she completed her turn he saw that her nipples had popped out to make twin buds standing firmly to erection at an angle several degrees above the horizontal. Each was the size and shape of a well grown raspberry, and about the same colour.

3

'Now I know why they call you "Pinks",' Henry remarked.

Poppy's blush grew darker still, while it had spread down her neck and begun to colour the flash of her cleavage, but she held her position, allowing them to inspect her naked body until her friend finally broke the silence.

'I hope you've all had a good gawp now?'

'Oh … yes, thank you, Hills,' Henry responded. 'Do sit down, Poppy. Well, gentlemen, ladies, I presume that concludes our game for the evening?'

'Oh no it does not,' Poppy responded. 'Deal the cards, please, Sergeant Gorski.'

'You don't have anything left to put up as a stake,' Henry pointed out. 'Remember, no tick, not today, unless you'd like to nip down to the main bar and strike a deal with Fat Babu? Go like that, why not, and he'll probably give you a better rate, or if you're embarrassed, stick a fez over each tit and another on your fanny. Goodness knows, we've enough to spare.'

Ginger laughed, Gorski showed a brief, faint grin, but Poppy responded with a look of pure fury, this time undiluted by arousal. Henry chuckled, then spoke again.

'No, I didn't think the idea would appeal. He drives a hard bargain, old Babu, and I hate to think what he does to girls who don't pay up on time. Whipping naked through the streets of Cairo, I wouldn't be surprised, and that's before the old bugger starts to get the horn for you. Anyway, chaps, what are we to do with these damn fezzes?'

As he spoke he jerked his thumb towards the row of bulging stacks they had placed along one wall. Each contained four dozen fez hats, purchased on good advice that they could be sold at a handsome profit in Algiers, where the local factory had been bombed. The first two trips had proved successful, so successful that for the third trip each of the seven-man crew had loaded two full sacks into the Lancaster's bomb bay, only to discover that the factory had reopened. The Cairo factory had refused to take back its goods, leaving Henry and his crew with nearly seven hundred of the distinctively shaped red hats[1].

'We could try Tunis?' Ginger suggested.

'Only if we can get the roster changed,' Henry pointed out.

'How about it, Pinks, do you think Daddy could be persuaded to put Jazzy Jess on the Tunis run?'

'Absolutely not,' Poppy replied. 'Now shall we play cards?'

'We must cut our losses,' Gorski put in, ignoring Poppy. 'Let Babu have the hats for arrack and girls. Take saucy pictures of the girls and sell them to the troops.'

'That's not a bad idea, you know,' Henry agreed, 'better still once we're back home. I mean to say, there's no shortage of Yanks, and they all seem to be grossly oversexed. Speaking of which, those are pretty stockings you have on, Pinks. American nylons, are they?'

'Certainly not!' Poppy snapped back. 'They're silk. Now please, can we continue the game?'

'You have no stake,' Henry pointed out once more. 'Unless, of course you'd care to volunteer to be the subject for Gorski's dirty pictures?'

'Certainly not!' Poppy repeated, her blush rising once more.

'She would sell well,' Gorski put in, running an appraising eye over Poppy's naked chest, which she hastily covered once more.

'She would,' Henry agreed. 'What d'you say, Pinks, ten shillings for a nudie set? Ginger could nip across to the base for Bunker's equipment and be back in under an hour.'

'Absolutely not!' Poppy insisted. 'What would my father say to see me in dirty pictures?'

'Don't show him,' Henry suggested. 'Come along, you're already out of your kit, so why be so modest?'

'Besides,' Ginger put in, 'you weren't so concerned for my sister, were you?'

'What did she do with Sally?' Henry queried. 'Not take saucy pictures of her, surely?'

'No,' Ginger responded. 'She spanked her, that's what.'

'Spanked her?' Henry demanded in fascination.

'Spanked?' Gorski asked. 'On her bottom?'

'Yes,' Henry explained. 'Spanked always means on the girl's bottom, or the boy's for that matter. If it had been across the face or something he'd say slapped or smacked, although those can mean on the bottom too, but spanked means on the bottom, always.'

The big Pole nodded, accepting Henry's explanation without comment or surprise, then began to shuffle the cards. Ginger carried on, his voice thick with indignation for his sister's fate as he explained what had happened.

'Yes, on her bottom, her bare bottom I might add, in the bunkhouse, with a dozen other girls looking on and laughing!'

'They weren't laughing,' Poppy interjected, 'or they'd have been given a dose of the same. Aircraftwoman 2nd Class Green had repeatedly ...'

'Oh, I'm sure she deserved it,' Henry broke in, grinning openly as he imagined Ginger's petite, flame-haired little sister wriggling bare-bottom across Poppy's knee as her fellow WAAFs watched her being spanked, 'but I'm sure you'll appreciate the irony, if not the justice, of you getting the same treatment yourself? So let's make that your stake, shall we, a jolly good, bare-bottom spanking against your clothes.'

'Absolutely not!' Poppy snapped.

'Then the game is over,' he told her, 'as that is the only stake I'm prepared to accept. Well boys?'

'Damn right!' Ginger agreed.

Gorski gave Poppy a brief, placid glance and nodded. Sarah remained silent, staring fixedly at the glass in her hand but Henry noted that she was having difficulty restraining a smile.

'I ... I do believe you'd enjoy it, you filthy goat!' Poppy stormed.

'And you didn't?' Henry replied. 'Pretty girl, Sally Green.'

'Why you ...,' Poppy began, only to break off, unable to find words to fully express her outrage at what Henry was implying.

'Look at it this way,' Henry went on. 'I now own all your clothes, including the stockings and cap you still have on, I might add. One way or another you're going to have to get them back, that or walk halfway across Cairo in the nude, which is likely to excite comment.'

'You wouldn't!' Poppy exclaimed.

'Oh but I would,' Henry assured her. 'Why not? As Ginger points out, you were very happy to show off Sally's bottom, so why should you object to your own getting an airing?'

'That was in barracks!' Poppy stormed. 'This is the Berkha[2], anything might happen!'

'We'd walk with you,' Henry assured her, 'and we'd probably get a cab most of the way.'

'And what about the sentries?' Poppy demanded. 'Everybody would find out!'

'Whatever would Daddy say?' Ginger mocked.

'Or,' Henry offered, 'you can get dressed and leave now. Not really the done thing, of course, but ...'

'Beasts!' Poppy hissed, interrupting him. 'Oh, very well then! I'll play, and if I lose, you may spank me, but you are to put up all my clothes as your stake, and I'll have you know, Henry Truscott, that you are a dirty, rotten old goat, a satyr, a filthy lecher, and no gentleman!'

'To the contrary,' Henry responded. 'My family pedigree is impeccable. Now come along, enough nonsense. We're supposed to be playing cards.'

Gorski dealt, with a fluttering agility that belied the clumsy appearance of his massive hands. Henry took his hand, holding the cards close to his chest as he looked to see what he'd been given. As he had hoped, the big Pole had used the distraction of Poppy's striptease and the ensuing conversation to make a few crucial adjustments to the order of the pack. He held three jacks, a two and a seven.

'Two, please, Sergeant Gorski,' Poppy asked.

Her face remained impassive as she took the new cards, her feelings betrayed only by a slight trembling in her fingertips. Henry had allowed himself a quiet smile, hoping she'd notice.

'Hills?' Gorski grumbled.

'I'll fold,' Sarah Hennigan responded. 'I'm not entirely sure what I would do if I won.'

'Well I'm in,' Ginger said, pushing coins into the centre of the table. 'After all, if anyone's going to spank Pinks it jolly well ought to be me. Three please, Sergeant.'

'One moment,' Poppy cut in, 'this is between Henry and I!'

'Not at all,' Henry told her. 'I agree to put your clothes in as my stake, but if somebody else wins then they get to give you

7

your spanking, and I keep your clothes. A game's a game, Pinks.'

'Yes, but ...,' Poppy began, glancing at Gorki's enormous hands, then at Ginger. 'I ...'

'She wants you to spank her,' Gorski remarked to Henry.

'I most certainly do not!' Poppy snapped, but her blush had deepened once again, to a furious crimson flush that covered most of her bare chest.

Whether it was true or not she was clearly agitated, no longer bothering to cover her breasts as she studied her cards, while her upturned nipples were stiffer than ever.

'Two please, Sergeant,' Henry said cheerfully and laid Poppy's clothes in the centre of the table.

His new cards were both tens and he immediately laid all five face down on the table. Gorski threw his own hand in, at which Poppy gave a faint sigh of relief, but she had set her lips tight as she looked up at Henry.

'Very well. What do you have?'

'You can't call me yet,' Henry pointed out. 'You either have to fold or raise, but yes, I see the difficulty. Tell you what, let's call a spanking two dozen smacks. Fair?'

'I supposed so,' she answered, her voice both hesitant and sulky.

'So you already have two dozen in,' he continued, 'and if you want to stay in you can raise Ginger and I another two dozen.'

Poppy responded with a quick, nervous nod.

'I'll raise,' Ginger said confidently and reached out to drop a cluster of coins in among the creases of Poppy's knickers where Henry had placed them at the centre of the table.

'Likewise,' Henry agreed. 'Poppy?'

'I ... I suppose I must.'

'Three twenty-fours, seventy-two smacks,' Henry remarked.

'I can count, thank you,' Poppy said.

Ginger made to reach for the small pile of coins in front of him, only to wince, hesitate and withdraw his hand. Henry realised that Gorski had applied a well-aimed boot under the table, but nobody else seemed to have noticed.

'I'm out then,' Ginger said. 'Pity.'

'Don't worry, old boy,' Henry assured his friend. 'You'll still be able to enjoy the view.'

'He will not!' Poppy answered.

'Oh yes he will,' Henry assured her. 'If you can spank little Sally in front of other people …'

'Other women,' Poppy pointed out furiously. 'I am not being spanked in front of your entire crew, Henry Truscott!'

'Only Ginger and Gorski,' Henry pointed out, 'and besides, you're already starkers.'

'Spanking is different,' Poppy stated.

'If you mean you'll be giving them a ruder show when you're over my knee, then yes, I suppose it is,' Henry agreed, 'but not much. We saw it all anyway, when you bent to take off your knickers, or at least, I did, Miss Fanny Adams and her little brown friend too.'

'You unspeakable pig!' Poppy gasped. 'Very well then, if you insist on being so utterly vile, you had better make the best of it and spank me properly! I'm raising you another two dozen!'

'Don't be so eager,' Henry laughed. 'I haven't won yet, and besides, I might chuck in. No, on second thoughts I'll risk a few more shillings.'

He put money into the pot, then again as Poppy gave a single, furious nod.

'Ninety-six smacks against your clothes and ten shillings,' Henry said. 'You can see me for another twenty-four.'

Poppy swallowed and nodded once more, only this time with more apprehension than anger. Henry began to put his cards down on the table, watching her expression change from concern to an odd mixture of relief and disappointment as he set down first two jacks and then the two tens.'

'Two pairs,' he said.

She had closed her eyes briefly as the cards went down and was shaking with relief as she laid out her own hand.

'Full house, fives over twos,' Gorski rumbled.

'Very good,' Henry admitted, 'but not quite good enough.'

He had laid down his remaining jack, and as he did so

pushed his chair back from the table, leaving his legs sticking out to make a lap. Poppy reacted slowly, the expression on her face flickering through a whole range of emotions that finished with her eyes wide and her mouth open. Henry waited patiently, enjoying her discomfort as she got slowly to her feet, her eyes wild as she threw one desperate glance towards the door and another to her friend, but Sarah Hennigan merely shrugged. Poppy's eyes met Henry's.

'Please?' she asked, not troubling to frame the rest of the question as she begged to be let off.

Henry shook his head and applied a meaningful pat to his lap. Poppy began to walk around the table, step by slow step, until she had reached his side. Again she hesitated, pleading now with her eyes, but the sight of her naked, trembling body and the subtle perfume from her skin was enough to make absolutely certain that she was not let off. Henry once more shook his head, and with a last, pathetic sob she laid herself across his lap, her feet and hands braced on the floor, her bottom lifted for spanking.

'Good girl,' Henry remarked. 'I see it's not your first time?'

Another sob escaped Poppy's lips in response, then a gasp of pure chagrin as Henry adjusted his knee to bring her bottom into greater prominence and so spread the firm little cheeks to show off her tightly puckered anus and the sweetly pouted lips of her cunt. She was wet, the flesh of her vulva puffy with arousal, the central hole of her vagina swimming with fluid, with more pooled on the taut skin of her hymen.

Henry gave a pleased chuckle to see the condition she was in, exchanged a knowing grin with the goggle-eyed Ginger, and began to spank. Poppy gave another of her weak little cries at the impact of his hand on her flesh, then again as Henry applied the second smack and began to count.

'Two, and three, and four … What a beautiful bottom you do have, Pinks. I mean to say, you need to be spanked, just for being so lovely.'

Poppy said nothing, now gasping and sobbing to each and every smack as her bottom began to bounce and quiver. Henry took a grip around her waist and raised his knee higher still, spreading her bottom as wide as her cheeks would go, her cunt and anus now flaunted to the room as the spanking continued. She still had her hands braced on the floor, but her feet had begun to kick to the sting of the slaps. Soon she was tossing her head and wriggling her bottom, so that as he spanked Henry could feel the soft rubbing of her belly against his cock, with inevitable consequences. He paused, his hand resting on her bottom as he began to knead her now heated flesh.

'Get off me, you pig!' Poppy spat after a moment of gasping in air. 'You won the right to spank me, not to fondle my bottom!'

Henry shrugged and immediately went back to spanking, catching her off guard and making her yelp and kick her legs. Her bottom was now a lovely rosy pink, while her juice was trickling freely down the slit of her cunt and smeared between her cheeks as they opened and closed to the pain of her spanking, helping to keep Henry's erection rock-hard against her flesh. He knew she could feel how hard he was, but she had begun to whimper and pant once more, perhaps accepting the state of his cock as an inevitable consequence of giving her punishment and so different to treating himself to a deliberate feel of her bottom.

'Sixty, that's half way,' Henry remarked as he applied an extra hard slap to her now blazing rear cheeks. 'Right ho, let's get you properly dealt with.'

As he spoke he had tightened his grip, locking his arm around her slender waist to hold her firmly in position as he began to spank faster and harder still. Poppy's cries grew louder, her fists began to beat on the floor in her frustration and pain, her legs began to kick with greater abandon, scissoring wide to show off her sopping cunt. Henry took no notice, spanking with all his force as he clung tight to the writhing, gaping girl while the others looked on, Ginger in open satisfaction, Gorski calm and apparently indifferent, Sarah Hennigan in shocked excitement.

'How does it feel to get a dose of your own medicine, Corporal Pankhurst?' Ginger asked.

Poppy burst into tears, great racking sobs that shook her

11

entire body, at which Henry stopped once more. Again he left his hand resting gently on one burning bottom cheek, to stroke and squeeze the resilient flesh, but this time there was no resistance, no demand for him to stop, only the soft noises of her crying as she hung her head in utter defeat.

'Let's get it over with, shall we?' Henry asked. 'Twenty-five to go, I think.'

She responded with a weak nod, then a yelp as his hand slapped down across her bottom one more time. Henry began to spank once more, still hard, but aiming slow, firm slaps to the fleshiest part of her bottom where her cheeks turned in to meet her thighs, and across her slit. She began to whimper in response, along with the occasional choking sob, and as Henry counted out the last few smacks she had gone completely limp, surrendering herself to her punishment.

'There we are then,' he said as he gave her a final, resounding smack, 'and I dare say that will teach you a lesson, if only to be careful who you play poker with. Come on now.'

He helped her to her feet, taking her hand as he too stood up. There was no resistance, the fight spanked out of her as he led her towards the door, her head hung low in shame and defeat, the tousled mop of her now dishevelled blonde hair concealing her face but her gentle snivelling giving away her emotions, while she had reached her free hand back to rub at one richly pinked bottom cheek. Henry paused to speak to Gorski.

'Tell Babu I'll need a room on the top floor for tonight. Oh, and have him send up a bottle of Red Infuriator and some olive oil.'

Gorski gave a grunt of acquiescence and followed as Henry led the still weeping girl from the room and up a flight of stairs to a crooked hallway illuminated only by the flickering oil lamps below. He pushed one door, which proved to be locked, but the second swung open to allow them into a small, bare room furnished only with a crude pallet on the floor. A tall window half-closed by ancient wooden shutters gave on to the Egyptian night, showing the rooftops of Cairo washed pale with moonlight. Poppy took no notice whatsoever and Henry allowed himself only a single glance before turning his attention to her as she sank into a squat on the pallet.

He freed his cock from the confines of his uniform trousers, offering it to her mouth. Poppy looked up, her tearstained face pale in the moonlight, her eyes wide in supplication. Henry merely shook his head and fed his half-stiff cock into her mouth. She took it in, and after a moment of hesitation began to suck, clumsy and reluctant, with none of the little tricks he'd come to enjoy from professional girls, but giving vastly more pleasure. He took her gently by the hair, tugging off the little air force cap and tossing it aside, to leave her naked but for her stockings, kneeling at his feet in an open kneed squat, her bottom pushed out behind as he fed his erection in and out between her lips.

At the sound of footsteps on the stairs he pulled out, leaving Poppy to lie back on the pallet as he inched open the door. Fat Babu himself stood outside, an oil lamp in one hand and a basket in the other. His great round head was split by a gap-toothed grin, while beads of sweat glistened on his forehead beneath the edge of his skull cap. Henry passed over a handful of coins and took both basket and lamp, turning once more to the room. Poppy now lay on the pallet, curled up on herself, but as he approached she once more rose, her pretty mouth opening to accept his cock. Henry ignored the invitation, instead catching her up under her knees to roll her onto her back, her thighs wide and the eager mouth of her cunt glistening in the yellow light.

'No, please ... I can't, I haven't ...,' she sighed. 'I'm a virgin!'

'I know,' Henry said gently. 'Don't worry. Just roll over.'

'Roll over?' Poppy queried. 'Oh no, not that. Henry, please ...'

'Hush,' Henry replied. 'Just roll over and lift your bottom.'

Poppy responded with a bitter sob, but she had done as she was told, rolling on to her knees with her beautiful bottom lifted and open to show off her virgin cunt and also the tight pink star of her anus. She had begun to cry again, sobbing into the blankets that covered the pallet, but as Henry knelt down to bury his face between her thighs her sobs quickly changed to gasps of sheer ecstasy. He'd begun to lick her clitoris, flicking his tongue over the tiny bud as he rummaged in the basket for the flask of olive oil he'd called for in order to lubricate her anus.

As he licked he was fully aware that Babu had not returned down the stairs and so was presumably watching through a slit in the door, but the idea of having the fat Egyptian bar owner watch while he sodomised Poppy was more appealing than otherwise. She either didn't know or didn't care, keeping her bottom lifted while he lapped at her cunt, and responding only with a resigned groan when he turned his attention to her anus. As the cool, slippery olive was poured out over her bottom she let out a low moan, which broke to a sigh as he began to rub it in, smoothing it over her hot, spanked cheeks, into the slit between and using his tongue to help it into the tiny, puckered hole into which he intended to insert his cock. When his fingers found her anus in turn she gave another protest, but weaker still, and she was merely whimpering as he began to probe at the tight, greasy little hole.

Henry took hold of his cock, nursing his erection as he gently opened up Poppy's bottom hole, pushing one finger slowly in and out before pouring yet more olive oil into the open cavity. The thick, golden liquid squeezed out as her anus closed, but this time his finger went in easily, as far as he could get it, drawing fresh moans and gasping noises from her mouth to express her ecstasy as much as her shame. Henry was grinning as he continued to work her anus open, adding fresh olive oil twice before he pushed in a second finger, for all that his excitement had risen to the point at which a few sharp tugs would have brought him to orgasm and spared her a buggering.

He did his best to ignore the sensation, working a third finger in up her now gaping anus and deliberately spreading the slippery little hole as wide as it would go before finally pulling his fingers free and rising into a lewd squat above her upturned bottom. Poppy gave another low moan as he pressed his straining helmet to her slippery rear hole, but she made no effort to escape. He pushed, gently, unable to hold back a sigh of his own as he felt her anal ring start to spread to the pressure of his cock. Another push and he felt her muscle give, admitting the full bulbous mass of his helmet past her muscle. A third and his cock was well in, her bottom hole squeezing on his cock shaft. Again and he began to slide up more easily, with Poppy now grunting and panting without restraint as her rectum slowly filled with erect penis.

At last he felt his balls squash to her empty cunt, with her ring stretched taut around the very base of his cock. A faint, rhythmic sound from behind him indicated that Babu was not merely watching Poppy being buggered but masturbating over the sight, but that only encouraged Henry to show off. Pulling his cock free to leave her anus a gaping red hole into her body, he once more sank himself deep, and again, only for the sheer joy of buggering her spanked bottom in front of another man to become more than he could bear. He cried out as his balls locked and he came; thick, white spunk erupting into her open anus and then over her raised bottom cheeks as he jerked frantically at his aching shaft, all the while with his eyes locked to the sight of his come bubbling from her well buggered bottom hole.

'You filthy, filthy pig,' Poppy sighed and she had collapsed onto the pallet, even as a grunt from outside the door signalled that Fat Babu also had achieved orgasm.

Chapter Two

HENRY CAME AWAKE ONLY slowly, his thoughts confused as he remembered the delight of buggering Poppy while supposing himself at Stukely Hall in Devon, with the real situation dawning only gradually as he first remembered that he was in Egypt, then discovered that Poppy was no longer with him. He swore softly as he pulled himself into an upright position. His head ached a trifle, as did most of his body, including his cock, which was painfully erect despite having come up Poppy's bottom and later over her breasts. Having given in so completely, and having drunk rather more than her share of the potent red wine he'd ordered, she had been obliging in the extreme, giggling as he taught her how to take a man's cock in her cleavage and making only a mild complaint when he had come all over her.

'Pinks?' he called out, only to realise that not only was she gone, but so were her clothes, and his.

'Bugger!' he swore once more, with rather greater emphasis.

He looked under the pallet, but it came as no great surprise to find that his clothes weren't there either. Nor could they be anywhere else in the room, which was bare but for the pallet, the two empty bottles standing forlorn in the middle of the floor and a small pool of olive oil.

'Bugger!' he repeated, this time with real vehemence. 'Pinks!'

There was no reply, but it was hard to accept that the girl who had cuddled up to him so sweetly the night before had really abandoned him, naked and miles from the RAF barracks.

He remembered that he'd threatened to do the same to her, but she had plainly been angling for a smacked bottom and a trip to bed all along, so surely she had realised that he was only bluffing.

'Pinks!' he called out once more, louder now. 'A joke's a joke, old girl!'

Rising from the pallet, he went to peer out on to the landing. It was deserted, the other doors locked. Faint sounds could be heard from downstairs and from the streets outside, but nothing to suggest that Poppy was about. Cautiously, he descended the stairs, to peer into the room where they'd been playing poker, half expecting to find her sitting at the table with a smug grin on her face. She wasn't there, nor anybody else, with the table bare but for the empty arrack bottle and five glasses. The bags of fezzes lay where they'd been thrown down as he, Ginger and Gorski led Poppy and Sarah Hennigan up to the room the evening before. Henry pulled open the nearest bag, muttering to himself as he extracted a fez.

'Damn it, Pinks, when I catch you, I'll … well, I already have, I suppose, but it'll be a damn sight harder next time.'

He put the fez over his crotch, looked down, shook his head and burrowed into the bag for a larger size. His cock was still obstinately erect, and yet he felt more of a fool with the ridiculous hat over his genitals than he had stark naked. Poppy had also taken his watch, which had been in the pocket of his uniform jacket, but the angle of the sun streaming in at the window showed that the morning was well advanced. His pass covered him until noon, no longer, which meant that he had to act without delay. Again he cursed, then moved to the door, listening to the voices coming from two floors below. Fat Babu evidently had customers, two men at the least, quite possibly more, and quite possibly including British soldiers, even airmen.

If he went down to borrow some clothes the story would be around Cairo in hours, leaving him a laughing stock, which was no doubt exactly what Poppy was hoping for. On the other hand his view from the window showed several lines of washing, one especially tempting, with a white gallibaya flapping in the gentle breeze. To reach it across the flat rooftops would be the work of a moment, and there seemed to be every chance of making it unobserved.

To think was to act, and Henry had quickly jumped down from the window onto the roof a few feet below. Clutching the fez to his still engorged genitals, he made quick progress from roof to roof, arriving at his destination apparently unseen and pulling on the gallibaya with a sense of relief not far short of what he had felt on returning from missions over enemy territory. Not that he was home and dry, as there was still the question of getting down from the rooftops, while even dressed and with the fez now on his head rather than concealing his cock, nobody was going to mistake him for an Egyptian.

An open window beside a neighbouring roof suggested a possible route to ground level and he peered cautiously within. The room was much like the one in which he had bedded Poppy, with a pallet on the floor, although it was decorated. It was also occupied, with a girl curled up on the pallet, plainly asleep, a blanket clutched in one hand and twisted around her upper body, so that the generous curves of her coffee-coloured bottom were half exposed to the light, and to Henry's gaze.

He spared a moment to drink in the view, his eyes flickering over the curves of her plump and resilient little peach, her shapely legs and pleasingly feminine curve of her hip. She was very pretty, with a soft, sweet face and long, jet black hair, while he couldn't help but wonder if the sheet clutched to her chest concealed a pair of boobies to match the rest of her body. His cock gave an involuntary twinge at the thought, but he was about to pull away from the window when he realised the implication of the bright light streaming through the bead curtain which hung across the door of her room. It could only come from an open door on the level below, which gave on to the street.

Still he hesitated, only to catch a glimpse of movement to one side. A woman had stepped out to take in her washing from the very line on which his stolen gallibaya had hung moments before. She was looking the other way, but only had to turn a fraction to see him. He climbed carefully into the girl's room, to freeze in motion as he realised that she was no longer asleep but looking up at him from huge nut brown eyes. He forced a smile, sure that she would scream at any moment and wavering between door and window as the best route of escape, but to his surprise she smiled back, sat up and spread her thighs in unmistakable invitation.

'Ah, it's a brothel,' Henry said to himself. 'Um ... no money.'

He patted his sides in an attempt to indicate that his pockets were empty. The girl didn't respond, but stayed where she was, with her smooth brown thighs still held wide to show off the treasure between as she looked up at him from half-lidded eyes, clearly aroused but oddly shy for a Cairene tart. Plainly she thought he was her first client of the day, an impression the state of his cock could only reinforce, with his erection creating a substantial bulge in the material of his gallibaya. She had noticed, and began to giggle, which was too much for him.

'Oh well, why not?' he muttered to himself and pulled up his gallibaya.

The girl's giggles took on a new, excited note at the sight of his naked cock and she immediately lay back, her thighs spread wide. Henry climbed on top, guiding his cock to her hole and in. Unlike Poppy, she was no virgin, her cunt tight but wet and receptive, so that his cock slid deep at the first push, all the way until his balls were pressed to the resilient curves of her bottom cheeks. He began to push inside her, his eyes closed in bliss for the feel of warm, wet cunt flesh around his cock. She responded with a gentle whimpering sound that quickly turned to the more familiar moans and gasps as he quickened his pace inside her, and before long her arms had come up to hold him close as they fucked.

With the passion of her response and the tightness of her sex it wasn't long before Henry felt the onset of orgasm. For a moment he considered trying to hold back, wanting to do far more than simply penetrate her and come, only to abandon the idea in the face of common sense and sheer ecstasy. Whipping his cock free, he let his gaze rest on the soft, enticing curves of her body as he tugged himself to orgasm, laying two thick lines of semen across her belly and chest before wiping the last of it off on her leg. She gave a happy smile in response, apparently unfazed either by his somewhat hasty use of her body or being spunked on. Henry responded in kind, rose and dropped his gallibaya over his now rapidly deflating cock as he reflected that she was definitely worth another visit.

'Henry,' he said, pointing to his chest.

'Jamila,' she replied, pointing to her own and then throwing him a look of mock reproof as she realised how badly soiled he'd left her body.

'Better a spot of spunk on the titties than a bun in the oven,' Henry said. 'I'll pay, um …'

He trailed off, as Jamila evidently didn't understand a word he was saying and seemed content with the situation. A glance through the hanging beads showed a long, narrow staircase leading to an open door, with the sunlit street beyond. With a smile and a wave for Jamila he slipped through the curtain and downstairs, to find himself in a hall occupied by a seedy-looking Egyptian and a British Army officer, Captain Nigel Smith, known as "the Gorilla" for his massive, hirsute body and bad temper.

'Smith,' Henry remarked, politely tipping his fez, and the next instant he was in the street.

When he looked back it was to find the seedy-looking Egyptian peering from the doorway. Again Henry tipped his fez, then hurried on as the man disappeared back into the building. A moment later and Henry had reached the front of Fat Babu's, where he glanced in. Babu himself was at the counter, busy preparing coffee, and beside him, neatly folded, was Henry's uniform.

'The little bitch!' he muttered, again reflecting on what he'd like to do to Poppy's bottom when he caught up with her.

He went in, ignoring Babu's look of surprise to see him coming in at the front and dressed in gallibaya and fez.

'I'll have some of that coffee,' he ordered. 'And I do think you might have brought my uniform up to me, given that I let you watch me with Pinks last night.'

'I was to bring your clothes,' Babu explained, pouring

20

coffee, 'but Corporal Pankhurst said to have them brushed and pressed.'

'Oh she did, did she?' Henry retorted. 'Including my underwear and cap, I suppose? Never mind. Did Sergeant Gorski speak to you about the fezzes?'

'Four dozen of arrack and I am to pimp you many girls.'

'For fifty-six dozen fezzes?' Henry demanded. 'That's outrageous!'

'Many girls,' Babu repeated. 'Many fine girls. Breasts like pomegranates. Bottoms like the finest watermelons.'

As he spoke he used his fat little hands to make gestures to indicate the roundness and size of the treasures he was promising

'They'd better be,' Henry told him, 'and you can start with little Jamila down the street.'

'Jamila?' Babu queried.

'You must know her, bouncy little trollop, ever so eager. From six or seven doors down.'

'Ah, that Jamila, yes. Ahmed al-Ashal's girl. She is perfection, but first she is promised to Captain Smith.'

'Well, yes, she has my sympathy, but I imagine she'll be right as rain in a day or two even after an encounter with the Gorilla.'

'He has paid well for her virginity,' Babu went on. 'Today he will take her for the first time, waking her from her sleep to feel his embrace. A very romantic fellow is Captain Smith. And for a fortnight she is his alone.'

'Her virginity?' Henry queried. 'In that case he's going to be disappointed ... very disappointed in fact. Damn! Look here, if he comes in, you haven't seen me, understood?'

Even as he spoke Henry had snatched up his uniform and made a dash for the stairs. In the room where they had played cards he dressed as fast as could, slapping his cap onto his head just as angry voices reached him from downstairs, first in Arabic, then in English, with Captain Smith's bass roar rising above Babu's high-pitched protestations.

For the second time in under an hour Henry left the establishment via the window, this time at full speed, hurdling walls and scrambling up parapets until he was sure he was out of sight and only then seeking out a way down to the street. Even when on solid ground he kept his pace at a fast walk, making his way through the narrow alleys of the Berkha until he was well clear of the Wagh itself, then making for the broader thoroughfares where he would be able to find a cab to take him out to Cairo West Airfield and the RAF barracks.

'Right arm up a bit, negligent like,' Bombardier "Bunker" Sloper called as he peered into his camera. 'Now say cheese.'

'Camembert,' Henry responded after quickly adjusting his position against the wheel of the Lancaster. 'Look, this thing is going to work, isn't it? I mean to say, it's meant for taking recce pictures.'

'Trust me,' Bunker assured him and triggered the camera, 'and besides, I've got my Bolsey as well. There goes. Nice composition that, Skipper, you an' Jess in the foreground and a line of buses behind. Very nice.'

'Put a naked girl in it and nobody would care if there was a line of pink elephants behind,' Henry responded.

'Oh no, always got to have a nice background, you have. We'd best take some up by the pyramids, and with camels and that.'

'Camels?' Henry queried. 'A bit specialist, I would have thought, but look, I've got to go. You can practise with Gorski, if you don't think he'll crack the lens.'

He had spotted Poppy, leaving the cluster of headquarters buildings and heading for one of the hangers, a sheaf of papers clutched in her hands. The Jazzy Jess was third closest of the line of Lancasters standing ready, and he soon caught up, slowing to enjoy the sharp click of her heels on the concrete and the way her bottom moved beneath her neatly tailored uniform before he accosted her.

'I say, Pinks!'

She turned, lifting her nose as she saw him.

'I want a word with you, young lady,' he went on. 'It was a bit rich, pinching my clothes.'

'You deserved it!' she answered him. 'You threatened to

22

make me walk naked through Cairo!'

'I was joking,' Henry explained.

'I didn't know that, and besides, you spanked me!'

'That was a bet, and besides, you were angling for it, and don't try to pretend otherwise. I thought we had an understanding, after last night I mean?'

'An understanding? You … you put your … your thingy up my bottom, and in my mouth!'

'Not in that order, damn it! For Heaven's sake, Pinks, now I've got the Gorilla after my blood, and …'

'Captain Smith?' she interrupted. 'What has he to do with it?'

'He …,' Henry began and then trailed off, realising that Poppy was hardly likely to sympathise with him for taking Jamila's supposed virginity. 'Never you mind, suffice to say that your little joke has got me into hot water, but nowhere near as hot as that little round bottom of yours is going to be the next time I get you alone.'

'I hardly think that is likely,' she answered him, tilting her nose another few degrees into the air.

'No?' he asked. 'Come on, don't tell me you weren't up for it last night, and don't tell me you're not angling for some more of the same.'

'Merely because you took advantage of me once is no reason to think that I will permit you to do so again.'

'Took advantage of you? Maybe I was a bit rough, but damn it, I've never seen a girl tease the way you did, and you're old enough to know what comes of that sort of behaviour!'

'I'm sure I don't know what you mean.'

'Oh yes you do, and by God if any girl every deserved spanking it's you, Poppy Pankhurst!'

'That's as may be,' she answered, 'but you will not be the one spanking me.'

She turned on her heel, to walk away with a deliberately taunting wriggle of her hips. Henry made to follow, thought better of it, and contented himself with a brief, muttered tirade on girls in general and Poppy in particular. Turning back towards the Lancasters, he had quickly rejoined his crew.

'Women!' he remarked. 'Toasty warm one minute, ice cold the next. Damn confusing too. D'you know, I have two sisters and no less than five aunts, six if you count my great-aunt Victoria, and I'm none the wiser for it.'

'She is in love with you,' Gorski remarked.

'Hardly!' Henry laughed. 'Or if she is, then she has a damned peculiar way of showing it.'

'Bed another woman. Then see what she does.'

'I might just do that, if only because just being with her for a few seconds leaves me fit to burst. Besides which, we need more girls to pose for Bunker, because God knows what Babu will dig up, and I'd rather not pay unless we have to, excepting Jamila that is, but she's worth the ackers, as you'll see. There's Sally, of course ...'

'I say!' Ginger interrupted.

'Don't be wet,' Henry told him.

'But she's my sister!'

'What does that matter? Of all the bluebirds on the station she's the best, Pinks excepted, maybe, and she's a good sport. And speaking of good sports, I seem to recall Hermione giving a sympathetic hand to a certain young airman who didn't expect to see the end of his thirty[3], so if my cousin can provide you with a happy ending I'm damned if I can see why I shouldn't take saucy pictures of your sister. So long as she's game, that is, which remains to be seen.'

Ginger had begun to blush and didn't answer. As they'd been speaking the remaining two members of the crew had joined the group; radio operator Al "Slick" Delaney, Brylcreemed hair glistening in the bright Egyptian sun, and "the Egg", their rear gunner, his hairless dome glistening just as brightly. Henry glanced across the six of them, fought back an instinctive pang of loss and regret for the absence of the seventh, then went on.

'That's the main thing, some girls to pose for us, and we want variety, to suit all tastes. We do it properly too, no playing silly buggers. Bunker takes the pictures, because he's the only one who knows what he's doing, and with one other chap there, probably me, or Ginger. Nobody minds Ginger. Gorski can cope with angry husbands or boyfriends, importunate pimps and that sort of thing, with the rest of us to back him up if need be. Slick, you're our salesman. All clear?'

'How about me, Skipper?' the Egg demanded.

'Frankly,' Henry answered, 'your skills lie elsewhere, and for God's sake don't try and collect any of the girls' knickers. None of your peculiar Wiltshire tricks, either. This is business. Oh, and it's strictly in-house. No outsiders, ever.'

All five men nodded their understanding and Henry carried on.

'Other matters. No outing today, but we have to stay on station. Gorski, Slick, I want you to go into town this evening and pick up the arrack from Babu. Don't let him slide back, and not on the girls either. We want popsies ...'

He continued, ticking off the points on his fingers while his mind took a rather different tack. The encounter with Poppy had left him with an urgent desire for more, but for whatever reason she was clearly not going to oblige. Sally Green was another matter. When the crew had been serving in England, Ginger had often shown round photos of his pretty little sister, first in civvies and then in her WAAF uniform. Her pert, snub-nosed good looks and riot of copper-coloured hair had intrigued him even then, and now that she was on the same base it was hard to resist the opportunity to take things further. He was also aware that he had a potential rival in Slick, which meant that he would need to make a quick move.

Having dismissed his crew and walked to the mess for a meditative drink he continued to allow his mind to roam on thoughts of Sally Green. One of the pictures in particular had always stuck in his mind. In it, she was somewhere in the Chilterns, where the family lived, as carefree as she was beautiful as she threw a stick for a terrier. Her dress had risen due to her exertions, or perhaps been lifted by a chance puff of wind, revealing one slender thigh with the hem of her stocking straining to the tug of a glimpsed suspender clip.

The picture had provided solace during many a gruelling mission, but had now been eclipsed by an altogether different and far less innocent image of the beautiful young redhead, that of her taking a bare-bottom spanking from her superior officer. Not that he had been anywhere near the WAAF huts when Sally Green had been punished, or even known about it until Ginger had passed on an indignant report, but that didn't prevent the picture being clear in his mind.

She would probably have been dealt with at the table which was invariable sited in the central aisle of the long, open-floored Nissan huts. Poppy would have sat down on the chair, allowing the other girls to get a clear view from the line of double bunks to either side. Sally would have been brought forward and given a brief telling-off for her delinquency, perhaps with her grey-blue uniform skirt already rolled up to show off her full knickers, girdle and stocking tops. When Poppy had made her point she would have taken Sally down across her knee, bottom lifted to the rest of the hut to make sure the other girls got a good view, trim little cheeks straining out the cotton of her knickers, either of the heavy blue, winter-weight cotton or lighter and white, but in either case full almost to bursting with perfectly formed female flesh.

The knickers would have come down, perhaps jerked roughly off, or peeled slowly down to increase Sally's humiliation, but in either case providing giggling amusement for the onlookers and agonising shame for the victim, but in all probability excitement too. After all, no complaint had been made, and there had long been rumours about Poppy's preference for girls, although as Henry had discovered it was far from exclusive. Very possibly Sally had egged Poppy on to dish out a spanking, just as Poppy had egged Henry on in turn, but that would have only gone so far to assuage her feelings as her knickers were pulled down in front of her fellow airwomen.

With Sally's knickers well down and her bare bottom flaunted to the giggling audience, she would have been spanked, hard, probably hard enough to make her kick and squirm the away Poppy had done, perhaps hard enough to make her cry. Whatever her reaction, it seemed certain that for such a slim girl in such a vulnerable position both her cunt and anus would have been on full view during the spanking, details that formed an important part of Henry's mind image. He closed his eyes to savour the vision, trying to decide whether it was more satisfying to imagine Sally taking her spanking in shamefaced defeat, resigned to her exposure and pain despite the sense of disgrace, or fighting every inch of the way in a futile and counterproductive attempt to retain what dignity she could. Both options were appealing, but less so than the idea of her first accepting what was being done to her as a necessary punishment only to discover that she was growing more and more aroused with every firm slap delivered to her resilient little cheeks. She would beg for it to stop, pleading with Poppy, but unable to bring herself to explain why for the sake of decency and so only succeeding in making sure her spanking was longer and harder still.

He could almost hear her voice as she begged Poppy to stop it, breathless and thick with shame, but in practice calm and demure as she spoke not of bare-bottom spanking but of the requisitioning procedure for staff cars. His eyes came wide as he realised that his erotic daydream had brought him to the edge of sleep, while Sally Green herself was directly outside the window, explaining details of her work to fellow WAAF clerks.

A swallow of coffee and he was on his feet, determined to make the best of the opportunity and arrange a rendezvous for as soon as she came off duty. As he hurried around the building it occurred to him that if she really had been angling for a spanking from Poppy then it was entirely possible that she had no time at all for men, only for the thought to be dismissed out of hand. As long experience had taught him, even those girls who took their deepest pleasures in each others' arms could usually be persuaded to try a spot of cock for a change.

His timing was perfect. As he rounded the corner of the building she was just stepping away from the other two girls, and immediately started towards him. A greeting, a friendly enquiry as to how she was getting on at Cairo West and conversation had been initiated. Some carefully chosen and sincere flattery delivered in a manner at once friendly and slightly paternal, a politely phrased question and she had

27

agreed to meet him later, at the Malqate Palace, a coffee bar on the edge of the city.

Sally's ready agreement to the rendezvous had left little doubt in Henry's mind that she was game for an evening of flirtation at the very least. As he sipped at a coffee surreptitiously laced with arrack his main emotion was one of anticipation, but it was tinged with guilt. Ginger was all too clearly unhappy about the idea of his little sister posing for saucy photographs, while it also felt not altogether suitable to be trying to winkle a girl out of her clothes for other people's satisfaction. Neither concern was overpowering, but after a period of examining his conscience he decided that the only fair thing to do was to place the facts squarely before Sally, including her brother's disapproval. That way she would be able make her own choice, and if she refused, then she refused.

Another consideration was whether or not to admit to her that he knew about the spanking she had taken from Poppy, and it was less easy to find a solution. She was sure to be embarrassed, but he knew enough to be aware that embarrassment was akin to excitement, as Poppy herself had shown so clearly the night before. He also wanted to spank her himself, and bringing up what had happened with Poppy would be an excellent way to introduce the subject into conversation, while if he didn't but then spanked her anyway, it might prove awkward if she discovered the full truth at a later date.

He was still musing on the conundrum when Sally herself appeared, riding the step of a three-hundredweight truck coming out from the airfield, which suggested remarkable self-confidence and also leant her a pleasantly dishevelled look as she walked towards him. She had quickly adjusted her splendid mane of copper-coloured hair, which she wore loose, more evidence of a defiant, tomboy's spirit, and sufficiently provocative to send a pulse of blood to his cock. He raised his coffee cup in casual salute and she returned a smile as she eased herself into the chair beside him, speaking immediately.

'Is this place dry?'

'Not if you know the proprietor,' Henry assured her, 'but

you mustn't be too showy about it. English coffee is the thing to ask for. Shall I?'

'Do,' she confirmed. 'What a day, absolutely beastly. I mean to say, who do these people think they are?'

'People?' Henry queried as he signalled for more coffee.

'NCOs,' she answered. 'I signed up to do my bit, not to be pushed around by some Whitechapel guttersnipe. Not that you'd know I suppose, being a high and mighty FO?'

'That's the services for you, I'm afraid,' he replied, 'and I dare say it's not so very different being barked at by a corporal or a Wing Co. I sympathise, believe me. I hear Corporal Pankhurst is among the worst?'

'Pinks? Oh no, she plays the game. It's the jumped-up ones I can't abide. Take this afternoon ...'

Sally carried on, describing her woes as Henry responded with sympathetic nods, but he was barely listening. The thought of the beautiful young woman beside him thinking of being given a bare-bottom spanking in front of her colleagues as "playing the game" was almost too much, and it was impossible to interpret what she had said any other way. Plainly Sally regarded what should have been an unbearably humiliating experience as a reasonable way to admonish her for whatever she'd done wrong, a thought that sent the blood pumping to Henry's cock so hard that for a moment he felt physically weak.

He pulled his chair closer in to the table in order to conceal his excitement, but Sally was far too involved in her denunciation of a Corporal Wolvis to notice. Finally she wound down, just as the waiter arrived, favouring Henry with a lewd wink as he placed fresh cups and a steaming pot on the table.

'English?' Henry queried, although very sure that the waiter would not have let him down.

'The way Sir likes it,' the waiter confirmed, grinning.

Henry poured, watching in fascination as Sally picked up the tiny cup she had been given and lifted it to her pert, freckled nose, which wrinkled in a delightful way as she took a cautious sniff.

'What's in this?' she demanded.

'Arrack,' Henry explained. 'Brandy flavoured with aniseed, or something of the sort.'

'It smells like turpentine,' she answered and swallowed the cupful at a gulp. 'Ah, that hit the spot.'

'Do that too often and it'll do more than hit the spot,' Henry pointed out. 'It's about half and half.'

'I can take my drink,' she assured him. 'So what's all this about dirty pictures?'

Henry had just taken a sip of his own coffee, and immediately found himself faced with the choice of spitting it back out or expelling it through his nose. He grabbed a napkin, clutching it to his face in a vain effort to retain at least some dignity.

'Wrong hole?' Sally asked, reaching out to pat him on the back.

'Something like that,' he admitted when he'd finally got his breath back.

'The pictures?' she reminded him.

'Ah, er … yes,' Henry answered, frantically trying to get his thoughts in order. 'Ginger said something, did he?'

'He says you're setting up some sort of wheeze to sell dirty pictures to the Yanks,' she told him, 'and you want me in. I'm game.'

'What about Ginger?' Henry asked.

'Ginger's like an old mother hen, always was,' she told him. 'He didn't want me to join the service. He doesn't even like me wearing lipstick. I never take any notice.'

'Well, um … I'm very glad to hear it,' Henry managed. 'You know it will all have to be on the KV, don't you?'

'Of course, that's half the fun.'

'And the other half?' Henry asked, somewhat dumbstruck.

'Taking my clothes off,' Sally answered.

Henry winced. His cock had finally given in to the provocation, expelling a healthy quantity of semen into his underpants. She had proved too much, her pale beauty, her carefree, tomboy attitude, her delicate scent, but most of all her casual joy in her own sexuality and all that implied. With some difficulty he raised his coffee cup in salute.

'Well, er … here's to you then. Shall we eat?'

Henry allowed his hands to slip down over the curve of Sally's bottom, lifting her slight frame with ease to sit her down on one huge block of stone among many in the crumbled ruin they had selected for privacy. She gave no resistance, and he had expected none. Long before their meal was over it had been very clear what was going to happen afterwards. It had been she who took his hand as they left the bar, and she who chose where to leave the Cairo Alexandria road, waiting until no lights were visible before scampering across the desert to the shelter of what had once been a temple.

She was already out of her jacket and skirt, with her bra turned up and her blouse unbuttoned to free her tiny, firm breasts. Nor had she been backward with him, tickling his erection through the material of his trousers with long, teasing strokes that made him glad he'd suffered his earlier accident, as otherwise he would have been unable to hold back. How his cock was out, standing stiff and proud from his fly in the pale moonlight as they kissed.

'Time your knickers were off, I think,' Henry whispered as he pulled back from her mouth.

Her response was a soft purr and to lift her bottom from the rock, allowing him to take hold of the hem of her knickers and ease them gently over her bottom and down to her knees. The moment she'd been stripped her arms went back around his shoulders, holding on to him as her mouth once more sought his. Their tongues met as he began to explore her bare bottom, lifting her under one small, soft cheek as the fingers of his other hand delved into her crease. He felt a shiver run through her body as he touched her anus, using the tip of a finger to tease the little hole until it had begun to squeeze in reaction.

'You're like that, are you?' she sighed. 'Oh well, if you have to.'

Henry didn't answer, not quite sure what she meant but hoping it was an invitation to enjoy her bottom to the full. Again they began to kiss, more passionately still as he moved his hand to cup the mound of her sex. She shook her head and he nodded his understanding even as he allowed a knuckle to brush the mouth of her cunt. As he'd expected, she was as tight as Poppy, her hymen creating a taut barrier to the otherwise willing hole. The thought went straight to his cock, tempting him to take her virginity then and there, only for him to push it away.

His cock was rubbing on her knickers as they embraced, and he quickly tugged them down to her ankles before taking a firm grip and using them to lift her legs, tipping her back onto the stone with her thighs rolled high and her bottom spread to his erection. Taking his shaft in hand, he began to rub his helmet in the wet slit of her cunt, making her sigh and clutch at the rock in ecstasy even as she shook her head in what could only be a plea not to have her virginity taken.

'You wouldn't stop me, would you?' he asked softly and once again she shook her head.

'You bad girl,' he went on, and he pushed his helmet to the mouth of her cunt, feeling her hymen taut against his flesh.

Again she shook her head, urgently, but she made no effort to move away. Henry gave a soft chuckle, pleased to be fully in charge of the situation at last, and happier than ever that he'd come in his pants and could now hold off as long as he pleased. Keeping his grip on her knickers, he rolled her higher still and once more began to rub his cock in the slit of her cunt, this time until she was gasping and squirming herself against him.

Her bottom was on full show, pale and round in the moonlight, her anus an intriguing dimple between her cheeks. He pushed his balls against her, rubbing them in her slit with his shaft rearing high over her undefended cunt, and with his hand now free he gave her a gentle, testing slap on one exposed bottom cheek. She gave out another little purr and he applied a second smack, a little harder than before.

'A very bad girl,' he said, and he began to spank her.

'Please, yes,' she sighed.

'Oh my,' he went on, 'so little Sally Green likes to be spanked, does she?'

'Yes,' she breathed. 'Spank me, Henry. Tell me what a naughty little girl I am and spank me ... spank me!'

'Hush!' Henry urged, as her last demand had been a scream, undoubtedly audible well outside their hiding place. 'Yes, you have been a naughty little girl, haven't you? Imagine letting a man take off all your clothes. Imagine touching his cock.'

He continued to spank her as he spoke, slapping each soft little bottom cheek in turn, but now took hold of her wrist to guide her hand to his erection. She took a firm grip, tugging up and down on his shaft and rubbing his helmet against her cunt as he went back to spanking her. Her mouth was wide, her eyes closed, her back arched tight. It was quite plain that she was about to come, and he didn't need to be told what to do.

'Naughty girl!' he chided, keeping a tight grip on her knickers as he began to spank her with all his force. 'Naughty, naughty girl! This is what you need, Sally Green, your knickers pulled down and your bare bottom spanked.'

She gave a little, choking sob and tightened her grip on his cock, rubbing the head hard in the wet slit of her cunt to make the fleshy ridges of his helmet bump on her clitoris.

'Spanked,' Henry said once more. 'Spanked on your bare, naughty bottom. Spanked like the bad little girl you are, Sally Green. Spanked like this, with your legs rolled up to show ...'

'As if ...,' she gasped, 'as if you're changing my nappy!'

'Changing your nappy?' Henry queried, then laughed. 'Oh yes, that's perfect, rolled up as if you were going to have your nappy changed! What a thought, and what a sight!'

Sally screamed, her body locking in orgasm and her slender fingers clutching his cock so hard it made him wince, but she obviously neither knew nor cared, using his helmet to rub herself off to the dirty words he'd put into her mind. He watched her come, delighted by her response and happy to wait until she'd done what she needed to do before retrieving his cock from her hand.

'My turn,' he said as he pushed his erection lower, pausing to rub it on her virgin hole briefly before moving yet further down.

She gave out a soft moan as she felt his cock press between the cheeks of her bottom, but gave no resistance. Henry grinned to himself as he prepared to bugger her, his grip still tight in her knickers to hold her open and vulnerable. Her anus was wet with the juice running from her cunt, making it easy to push the head of his cock into the soft, slippery little hole. She was tight but willing, pushing out to take him, and to make him wonder if he was the first man to be allowed to insert his penis in her bottom hole.

With the head of his cock inside her he began to work it slowly in and out, pushing a little deeper each time and watching as bit by bit his cock shaft sank in up the straining ring of her anus. She took it well, gasping and panting a little, with her head turned to one side and her mouth wide. Her hands had gone to her chest, each on one tiny breast, massaging gently with the taut nipples sticking up from between her fingers, and unlike Poppy she stayed quiet, allowing him the pleasure of her bottom hole without complaint. Only when the full mass of his cock was in her rectum and he had begun to push harder did her little gasps and pants grow louder, encouraging Henry to slap her bottom as he buggered her, and to rub his balls in the soft valley between her cheeks.

'That's nice,' she sighed. 'Spank me while you do me. Spank my naughty bottom, Henry. Spank me hard and tell me how you'd punish me, how you'd spank my naughty bottom and put me in a nappy ... how you'd spank my naughty bottom and make me go around in a nappy, so everyone could see I've been spanked ... so everyone could seen how I'd been punished for being such a naughty little girl ...'

She broke off with a long sigh. Henry could hold back no more, with the picture of how she'd look burning hot in his mind and he took hold of his balls and the base of his cock to masturbate into her anus. He could feel the heat of her smacked cheeks against his hand, as he imagined those same little red cheeks peeping out from around the edge of a thick, towelling nappy, wrapped around her hips after she'd been well spanked and then put on parade in front of her colleagues.

He came, pumping his spunk in up her bottom as he imagine her on parade, her top half in her immaculate blue-grey uniform, her bottom half naked but for a nappy that didn't quite cover her bottom, leaving it very plain that she had been spanked. She was purring as he did it, her pretty mouth set in a happy smile, even as he pulled out to squeeze the last blob of spunk from his cock into her gaping anus.

'That was lovely,' she sighed. 'Now could you clean me up?'

'By all means,' Henry responded, digging into his pocket for a handkerchief. 'Yes, that was rather splendid, but I should be the one thanking you.'

Sally didn't respond, but stayed as she was, her eyes closed in bliss as Henry wiped her bottom and dabbed the juice from her sex. His cock also needed attention, and by the time he was finished she had pulled her knickers back up and was putting her uniform back on.

'We'd better get back,' Henry suggested. 'With any luck we can pick up a truck.'

They walked back to the Alexandria Road, but it was empty, leaving them with a long walk across the moonlit desert before they reached the gates of Cairo West Airfield. Their evening passes were still good, but it was past the hour at which the junior WAAFs were supposed to be back in barracks.

'Will you be all right?' Henry asked as he drew away from their goodnight kiss.

'Don't worry,' she assured him. 'Pinks is on duty. She'll let me in.'

She reached up to press her lips to his in a last, firm kiss before moving swiftly away, leaving Henry wondering if there was going to be another spanking that night.

Chapter Three

As HENRY STEPPED OUT into the bright morning sunlight he clapped his hands together for the sheer satisfaction of being alive. Having buggered the two prettiest girls on the station within twenty-four hours of each other, and fucked the delightful Jamila in between, it was difficult to find any fault with life whatsoever. Admittedly the fez operation had gone disastrously wrong, leaving him and the crew out of pocket, while he knew that eventually he would have to deal with the wrath of Captain Smith, but neither problem seemed to matter. Indeed, since the wheels of Jazzy Jess had touched the ground of Lincolnshire on the tenth of April the previous year with their last raid complete he had seldom felt anything really mattered, given what he had come through alive.

Striding towards the officers' mess he caught the inviting scent of frying bacon and once more smacked his hands together, this time in anticipation of a decent English breakfast. Other officers were also approaching the mess and he quickly fell into conversation, although neither Ginger nor Bunker were in evidence. As he ate he learnt that their flight plans were being reshuffled, and there was a great deal of speculation about who would be going where. Henry concentrated on the plate of bacon and eggs in front of him, reasonably confident in getting a short enough run to allow him to get the picture project off the ground and also see plenty of Sally, who was plainly going to require a great deal less hard work than Poppy.

Having finished and taken a leisurely coffee while listening with half an ear to talk of the recent protests against British rule in Egypt, he strolled over towards the main buildings. Sarah

Hennigan was behind the desk as usual and rather than join the knot of airmen around the notice board, Henry went to sit on her desk, casting an appreciative glance at the swell of her bosom before speaking.

'Morning, Hills. What do you have for me? Tunis? Benghazi?'

'You'll see,' she answered with a bright smile.

'What then?' he demanded, feeling a sudden tremor of concern. 'There's no need to be so mysterious. We're not on the Blighty run, are we?'

'No, no,' she reassured him, still smiling.

She seemed intent on teasing him, so Henry turned to the board, peering over the shoulders of the others until he managed to find the correct reference for Jazzy Jess and her destination. He read what it said, then a second time to make sure his eyesight wasn't failing him, then a third time, out loud.

'Ascension Island, via Algiers and Dakar. Ascension Island, via Algiers and Dakar!? Hills!'

'Yes?' Sarah asked sweetly, glancing up with big brown eyes.

'This is a joke, isn't it? I mean to say, of all the God-forsaken spots on Earth … Hang on, this is Poppy's doing isn't it? She's managed to convince her idiot of a father that I'm the right man to be sent halfway around the world, no doubt on some damn fool errand.'

'You're taking out anti-aircraft guns,' she informed him.

'To Ascension Island? Who do they imagine is going to attack the place, a school of dolphins?'

'I'm not privy to that sort of information,' she told him. 'I just follow my orders, and so should you.'

'Yes, of course,' Henry admitted, 'but … oh, the Hell with it. Pass me the bumph then, but you can tell your scheming little friend that I'll be getting my own back on her without fail. Besides which, what have I done to deserve this treatment in the first place?'

'I'm sure I don't know what you mean?' Sarah responded.

'Don't play the innocent with me,' Henry responded. 'I imagine the conversation in detail. There's old Sir Pomeroy, wondering which idiot to send to Ascension Island and up chirps his little angel, recommending dashing, reliable Henry Truscott. But why, that's what I want to know?'

'Do you really have to ask then?' Sarah queried.

'Yes,' Henry responded. 'Not because I ... you know, surely not? Unless it's about Sally, and ...'

Sarah gave a shrug and a sigh, as if to express astonishment that men in general and Henry in particular could be so obtuse. A queue had begun to build up, and she quickly dealt with two other pilots before handing Henry a dull green folder. He took it and left without further comment. Given the distances involved and the obscure places at which he had to touch down to refuel, it seemed unlikely that he would be back from Ascension Island in less than a week. That brought him perilously close to the date on which the squadron was due to be relieved, leaving little time either to enjoy himself with Sally Green or to get together a decent selection of photographs.

Unfortunately there was nothing to be done about it, as he could hardly lodge a protest. To suggest to Air Commodore Sir Pomeroy Pankhurst that he shouldn't allow his decisions to be influenced by his daughter was unthinkable at the best of times, without having to explain that her reasons for being upset involved being spanked, buggered and then jilted when she began to play hard to get.

Outside, trucks and other service vehicles were already beginning to cluster around the Lancasters, including a long low-loader with what were presumably the anti-aircraft guns for Jazzy Jess beneath tarpaulins. Gorski was nearby, watching operations with a critical eye, and Henry made straight for him, attracting the attention of his flight engineer with a cough as he approached.

'Brilliant!' he announced. 'Bed another woman, he said. See what she does then, he said. I'll tell you what she's done, Gorski old boy. She's got us sent to Ascension Island, that's what she's done.'

'I did not mean you to bed another woman,' Gorski began to explain.

'I know, I know, you were speaking rhetorically,' Henry broke in. 'You know what happened then?'

'You took Sally Green to town.'

'Rather more than that, and when we got back Pinks turned out to be the duty corporal. Gather everybody up, would you? Briefing time.'

The other members of the crew were all nearby and had soon gathered around Henry beneath the tip of one huge wing.

'It's an easy job,' Henry explained. 'Dull as ditchwater in fact. We fly out to Ascension Island, touching at Algiers and Dakar, nothing simpler. The problem is that it'll take the best part of a week, which more or less scotches our little enterprise. Any suggestions?'

'There's some fine bints in Dakar,' the Egg put in. 'We could take some pictures of them. Get a bit of variety too, that way. I like a bit of variety.'

'So we hear,' Henry responded, looking doubtfully at the squat, bald rear-gunner. 'But I don't imagine we'll be there long enough.'

'These things can't be rushed,' Bunker insisted. 'You need to talk a girl round, get her in the mood. You know the form. Then there's location. You can't just ask 'em to strip off in the local bar, not in most places.''

'He's right,' Slick agreed.

'How about Algiers then?' the Egg insisted. 'There's some fine bints in Algiers.'

'We have the same problem,' Henry objected. 'Not enough time. Ascension Island's another matter. What are the girls like there, Egg?'

'Wouldn't know,' the Egg admitted. 'Never been there. Black girls, I'm guessing, like in Jamaica maybe, with titties like fucking footballs an' big, round bums that wobble when they walk and make you want to stick your joystick right up between, all the way in, to fuck 'em good before you pull out and do the goo right in their faces an' make 'em lick it all up, and maybe ...'

He went quiet as he realised that everybody was staring at him.

'Well, quite,' Henry said, 'only we can't count on that, can we?'

'How about we ship some back?' Bunker suggested.

'Back here?' Henry queried.

'Yeah, why not?' the bombardier went on. 'That way we get to know them on the way, and there's plenty of room in the bus, 'specially if we've got no load coming back, and I don't see how we will. We could get six, easy, maybe eight.'

'And what do you suppose Air Commodore Sir Pomeroy Pankhurst is going to say about it when we come back with a cargo of native girls?' Henry demanded.

'He doesn't have to know, does he?' Bunker pointed out. 'All we have to do is fix it so we land after dark, an' when we're down you turn Jess nice and slow at the end of the runway while we get the girls out. Off we go into the desert and Bob's your uncle, free bint 'til relief and all the saucy snaps you could want.'

'He's finally flipped,' Ginger suggested.

'What have we got to lose?' Bunker insisted. 'Even if we get caught they ain't going to shoot us. Dishonourable discharge, maybe. Big deal. We're all up for demob, ain't we?'

'Yes,' Henry admitted cautiously, 'that's true, except for Gorski. But how do you propose to get the girls aboard in the first place? I'll be damned if I'm ending up on a charge of kidnapping.'

'Nothing like that, Skipper,' Bunker assured him. 'We just ask 'em aboard. Girls is always up for a bit of adventure. It'll be a piece of cake.'

'It'll be a bloody disaster,' Ginger responded.

'I suspect Ginger is right,' Henry stated, 'but we'd better get a move on or we'll be holding up the rank.'

They climbed aboard the plane, Henry settling himself at the familiar controls while the others dispersed to their stations. Flight checks were equally routine, and he soon had all four of the great Merlin engines turning over as he waited his turn to taxi out on to the runway. As Marley's Ghost turned out of line in front of him he followed, in slow procession, to watch each aircraft rev up and then take to the skies. When his own turn

40

came he could feel a tightening in the pit of his stomach, for all that the mission was as safe as it was simple, but as always he showed nothing of his emotion.

As Jazzy Jess rose from the ground he slowly relaxed, allowing himself to enjoy the magnificent view across the Nile Valley as he gained height. The pyramids at Giza had been visible briefly as he taxied, imposing despite the distance and the hazy air, but now seemed tiny as he banked the Lancaster in a slow, lazy turn to the southwest, as if a child had been playing with toy bricks, and dwarfed by the sheer scope of the desert itself. Movement caught his eyes, beyond the pyramids, where the Giza Road struck out into the desert, a multitude of moving dots, their colour little different to that of the sand but each accompanied by a splash of black shadow from the morning sun.

'Camels,' he yelled to Gorski, pointing down. 'Must be a thousand of the buggers.'

On sudden impulse he pushed the Lancaster into a dive, ignoring the cries of alarm from his crew and pulling up a bare two hundred feet from the ground, to send the massive bomber screaming over the herd of camels at what he knew from experience must have seemed little more than head height. The animals scattered in every direction, running in blind panic, to Henry's delight, and as he began to climb again he was rewarded with the sight of a camel herder shaking his fist at the plane. For a moment there was only the roar of the engines as he sought for height once more, before Bunker's voice sounded from his headset.

'Got you your first arse shot there, Skipper. Fifty of 'em, all in a row and as brown as berries. Bit ugly mind.'

Both Algiers and Dakar proved disappointing, the first a brief relay stop with time only for refuelling and routine checks to the Lancaster, the second bustling with American airmen but a good distance outside the city, while none of them could find the energy to chase after girls in any event. The next morning they set off for Ascension Island, now flying almost due south over blue ocean and with a United States Air Force colonel aboard, Millard Jackson, a large man with an effusive but pompous manner who insisted on being addressed by his full rank. By the time Green Mountain came into view Henry was seething with poorly suppressed irritation for the man's attitude, and it was with great relief that he brought Jazzy Jess to a standstill on the concrete of Wideawake Airfield at the end of a trio of USAF Liberators. Nearby, a Stars and Stripes flapped briskly above the cluster of buildings.

'Ascension Island's ours, isn't it?' Ginger queried as he climbed down from the Lancaster.

'American flag, American bombers,' Colonel Jackson told him. 'Looks American to me.'

'I imagine we're letting them use it,' Henry remarked, glancing around.

The air was hot but fresh, the island sky wide and a rich blue, strangely open after Egypt.

'You Limeys ain't got a lot of say in that kind of thing, not nowadays,' Jackson answered him. 'OK, now I've hitched a ride with you boys I've got a day to see me the sights. I need a driver. Truscott, you'll do.'

Henry was about to give the demand a curt retort when he caught a signal from Bunker.

'That would be an honour, Colonel, sir,' he managed.

'Damn right it would,' Jackson answered him.

'May I suggest a couple of my men as an escort?' Henry suggested, responding to Bunker's continuing signals. 'Pilot Officer Sloper and Sergeant Gorski perhaps?'

'Yeah, why not?' Jackson responded. 'Sort out your papers and get back here on the double. You, Gorski, get me a jeep.'

Gorski saluted and started for the airfield buildings at a smart walk, while Henry went to greet a group of men approaching from the same direction. With the formalities complete he made his way to where Gorski was climbing out of a jeep marked with a white US star. He took the driving seat with Gorski beside him, still wondering what Bunker had in mind as they made their way from Wideawake Field and towards Georgetown.

The town proved to be tiny, no more than a collection of

low white houses around the nineteenth-century fortifications, but far busier than Henry had expected, with great numbers of servicemen, mainly US Army but also air force and a fair few British. There were several bars, including the Long Beach Shack, outside which he was ordered to park and wait. The moment the Colonel had disappeared through the doors he turned to his companions.

'So what's the game?'

'Can you imagine what GIs will pay for snaps of one of their own bigwigs on the job?' Bunker answered. 'An' he's a right bastard an' all.'

Henry considered the proposition for no more than a moment before replying.

'We've got to try. Have you got your Bolsey?'

'Never without it.'

'Right. Here's some money. Find a girl. Bribe her to make a pass at the Yank and we'll take it from there. Gorski you go with him. We don't want any trouble with pimps.'

Both men left, disappearing behind the Long Beach Shack while Henry stayed at his post. Ten minutes passed, and half an hour, with no sign of either his companions or the Colonel, when Bunker suddenly appeared from the direction of the beach, sliding into the seat beside Henry as he spoke up.

'She's called Maria, Brazilian girl with a pair of knockers I'd give a week's pay just to see, ten for a feel. Works at in the kitchens at Fort Thornton, but she seems game.'

'Where?' Henry demanded.

'In the bar,' Bunker replied. 'She knows the staff. Gorski's in there too, keeping an eye on things.'

'Well done,' Henry told him. 'Now all we have to do is wait.'

An hour passed, and a second, before Colonel Jackson finally emerged from the Long Beach Shack. He had a bottle in one hand and his other arm around the waist of girl with skin the colour of mahogany and a spectacular bush of crinkly black hair. Bunker's description of her breasts hardly did them justice, while her full, swaying hips implied an equally fine bottom behind. She was also taller than Jackson and was clearly helping to support him as he approached the car. All she seemed to have on was a short, canary yellow dress and a pair of flat, cork-soled shoes, because from the way her breasts moved under the light material it was obvious she had no bra on, making him wonder if she had no knickers either.

'Make way for Colonel by-the-grace-of-God Millard Jackson,' Jackson called. 'Hey you, what's-yer-name, the Limey flyboy, find me a hotel. This piece of cute black tail is gonna get a portion of Texas beefsteak, oh yes she is!'

He flung himself down in the car, pulling the girl, who was presumably Maria, in behind him so hard that instead of landing on the seat she sprawled across his lap, causing her dress to fly up and briefly exposing her well-fleshed black bottom, clad only in the smallest and tightest pair of knickers Henry had ever seen, made from the same bright yellow cotton as her dress and stretched taut across the bulging curves of her cheeks, to which the Colonel immediately applied a resounding smack. Henry had turned to look and found himself unable to restrain a grin.

'You keep your eyes to yourself, boy,' Jackson told him. 'This ain't for the likes of you, is it doll?'

Maria didn't answer, but was smiling cheerfully and teasing the Colonel's leg as they set off. Henry had no idea where he was going, but he had no sooner turned the corner at the end of the road when he saw a hotel sign up ahead, with Gorski standing beneath. Once more he drew to a stop, leaving Jackson doing his best to get Maria's dress off as he went in to book a room. The tiny foyer was crowded and the owners plainly used to the behaviour of drunken and amorous guests, making no difficulty about Henry's request for adjacent rooms even with Jackson openly fondling Maria's bottom as he pushed in through the doors.

Henry took the keys and quickly made his way up to the second floor, opening the door of the room he'd booked to let Jackson and Maria fall inside. No sooner had the door slammed than Bunker and Gorski appeared at the top of the stairs, both hurrying to join Henry. Inside the room Jackson's voice was clearly audible, praising Maria's chest, which was presumably now bare.

'Ooh booby baby! Come to Papa! Oh boy!'

'Not yet!' Henry hissed as Bunker began to ready his camera. 'I've got the next door room and there are balconies. See if you can climb on to theirs and with a bit of luck you'll be able to get a decent shot, maybe several.'

The three men quickly made their way through the adjoining room and out into the warm Atlantic breeze where the balconies hung over the street below. To Henry's relief the Colonel had failed to shut his curtains, although it was no surprise that he'd left the light on, given what he was doing. Maria was standing in front of him, her magnificent dark body nude but for her little yellow knickers, while he was holding one full black breast in each hand and squeezing them around his face while making delighted bubbling noises.

'Good,' Henry whispered to Bunker, 'but not good enough. They'll never recognise him, not with his face buried between those things.'

'Not through this glass anyway,' Bunker answered. 'It'll all be reflections. You pull the door open and maybe I can get off one good shot.'

Henry nodded and crouched low, watching as the Colonel continued to mould Maria's breasts against his face. She was taking it well, or at least patiently, with her hands on her hips as he nuzzled her, but as he turned his attention to one big, jet black nipple and began to suck her eyes had closed and her lips parted a little in involuntary reaction.

The Colonel's hand had gone to his crotch as he suckled on Maria's chest, to pull a thick, pale cock from the fly of his uniform trousers. He began to masturbate as he sucked and licked at her nipples, with his eyes wide in his gradually reddening face as he tried to take in all the sensation he could from the twin glories he was enjoying. Maria reached out a hand, to take hold of his cock, peeling the thick, rubbery foreskin back to reveal the wet pink glans within.

'That's right, honey child,' he sighed, 'you get the big boy ready, and then I'm gonna fuck these big black boobies, an' fuck your sweet lil' pussy, an' fuck your sweet lil' tail …'

He broke off with a groan, smothering his face between Maria's breasts once more. She'd got him hard, using evidently skilled fingers to stroke at his fat white balls and thick cock until it was straining upright from his fly. Taking it more firmly in her hand, she began to masturbate him, tugging hard and fast at his shaft as if determined to make him spunk before he could carry out his erotic threats. Henry tightened his grip on the handle of the glass paned door that led from the balcony into the room, keen to capture the moment when the colonel spunked all over Maria's belly, which seemed inevitable.

'Not just yet, booby baby,' the Colonel gasped. 'I ain't had my money's worth, not by a long way. Now you just sit down on the bed, honey child, and push those fat black mamas together to make me a slide. I'm gonna fuck your titties, and I'm gonna fuck 'em good!'

Maria made a face but obeyed, sitting down to squeeze her breasts together around the Colonel's cock. He immediately began to fuck in her cleavage, with the fat red knob of his bloated cock popping up and down between the soft, dark pillows of her breasts.

'That's the way!' he crowed. 'Ride 'em cowboy, ride them big black puppies to Heaven and back! Hell, you are something! I swear it, you are! You are the best damn bit of juicy black tail this side of New Orleans, with your big black titties an' your fat black ass. Wee doggie, am I gonna have fun tonight!'

His face was a picture, red and glossy with sweat, his eyes wild and his mouth running with drool, while they also had a fine view of Maria, with her huge breasts in her hands and her back pulled in to show off the elegant dip of her spine and the swell of her well-fleshed bottom, with the tiny yellow knickers doing more to accentuate her curves than to conceal them.

'This is the right time,' Gorski suggested.

Henry nodded, pulled the handle gently down and eased the door wide. Bunker moved forward, the camera flashed, capturing the scene at what seemed the perfect angle. The Colonel didn't react, still plunging his cock up and down in Maria's cleavage, mumbling about black tail and black titties as his thrusts grew ever faster, oblivious to all else, his eyes now tight shut and his jaw clenched.

'Again!' Henry hissed. 'He's coming!'

Bunker was already fumbling the new flash bulb into place and an instant later had raised the camera. Once more the room exploded in a blaze of light, at the exact instant a great gout of thick, white spunk erupted from the Colonel's cock to splash in Maria's face and over the fat brown pillows of her breasts. Still he failed to notice, his face set in ecstasy as he finished himself off, now easing his cock slowly up and down in the now slimy tunnel of Maria's cleavage.

'One more,' Bunker said, raising the camera just as the Colonel finally realised that something was amiss.

The flash bulb burst just as the Colonel stepped back, his glistening, slippery cock on full view, his face set in an expression of outrage and surprise. For a moment the scene held, before the Colonel found his wits, charging forward with one arm already drawn back to drive a fist into Henry's face. Henry ducked. Gorski's own fist shot out, a single, clean blow that connected with the American's jaw and knocked him back onto the bed, where he stayed.

'Thank you,' Henry told the big Pole, 'and thank you too, Maria. An excellent performance if I may say so. Give the lady a handkerchief, somebody.'

Maria had barely reacted, save to cover her naked breasts and then regret the impulse as she discovered just how badly soiled the Colonel had left her. Taking the handkerchief offered by Gorski, she began to mop up, while the others considered the unconscious American.

'I expect he needs some fresh air,' Henry suggested, 'preferably somewhere a long way from the airfield, and the town. With any luck we'll be in the air before he wakes up.'

'English Bay,' Maria suggested. 'I'll show you. What a rude man he is, speaking to me like that!'

She had given the Colonel's now flaccid cock a contemptuous little flick of her fingers as she spoke, then returned to her toilette.

'Absolutely,' Henry agreed. 'No manners at all.'

*   *   *

Henry was grinning as he pushed the throttles of Jazzy Jess home. Revenge, he reflected, might not be the most noble of motives, but it was immensely satisfying. They had left Colonel Jackson asleep at the top of the beach by English Bay, stark naked but with Maria's diminutive yellow knickers tied around his cock and balls. The memory made Henry laugh, and not for the first time he wondered if the colonel would choose to walk back to Georgetown naked or in nothing but a pair of very obviously feminine knickers.

What did seem certain was that their escapade would not be reported, simply because of the level upon level of embarrassment Jackson would have been forced to bring on himself had he done so, to say nothing of the photographs now resting safely in Bunker's camera. In fact the evening had been highly satisfying all round, his sole regret that there had been no opportunity to indulge himself with Maria, whose glorious curves and easy, playful manner had left him badly in need of relief.

With Jazzy Jess safely at cruising altitude and the noise of the Merlins a steady, rhythmic roar, he once more allowed his mind to wander, reflecting on the beauty of Maria's body. Having left Ascension Island as soon as they could get clearance, they were now ahead of schedule, which meant they would be able to spend a day in Dakar without arousing disapproval. The rest of the crew were keen, and despite his desire to get back to Cairo and Sally Green, Henry was tempted, because having missed out on Maria he knew the regret would linger at least until he had managed to thoroughly indulge himself with another tall, well-fleshed black girl. Just the thought sent the blood to his cock and he spoke into his microphone.

'All right, overnight in Dakar it is.'

The crew responded clearly, all but the Egg, who had been the most determined to have a night in the African city.

'Did you catch that, Egg?' Henry asked.

Still there was no response.

'Rear Gunner?' Henry queried. 'Sergeant Filbert, answer

me will you!?'

'Maybe he's asleep again?' Ginger suggested.

'That or the silly bugger's fallen out,' Henry replied. 'Take over, will you, Gorski. I'm going back.'

He left the flight engineer to take over the controls and moved back down the fuselage of the Lancaster, nodding to Slick at the radio operator's table and climbing over the spars to where he could see into the tail. The Egg was there, only not in the rear turret where he belonged but seated on the Elsan. His trousers were around his ankles, along with a pair of issue underpants, while his legs were well spread, as if he were really on the loo, although the expression on his face suggested a level of ecstasy far beyond simple relief. This was hardly surprising, as between his open thighs knelt Maria, her yellow dress turned up under her armpits, her full, dark bottom thrust out towards Henry, her big boobs bouncing to the rhythm as she bobbed her head up and down on the Egg's cock. His eyes were closed and he was plainly oblivious to Henry's presence.

Annoyance, amusement and lust were all vying for first place among Henry's emotions as he took the scene in, but from the way the blood was moving to his cock it was plain which would win. Seen from behind, Maria was an alluring sight, the full, dark moon of her bottom resting lightly on her ankles, her cheeks wide enough to give a clear view of the neatly puckered star of her anus, while the swell of her cunt would have been on equally full show had she not had a hand between her legs to massage her wet, pink slit as she sucked on the Egg's cock. He, in sharp contrast, was small, hairy and quite exceptionally ugly, making Henry wonder how he had persuaded her to perform such an intimate act, and on such short acquaintance. Only one solution seemed to fit the facts, and as Maria finally realised that she was being watched and came off the Egg's cock with a gasp of surprise, Henry responded with a smile.

'Paying for a trip to Cairo, my dear?' he called out, lifting his voice above the roar of the engines with difficulty.

The Egg began to splutter out an explanation, but it was neither audible nor comprehensible and Henry raised a hand to cut him off before addressing Maria once more.

'Not that I mind, you understand, but it's traditional to come to terms with the pilot rather than the rear gunner.'

Maria nodded her understanding and reached out as if to unzip Henry's trousers, clearly happy to oblige. It was exactly what he needed, and after a single dubious glance at the gnarled and crooked erection sticking up out of the Egg's fly he let her get on with it, pulling his cock and balls free to lick and kiss at both while she used her hand on the rear gunner's already excited tool. Henry closed his eyes, trying to ignore the presence of the Egg as his cock began to stiffen to the ministrations of Maria's tongue. She was skilled, and obviously experienced, knowing exactly where to lick to give the most pleasure, so that in no time at all he was rock hard.

She took him in hand, transferring her mouth to Egg's cock, taking him deep only to pull back and with a sudden motion press down once more, allowing his straining helmet to penetrate the full, tight purse of her lips. The Egg gave a startled grunt, then another as Maria once more took him deep, to suck down what he had done in her mouth and swallow, all the while with her hand still working on the shaft of Henry's erection. He was nearly there himself, holding back from orgasm only by an effort of will, but determined to take full advantage of her willingness and evident delight in men's cocks.

Maria once more took Henry in her mouth, leaving the Egg grinning happily as he put his cock away. She was squatting down, one hand between her thighs, playing with herself as she squeezed at his balls with the other, all the while doing wonderful things to his cock with her lips and tongue. Suddenly he could hold back no longer. His cock jerked, Maria's grip tightened on his balls even as she took him deep and he had come, spunking up down her throat to have her swallow and swallow again, even as she herself came with a powerful shudder that ran right through her body.

'I say, but you Brazilian girls really know what you're doing,' Henry sighed as he slid down onto the spar.

'You like me then?' Maria asked, smiling.

'Absolutely, top notch,' Henry replied, 'and you've certainly earned your lift to Cairo, although as skipper, and in the interests of fair play and all that sort of thing, I don't suppose you'd be frightfully kind and share the benefits of your experience with the rest of my crew?'

'You want me to suck their penises?' Maria asked.

'Er … yes, if that's all right?'

Maria merely shrugged, and as Henry turned back to the front of the plane he realised that there was already a queue, with Slick, Ginger and Bunker all waiting expectantly in line.

Chapter Four

'JOLLY GOOD SPORT, THAT Maria,' Ginger said as the six crew members set out from the gates of Dakar Airfield. 'I mean to say, six chaps in a row!'

'Quite an appetite,' Henry agreed, 'and she was certainly enjoying herself. Some girls are like that, of course, can't get enough.'

'Took me three months to talk my missus out of her knickers,' Bunker put in, 'and God knows how many boxes of chocs.'

'I must have spent a fortune on chocolates over the years,' Slick agreed, 'and half the time all you get is a peck on the cheek.'

'Yes,' Ginger sighed, 'and not to mention roses, and dinners, and trips to the cinema.'

'You English,' Gorski said. 'In Poland, the girls are not such prudes.'

'I knew a girl once,' the Egg supplied. 'Queenie her name was. Her old man was a farmer over Shrewton way. If I bought her a box of chocs she'd let me stuff half of 'em up her fanny and lick up the melted chocolate. She'd eat the other half while I was busy, and if she was in a dirty mood she'd let me do it from the back, so I could pop some up her arsehole and all. Good that was.'

There was a long moment of silence.

'Right,' said Henry. 'Well, if that concludes Sergeant Filbert's reminiscences, we ought to discuss the operation. The first thing is, this is Frog territory, so most of the girls won't be able to understand a word you say. On the other hand there are sure to be plenty of knocking shops. Dirty bastards, the Frogs. So what I suggest we do is find ourselves a decent-looking establishment and Ginger and I will try to fix a party rate. How's that?'

'What about girls for the pictures?' Bunker asked.

'I'll fix it so that we can swap round,' Henry told him. 'That way you'll be able to get a few shots of each girl.'

'How about bringing 'em back?' Bunker went on.

'I'm not sure about that,' Henry told him. 'I mean to say, Maria's aboard already, so no harm in it if you do find a willing girl, as long as she's pretty enough, and preferably speaks English. But it's a shaky do at the best of times, what with the snowdrops on the gates and having to get them out once we're back. Then there's a chance we'll be told to pick up another passenger.'

'How about Maria then?' Ginger queried.

'We'll stick her in the bomb bay if we have to,' Henry told him, 'but let's hope it doesn't come to that. Now if we can just flag down one of these trucks we'll be there in no time.'

Henry watched, smiling happily to himself as the two girls kneeling in front of him applied agile tongues to his cock and balls. They were as skilled as Maria, perhaps more so, which was no surprise when they were working at Les Mademoiselles d'Afrique, the most exclusive brothel in Dakar. The crew had had the good fortune to pick up a truck driven by a man who'd been chauffeur to a local commander and knew the city in detail. He'd made several recommendations, from which Henry and Ginger had chosen Les Mademoiselles, although they'd been unable to get a party rate, leaving the others to try less expensive establishments a little further down the road, with the French driver now acting as comrade and translator.

The brothel was a fine, four-storey building in the French colonial style, and clearly prosperous, while their reception had been positively genteel. A doorman of imposing bulk but immaculate manners had ushered them inside to a large reception room upholstered in crimson plush, gilt and mirrors. They had been served glasses of champagne, which even seemed to be the real thing, while fourteen girls had been lined up for their inspection. It was not an easy choice, with girls of every colour and figure, but not one of them unappealing. Each had introduced herself with a curtsy and a smile, save one, a stately Amazon clad in skin-tight leather and holding a long, single-tailed whip who stood back with her arms folded beneath her impressive chest and a faint sneer on her lips.

Ginger had spent a long time in goggled-eyed admiration, apparently tempted by the Amazon but finally selecting Michelle, a tiny, pale waif with an appealingly fragile body, huge dark eyes and black hair in a bob-cut but a brisk, no-nonsense manner. Henry took longer still, sipping his champagne as he considered his options. None of the girls were actually naked, but some were in no more than heels, stockings and corsets, leaving breasts, bottoms and sex bare, while others had on flimsy peignoirs or dishevelled day dress. The leather-clad dominatrix had a certain appeal, but while a whipping was always stimulating it wasn't clear whether or not he would be able to dish out the same in return, which would have spoiled the fun.

Several of the girls were clearly locals, tall, elegant women with skin darker even than Maria's but long, straight hair caught up in ornaments of silver or ivory, very different to either European girls or the Cairene tarts he was used to. Two in particular stood out, Aissatou and Khadija, the tallest of all and so alike they might well have been twins, which proved to be the case. A brief word with Madame Rossignol, the proprietress, an exchange of currencies and they had been his for an hour, so that as they knelt to lick his genitals in a comfortable room on the second floor he was reflecting on how much easier sex was when one simply paid for what one wanted.

'I'm ready,' he announced when they had taken him to the point at which he had to stop or simply come in their faces. 'On the bed with you.'

Neither girl spoke English, but pidgin French and a few hand signals, finishing with a slap to Aissatou's neatly turned rump, quickly got his meaning across. With two girls to play with it seemed sensible to go underneath, so he quickly stripped off his remaining clothes and lay down on the bed, holding up his erection as he beckoned to them. Both were kneeling beside him and immediately crawled forward – Khadija to throw one long leg across his middle and ease herself down on his cock, Aissatou to straddle his face, presenting him with her bare black bottom as she looked back and down over her shoulder with a quizzical expression. Henry nodded.

'That's the way, my girl,' he said, 'you just sit yourself down, right in my …'

He didn't finish, as she had lowered her bottom onto his face, giggling as she spread her muscular little cheeks to his mouth and letting out a little, pleased cry as his tongue found her anus and he began to lick. Khadija was also enjoying herself, bouncing enthusiastically on his cock, with both girls gasping and giggling as they rode him. Henry was in heaven, his cock deep in one girl's cunt and his tongue up another's bottom hole, which left both hands free to explore their elegant, slender waists and firm, pointed breasts.

Aissatou began to grind her bottom in his face, then abruptly pushed back, pressing her sex to his mouth and spreading her cheeks to his gaze, so that as he began to lick cunt the glistening black knot of her anus was directly above his eyes. It was too much for him. Already he'd begun to push up into Khadiya's willing hole, and as her sister began to come, so did he, only for her to dismount at the last instant, grab his cock and take it deep in her mouth, sucking urgently and swallowing her mouthful of come.

As his orgasm began to fade Henry was still licking Aissatou's cunt, happy to give her the pleasure she wanted and flattered that he had brought a professional girl to orgasm. Even when she was done she stayed siting on his face for a long moment, wriggling her bottom to encourage him to lick her anus as she chattered excitedly to her sister in their native language. Henry obliged, massaging his still half-stiff cock as he licked at the tight brown dimple between her cheeks, wondering if he could manage to come a second time before his time was up.

'*Fais moi une pipe*,' he ordered, pointing at his cock as Assiatou finally dismounted, only for Khadija to immediately throw a leg over his head, evidently wanting the same treatment he'd given her sister. 'Oh … well, anything to oblige.'

Khadija settled her bottom into his face, anus to mouth and he began to lick, the girls now giggling openly together for what they were doing, until Assiatou went quiet as she took Henry's penis into her mouth. He relaxed, enjoying Khadija's bottom as his cock began to grow once more, slowly but surely swelling up to the skilled motions of Assiatou's tongue and the pleasure of licking her sister's anus. Before long he was hard again, and now sure he could make it, when Khadija abruptly rose and turned to present him with her cunt, talking urgently in her own language and pointing at the bright pink bud of her clitoris as she held her lips apart to show herself off.

Henry obliged, lapping at her slit while her sister continued to work on his cock, now with one hand on his balls and a finger down between his cheeks, squeezing and tickling to keep his excitement up while he brought Khadija to orgasm. She came quickly, rubbing her cunt on his mouth and squeezing her breasts, her eyes closed in ecstasy as she cried out to her sister. Assiatou immediately rose up, to take Khadija in her arms, holding her until she had spent her orgasm, when their lips met in an open mouthed kiss.

Khadija dismounted, still in her sister's arms and Henry rolled to the side. His cock was still stiff, although aching a little, and as he watched the two girls kiss his erection showed no signs of going down. They saw that he was ready and turned him quizzical looks, but he nodded and motioned for them to carry on. Both smiled and returned to their embrace, leaving Henry to return to the chair where he'd first sat down for them to bring him to erection.

He had ordered up a bottle of iced Beaujolais, and poured himself a glass, taking a good swallow before settling down to play with his cock and sip wine while he watched the two sisters cuddle. They obviously knew what he wanted, and seemed keen in any case, their caresses quickly growing less comforting and more sexual as they began to stroke and kiss each other's breasts and bottoms. Henry stared entranced, his own arousal growing with theirs as eager fingers found wet cunts and tongues began to lap at hard nipples and between ready slits.

Before long they'd gone head to tail, faces buried between each others thighs, licking eagerly, with Assiatou on top, her trim black bottom poised over her sister's face, and as she began to tickle Khadija's anus Henry could wait no more. Rising quickly, he crossed to the bed, to push his straining erection in up Assiatou's cunt, fucking her deep as her sister began to suck on his balls. His hands went to Assiatou's hips, pulling himself in as deep as he could go, then to her bottom, to spread her lithe black cheeks and admire the tight little hole he had taken so much pleasure in licking, along with the junction between his cock and her straining cunt.

He began to spank her, drawing a squeak of surprise muffled somewhat because she had her face buried in her sister's cunt, but she immediately pushed her bottom back and up, offering herself for more. Henry obliged, slapping her cheeks turn and turn about as he fucked her, now with his balls deep in Khadija's mouth. With that he felt himself start to come, an irresistible urge accompanied by a wrenching sensation as his balls gave up their load for the second time in quick succession. His teeth were gritted as he filled Assiatou's vagina with spunk, but it felt too good to stop and he kept himself deep inside her, ignoring a plaintive squeak from Khadija as the mess squashed out of her sister's hole and into her face.

As Henry stepped out into the street the brief African dusk had begun to descend on Dakar, with lights coming on in the windows and a sudden coolness in the air. He glanced up and down the street, unsure what to do with himself. At the end of his hour with the two girls he had come back down to the foyer, only to find that Ginger had paid for a second hour with Michelle, while he had no idea which of the other local establishments the driver and the rest of the crew had decided to patronise. Bunker had said he would come back with his camera to see if was possible to get some pictures, but there was no sign of him.

A bar and restaurant across the road looked promising, as the vigorous sex had left him hungry, while the champagne and Beaujolais had provided just enough alcohol to leave him wanting more. He walked across, to settle at a table on the open street, where he was presently served with a carafe of white wine and a plate of the local speciality, *thiéboudienne*, which proved to be like a thick bouillabaisse and quite delicious.

By the time he had finished his meal he was feeling pleasantly relaxed, with his hunger for both sex and food thoroughly satisfied, while the wine he was still drinking had brought him a happy flush. None of the others had returned, but he was rather glad, enjoying a rare moment of solitude, and when Ginger finally emerged from the doors of Les Mademoiselles, Henry raised his glass in lazy salute.

'Care to join me?' he offered.

'Brandy, please,' Ginger answered, plainly agitated. 'Look, we're bringing Michelle back to Cairo. That's all right, isn't it?'

'Your pretty little French piece?' Henry answered. 'Yes, I should say so, as long as we can get her safely aboard. What's the gen?'

'She was a secretary with the Vichy officials over here,' Ginger explained, 'so she figures that if she goes home she's likely to get her head shaved for her and goodness knows what else, while she doesn't want to stay here either.'

'Fair enough,' Henry agreed. 'A damsel in distress and all that. I take it you told her we'll need some dirty pictures?'

'That's fine,' Ginger assured him. 'The problem is getting her clear. Madame Rossignol's a right old battleaxe, apparently. She canes the girls for the slightest infraction.'

'Oh yes?' Henry queried, intrigued by the thought of the petite Michelle bending to have a cane applied across the cheeks of the pert little bottom she had wiggled so temptingly at them to draw Ginger's attention.

'Yes,' Ginger went on, 'and in front of customers, more often than not. They're not even allowed out alone, but have to go in twos or threes, and never for more than a couple of hours at a time. Whoever comes out with her is sure to get the cane if they're separated ...'

'Six of the best isn't so bad,' Henry interrupted.

'... so I suggested she chose a girl who wants to come too,' Ginger finished.

'Two girls?' Henry queried. 'Well they're lookers, no question there, but ... all right, in for a penny and all that. Where are we meeting her?'

'Down the road, on the corner of the Rue Mangin,' Ginger answered, glancing at his watch, 'in ten minutes?'

'Ten minutes?' Henry demanded.

'Apparently the place gets busy later and they won't be able to get out at all.'

'Very well,' Henry agreed, 'but we'll have to get them straight back to the airfield. Madame Rossignol's bully boys may be polite, but they look tough and I'm damned if I'm spending my evening playing hide and seek with them around the streets of Dakar. The others will just have to get back under their own steam.'

He joined Ginger in a glass of brandy and paid the score before they made their way to the agreed rendezvous. Michelle was already their, her tiny figure unmistakable despite the long coat she now wore. With her were Assiatou and Khadija. Henry gave each a polite nod before speaking to Michelle in his best schoolboy French, only to have her respond in rather better English.

'We thank you, Mr Truscott, Mr Green.'

'Thank us when we're in the air,' Henry responded, 'first we have to get past the snowdrops and inside Jazzy Jess.'

'Excuse?' Michelle responded. 'I do not understand.'

'Never mind,' Henry told her. 'Just come with us and do as I say.'

He stuck his hand out to signal what appeared to be a cab, an ancient phaeton drawn by a mule and driven by a grinning local who was clearly in no doubt about the girls' profession despite their cloaks.

'Airfield,' Henry ordered as they climbed aboard, 'but not the main gate, er ... *au bord de la ... à la côte de l'aéroport* ... what the Hell, just go where I point.'

He jabbed his finger in the general direction of the airfield and the driver responded with a lewd wink as he gave the mule a flick of his whip.

'One thing's for certain,' Henry stated as he squeezed himself in between Assiatou and Khadija, 'when I signed up for this show I never expected to be smuggling tarts out of Senegal. They ought to have put it on the recruiting posters.'

Ginger responded with a nervous nod, clearly worried about pursuit, but the streets were bustling with people and vehicles and it seemed to Henry highly unlikely that the absence of the girls would have been discovered. Sitting back in his seat, he put an arm around each of his companions, and as Michelle nuzzled up to Ginger's side he too had begun to relax.

The trip out to the airfield was uneventful and Henry had quickly directed the driver out onto a dry, scrub-grown waste where a rickety fence was all that separated them from the line of aircraft drawn up in readiness for scheduled departures. The Jazzy Jess was one of three Lancasters, and was shadowed by the bulk of an equally massive Short Stirling, making it easy to get the girls aboard so long as they managed to avoid the sentries. These worked in pairs, bored-looking French servicemen with their rifles at the slope and cigarettes in their hands as they sauntered along the inside of the perimeter. Despite the night, a gibbous moon and light from the airfield buildings made it next to impossible to cross the fence without being noticed.

'Bribery?' Henry suggested.

'I haven't a great deal on me,' Ginger protested, patting his pockets.'

'I don't mean with money,' Henry told him. 'We're British airmen, aren't we? They'll realise we're out on a lark, so as long as we keep them happy they're not going to make any fuss. Michelle, if you would be so kind ...'

He left the sentence unfinished, but she had understood,

responding with a brief grimace and shrugging her cloak from her shoulders. Underneath she wore only shoes, stockings and a satin corset that showed brilliant green gleams from the distant lights, along with a matching collar.

'It was the easiest way for her to get out without arousing suspicions,' Ginger explained.

'I'm not complaining,' Henry responded, 'it's a very fetching outfit, and just the thing for our purposes. 'Er ... Khadija, Assiatou?'

He gestured to the two black girls, who promptly opened their own coats to reveal similar outfits, save that their corsets were banana yellow and scarlet. The guards had seen them and were approaching at a run, worrying Henry but only for a moment. Michelle addressed them, her voice cool and teasing, and after no more than a brief exchange all five of them had been helped over the fence and onto the airfield.

Henry and Ginger walked over to lean on one of Jazzy Jess's huge wheels, talking quietly together as they listened to the muted giggles and soft slurping sounds coming from the shadows beneath the wing of the neighbouring Short Stirling. All three girls had gone with the guards, and were obviously sucking their cocks, although it was impossible to see who was doing what, while Henry had barely recovered from his own exertions and felt more gratitude than arousal for what the girls were doing.

'We're going to have to go back over the fence and come in again through the front gates to have our passes stamped,' he explained to Ginger. 'Still, they seem sensible girls, so once they're in I think we can rely on them to lie doggo until the morning. Besides, Maria will look after them. Algiers shouldn't be a problem, which just leaves getting them unloaded at Cairo. Four girls, eh? Best damn cargo we ever carried.'

From the darkness beneath the Short Stirling's wing a grunt and an odd, wet sound indicated that one of the guards had come in a girl's mouth.

The rest of the night passed without incident and Henry was

pleased to discover that the gossip in the officers' mess involved neither aggrieved American colonels nor girls in brightly coloured corsets and very little else. He had quickly secured permission to leave, with neither passengers nor cargo, but lost no time in assembling his crew in case something came up at the last minute. Even as they walked out towards the Jazzy Jess he couldn't help but glance back over his shoulder, but if there was anything amiss he could see no evidence of it.

'Good time last night, Skipper?' Bunker asked as they fell into step.

'Yes,' Henry responded. 'Excellent in fact. And you?'

'Cracking.'

'Did you get any pictures? I thought you were going to come back to *Les Mademoiselles d'Afrique* to take some?'

'We were too busy, Skipper, if you know what I mean.'

'I can imagine. Not that it matters anyway, because I had two exquisite local girls and Ginger hooked up with a sweet little French piece called Michelle. They were keen to get out of here, so we've signed them up for your pin-up parade. They're in Jess along with Maria. Michelle's tiny, but perfect, like a little porcelain doll, and you wait until you see my two. They're twins; tall, slender, skin like ebony and the roundest little bottoms ...'

'I know. I've met 'em.'

'You have?'

'Sure, when we came back last night.'

They had reached Jazzy Jess and Bunker pulled the door open, climbing aboard before Henry could ask further questions. A last glance back across the concrete and Henry followed, to find himself face to face with a girl, and not one of those he'd expected to see. She was small, compact, with an olive complexion, huge dark eyes and a great deal of black hair piled on top of her head and decorated with a large, red flower. Two small, pert breasts showed between the sides of the sheepskin flying jacket which appeared to be all she had on.

'Who the Hell are you?' he demanded, more or less by instinct, and as his eyes adapted to the dim interior of the Lancaster he realised that she was far from alone.

62

'She's called Jacinta,' Slick volunteered. 'She was dancing in one of the bars we visited last night. She's Portuguese. And this is Zokie, from Benin, who does this amazing trick with a snake, and this is Lola, who was recommended by Jean-Pierre, you know, the French fellow who was driving us last night, and at the back is Ainikki, who … I'm not really sure where she came from, but we were a bit tiddly by then.'

'Plastered, more like,' Henry responded. 'That means we're carrying eight girls, Slick, which is rather more than I had anticipated.'

'You did say …,' Bunker began.

'I know what I said,' Henry retorted, 'but I was expecting one or two extra, not seven!'

'Don't you like them, Skipper?' the Egg asked, sounding hurt.

'I like them,' Henry responded, 'but don't you think eight is rather more than we need?'

'No,' the Egg answered, the tip of a sharp, greyish pink tongue flicking out briefly to moisten his lips.

Henry shook his head and moved aside to let the rest of the crew aboard as he appraised the new girls. There was no doubt the crew had chosen well, especially allowing for the influence of drink. Zokie not only had classically feminine proportions but skin even darker than the Dakar girls, almost true black, with a lustrous tone that hinted more at midnight blue than brown, while her large eyes and a slight pout to her full lips added an exciting touch of vulnerability to her appeal. Lola appeared to be French, or possibly Spanish, with warm, Mediterranean looks and a challenging glitter to her eyes, while Ainikki was tall, svelte and blonde, with her luxurious hair curled in plaits above each ear.

'She's not German is she? Ainikki, I mean,' he demanded as Gorski climbed aboard.

'Finnish,' Gorski explained.

'Which is what we'll be if their Airships catch us. Oh well, we'd better get off the ground, and fast, before some nosy blighter decides to interfere. And another thing, we can't have them running loose during take off, or we're likely to end up in the drink, on this runway. Where's Maria? Leave her alone, Slick.'

The Brazilian girl came back from where she'd been perched on the radio-operator's table, with Slick apparently intent on talking her out of her dress once more.

'You seem a sensible girl,' he stated. 'Keep an eye on the others, will you? I don't suppose you speak French though, do you? All right, you're the boss girl. Let's make you a Corporal. And Michelle, you seem to be the only one who can speak to everybody, so you're Lance-Corporal and Maria's two-I-C. For now, keep them in the middle of the aircraft, between the front two spars, and keep 'em still. All clear?'

Both girls nodded their agreement, allowing Henry to move forward, only to find Bunker still not at his station.

'How about some pictures, Skipper?' the bombardier suggested. 'Once we're in the air, I mean. I reckon every bomber boy in the pack'll pay for a shot of a naked bint at his station, and a lot more besides. I've got plenty of film.'

'That's true,' Henry admitted. 'Once we're under way then.'

He settled himself into his seat and began the familiar routine of preparing for take-off, doing his best to put the girls out of his mind, although even when the roar of the Merlins had drowned out the excited chatter from behind him the rich tang of their mingled perfume made it difficult to think of anything else. Fortunately Maria and Michelle seemed to have the others in good order, while their combined weight was insignificant compared to a normal load, allowing him to pull Jazzy Jess into the air without difficulty. No sooner were they at cruising altitude than Bunker popped up from his position in the front turret, his homely face set in an expectant grin. Henry merely jerked a thumb back down the length of the fuselage, receiving a hurried salute in return.

Several hundred miles of scrubland and then open desert had passed beneath them before Bunker appeared once more, now grinning from ear to ear and with his uniform jacket half undone, also his fly. Behind him was Michelle, also smiling, and stark naked.

'Your turn, Skipper,' Bunker shouted. 'How about some with little Michelle on your lap? Then you can hand over to George and we can pretend she's flying Jess.'

'You're going to get me court-martialled, Bunker,' Henry replied, but Michelle was already wriggling her bottom into place on his lap.

She felt warm, soft and very much alive, causing his cock to react on the instant, which made her giggle just as Bunker took the first picture. For the second she put her hand to the top button of his uniform, and for the third swung her legs across his to sit facing him as if his cock were inside her, which by then he was earnestly wishing it was. Bunker gave him the thumbs-up and Michelle climbed off, allowing Henry to set the autopilot so that she could take his seat. More pictures followed, before she transferred herself to Gorski's lap and Henry was able to resume his place at the controls, only to find that Michelle's presence had left him with a need too strong to easily be denied.

'Keep us level,' he ordered Gorski. 'I say, Michelle, you wouldn't mind giving me a helping hand, would you? You've rather, um ...'

Her smile was all the answer he needed, but as they moved back down the fuselage he quickly discovered that he wasn't the only one who'd reacted to the warmth and nearness of the girls. Ginger was at his station, rather shyly fondling Jacinta's bottom as she stroked at his cock through his trousers, but Slick had no such reserve, with his back to his table and a long, pink erection and a pair of rounded balls protruding from his fly as the twins gave him their skilled attention. Zokie and Lola were watching, while both Maria and Ainikki were attending to the needs of the Egg, who had them bent over the tail spar as he licked and groped at their bottoms while tugging frantically on his crooked erection.

With the exception of Ginger, none of them seemed to have the slightest concern for modesty, which made it a great deal easier for Henry as he made himself as comfortable as possible on the rear wing spar and tugged down his zip to allow Michelle to get at his cock. She perched herself on his lap with an encouraging wiggle of her bottom and took him in hand, rolling his foreskin back and forth over the sensitive head within as she smiled down at him. Henry kissed her, then took a handful of her bottom, which she stuck out obligingly, allowing him to fondle her at leisure and as intimately as he pleased while she masturbated him. She was so small that his hand cupped the full width of one fleshy little cheek, allowing him to burrow a thumb between her thighs and tease her cunt as his cock grew in her hand.

He was soon stiff, while the wetness of her quim told its own story, but he was still surprised when she suddenly rose and swung her bottom across to the centre of his lap, still holding his cock so that she could guide it up into her body. Henry let her control the pace, her little bottom bouncing in his lap as he reached around to cup her tiny breasts, letting them jiggle and rub against his hands. Her own hands were between her legs, rubbing at her cunt and squeezing his balls as she rode him, so that in just moments she'd brought herself to orgasm on his cock.

Henry was ready himself, and was tempted to bugger her, using the copious juices from her sex to lubricate her anus, only to find her too fast for him, quickly sinking to her knees to take his cock into her mouth. He made no effort to stop her, watching as she first sucked up her own juices and swallowed, then set to work on his erection, using her tongue and lips and teeth to lick and kiss and nibble at his cock with her hand clasped tight around the bottom of his shaft to masturbate him into her mouth.

It took just seconds before a fountain of spunk erupted from his cock, full in her face, splashing her forehead and one eye to leave mascara running down her cheek in a thick, sticky tear as she took him deep in her mouth to swallow the rest. Even then she was still tugging at the base of his cock, until Henry signalled her to stop and relaxed back with a long, satisfied sigh.

The stopover in Algiers passed with no more event than on the way out, although Henry once more found himself immensely grateful to be airborne. A carefully judged paperwork query allowed them to leave at a time which meant they would touch down in Cairo well after dark, but as they flew high over the African coast Henry found himself growing increasingly nervous. He did his best to distract himself, leaving Gorski at the controls while he took Zokie and Ainikki to the middle of the aircraft to have his cock sucked once more. Zokie proved to have all the skill he would have expected of a girl trained in a Dakar brothel, using her pointed pink tongue on his balls and penis with a level skill he was starting to get used to, while Ainikki seemed more of an enthusiastic amateur, enjoying his cock but equally keen on her own pleasure.

With the noise of the engines and their lack of a common language it was impossible to communicate save by action, so that before long he was sat sprawled on the floor on the Lancaster with Zokie curled up beside him, his cock in her mouth while he explored her body, while Ainikki had her bottom pushed out into his face to have her cunt licked from behind, with her pale, smooth cheeks spread wide in his face and her anus pushed to the tip of his nose. He came first, giving Zokie a mouthful of spunk which she obligingly swallowed, but made a point of continuing until both girls had also come, which left them smiling and grateful.

He felt somewhat better once he had returned to his seat, telling himself that the worst which could possibly happen would be a dishonourable discharge, and that as he had no intention of making his career in the RAF it wasn't even important. Nevertheless he remained on edge, and when the lights of Cairo finally appeared on the horizon he leant across to talk directly into Gorski's ear, speaking with what he hoped sounded like real confidence.

'Piece of cake, eh? No flak, no night fighters, unless you count our own cargo. Now look, you've got more common sense than the rest of them. I want you to bail out with the girls. You go first, to make sure they keep away from the props, but brief Maria and Michelle and have Slick standing by at the door. Head north-west until you hit the Khatatba Road and lie doggo until I come for you. Clear?'

Gorski nodded and rose to make his way back down the fuselage. Henry replaced his mouthpiece and spoke again as he turned his attention to the instruments.

'Okay, boys, one more time.'

He called for the attention of the Cairo tower and began to bank Jazzy Jess into a long, slow curve towards the south. The runway lights came into view, bright points against the utter blackness of the ground with the blaze of the city growing ever brighter to the east. Every element of flying the Lancaster had become routine, but landing never failed to put his heart in his mouth and as the lights came up to meet him he found himself mumbling the same familiar prayer he had said each night at his bedside when a child.

The wheels hit with a jolt, then again and they were down, allowing him to throttle back, but only slowly, keeping the Lancaster rolling until the turning circle at the far end of the runway. Adjusting the throttles, he made what seemed a painfully slow turn, bringing Jazzy Jess around almost on her own axis before once more starting down the runway, still at a crawl until Slick's voice came loud into his headset to confirm that all had gone well.

With the girls on the ground and Jazzy Jess safely in her place at the end of the line of Lancasters, Henry felt a great deal more cheerful. All he had to do was get hold of a truck and meet Gorski at the agreed rendezvous, a task easily accomplished once he had been debriefed, as nobody would be surprised that he wanted to go into the city for the rest of the evening.

All went well, and within an hour he and Ginger were moving out towards the Alexandria Road in a three-hundredweight truck. There was nobody to see that he turned north into the desert instead of towards the city, and before long they had pulled up beside the empty Khatatba Road. He flashed the lights to signal Gorski, who rose from behind a clump of straggling bushes like a well attended genie, with the eight girls behind him. Most were in sheepskin flying jackets or wrapped in blankets, but there was still a great deal of naked flesh on display, once more quickening Henry's pulse. He stepped out to help them into the back of the truck, allowing himself a good feel of nubile bottoms and legs, which they didn't seem to mind at all, so that by the time they set off once more he was firmly in the mood for mischief.

'As I said, a piece of cake,' he said happily. 'Well done, boys and girls.'

'Where shall we go?' Ginger asked.

'Not Babu's,' Henry told him. 'I don't want to run into the Gorilla. How about one of the house-boats[4]?'

'With our own girls? Gorski queried.

'Good point,' Henry agreed. 'They'll charge us corkage.'

'El Khalili market?' Ginger suggested. 'We can hire a room above a shop. Besides, the girls will need clothes, and food, and somewhere to stay.'

'Very true,' Henry agreed, 'we mustn't forget the logistics, and everything in its proper order. So who's for a beer, or a perhaps a drop of something stronger?'

Chapter Five

HENRY SWALLOWED A TOT of arrack at a gulp. In front of him stood all eight girls, as if on parade. As NCOs, Maria and Michelle were a little to one side, while the others were lined up in what he, Ginger and Gorski had decided was the most aesthetically pleasing order. To the extreme left was blonde, Finnish Ainikki, followed by the two Mediterranean girls, Lola and Jacinta. Next came Assiatou and Khadija, as like as two peas in a pod, and lastly Zokie. All eight were in matching uniforms, peaked military caps with a scarlet band, smart scarlet dress jackets with the top three buttons undone to allow for the comfort of their breasts and incidentally show off intriguing slices of cleavage, heels and nothing else. Below the hem of each uniform jacket showed the furry triangle of the girl's cunt, with her bottom cheeks peeping out enticingly from behind, a display which had led to a great deal of giggling and quite a few smacked cheeks as the corporals tried to get them into line.

Ginger's suggestion had proved to be a good one. Not only had they found a clothes shop with a large, airy room two floors above, but the proprietor, Nabil Sidqi, supplemented his trade by procuring girls for the more modest British officers and so made no objection to helping herd eight partially naked girls into the rear of his premises. He was also an ex-soldier, with stock that included an impressive amount of gear from General Allenby's army of the First World War, including the dress uniforms the top halves of which the girls now had on. There had been one or two objections at first, but the promise of more practical garments and a plentiful supply of drink had quickly sorted these out, leaving Henry with the smart parade of half-naked girls he had envisioned the instant he'd seen the uniforms piled at the back of the shop.

'Now that's what I call a review,' he remarked. 'Damned smart. Turn 'em about one more time, Maria.'

Maria, fully familiar with the military way of life, barked an order, which Michelle translated. The girls turned, and if their timing was less than perfect the fault was more than compensated for by the resulting view, of six pairs of neatly turned bottom cheeks on display beneath the hems of their jackets. Not one tried to cover her bottom, and most were stifling giggles, tempting Henry to demand a yet more intimate display and in doing so test their willingness to do as they were told.

'Have them touch their toes, Maria,' he suggested.

'Sir,' Maria responded, promptly and smartly, but with a flicker at one edge of her mouth which hinted as a cruel grin. 'On the order, squad are to touch their toes. Lance-Corporal Boudin?'

Michelle relayed the order in French. Assiatou and Khadija promptly bent to touch their toes, making their jackets lift to show off the full glory of their tight black bottoms, each with the rear of her neatly turned cunt and the jet black dimple of her anus on full show. Zokie and Ainikki hesitated only an instant before they too had put their bottoms on show in the same, lewd pose, one dark, one pale, but both so beautifully formed to tempt any man's cock. Lola and Jacinta took a trifle longer, sharing a grimace of mingled embarrassment and shy humour before bending down to touch their toes and put the most intimate details of their bodies on display. Once down, all six girls stayed in place, a parade of bare bottoms that sent the blood pumping to Henry's already half-stiff cock. The two NCOs were clearly enjoying the view as well, also their authority, Michelle cool and poised but smiling, Maria no longer troubling to hide her cruel grin. Seeing the pleasure the Brazilian girl was taking in the exposure of the others, Henry found his own mouth twitching into a similar expression.

'Corporal Esposito, Lance-Corporal Boudin, you too,' he

ordered.

Maria's expression changed to shock and embarrassment, but she did as she was told, turning her back and bending low to show off the full, brown globes of her bottom, her cunt and anus clearly visible between, now no more dignified than the others. Michelle had also obeyed, but was looking back with a coquettish smirk as she showed off, then a wink. Henry adjusted his now rock solid erection to make himself more comfortable, refilled his glass and took another swallow of arrack, all the while with his eyes lingering on the line of eight bare, female bottoms in front of him. Each and every one offered two tempting little holes, and to know that he had the choice which to fuck and how gave not only arousal but a wonderful sensation of power.

'Very good, Corporal Esposito,' he said. 'Back to attention.'

Maria gave the orders and the girls returned to attention, facing front and with their hands to their sides. Some now looked embarrassed, others flustered, while the twins were clearly amused by being made to show themselves off so intimately. Only Michelle seemed fully cool and poised, while Maria clearly had mixed feelings, enjoying her own power more than being part of the display.

'Do you think they should have rifles or something?' Ginger suggested. 'Little whips perhaps?'

'Michelle and Maria, certainly,' Henry agreed, 'the others, I think not. Sidqi has plenty of camel whips, why don't you nip downstairs and borrow a couple?'

Ginger gave a brief, urgent nod and walked quickly from the room.

'I know what he wants,' Gorski remarked.

'Each to his own taste,' Henry replied, 'although I prefer to dish it out myself. Very well then, squad dismissed. Maria, Michelle, I trust you can look after Ginger? And that leaves us three each, Gorski old man. Hmm ... let me see, each is more desirable than the last, but ... yes, why not? Ainikki.'

The Finnish girl smiled and came over to perch herself on his lap, draping one arm around his shoulders. He put one hand to her bare bottom as she settled onto his knee and gestured to

Gorski with the other.

'The twins,' Gorki stated without hesitation and both black girls skipped over to seat themselves on his legs.

'The next two choices to me then, I think,' Henry said. 'Let me see ... Zokie, for one, and for the last, impossible to choose between two such lovely girls, but we can always swap later, so I shall start with Lola.'

Zokie had already come to him, to stand by his chair. He let a hand stray up her leg as Lola joined them, stroking her smooth black flesh, which felt remarkably muscular. They had ordered pallets to be laid out at either side of the room, and he rose to lead the three girls over to one corner, where the lamps at the far end of the room shed just enough light to allow him to see what he was doing.

The four of them cuddled up together, the girls' hands moving to his body as his moved to theirs, so that his cock was soon out, with Ainikki tugging up and down on his shaft as she fiddled with her buttons. Zokie had already undone the remaining buttons of her jacket, showing off two firm, dark breasts nearly as full and heavy as Maria's. Henry took one stiff nipple in his mouth, suckling eagerly as his trousers were unfastened and pulled down. Lola was waiting to one side and he put an arm out, cupping her bottom and kneading gently as he drew her in.

He went down on the pallet, the three girls moving close, Ainikki to take his cock into her mouth and Zokie smothering his face between her breasts as he continued to fondle Lola's bottom. Ainikki's hand closed on his balls, squeezing them, with one finger pushed down to tickle his anus as she sucked and wanked on his erection. Zokie moved up, to swing a leg across his body and sit down on his face, smothering him once more, but now in between her muscular black bottom cheeks. Henry stuck out his tongue, lapping at her cunt and anus as she wriggled herself into her face, while his fingers had slipped between Lola's thighs to tickle her bottom hole and tease her cunt.

Already he was on the edge of orgasm, but struggling to hold back and not waste himself too early. He could hear voices from across the room and concentrated on what was being said in an effort to resist the exquisite things Ainikki was doing to his cock and balls and the pleasure of having Zokie's bottom spread in his face. Maria was the one talking, her voice cool and imperious, while Michelle was laughing. Ginger responded in soft, breathless tones followed by the smack of a whip on flesh and a cry of mingled pain and ecstasy. Again Michelle laughed, and again came the smack of leather on skin, at the same time as a delighted giggle that might have been any one of the three girl playing with Gorski.

Zokie was getting urgent, her cunt pressed firmly to Henry's mouth, while Ainikki had begun to twist at his cock as she sucked his helmet, with one finger in up his bottom. It was more than he could bear. His cock jerked and he'd come in her mouth, one eruption of spunk and then a second as she took him deep into her throat, swallowing as best she could as her fingers locked tight on his balls. He cried out in ecstasy, heavily muffled by the wriggling Zokie, who was now saying urgently, in her own language, what he took to be demands for her own orgasm.

He did his best to oblige, licking eagerly until her words changed to gasps and cries of pleasure as she squirmed her bottom in his face. Her bottom cheeks tightened across his mouth, he felt her anus start to pulse against his nose and she was coming, riding his tongue until she'd taken her full satisfaction and only then allowing herself to topple slowly to one side. Henry spent a moment gasping for breath, then managed a nod for Lola, who was watching in both shock and fascination. She had already undone her jacket, showing off her little round breasts, and she hesitated only a moment before taking Zokie's place, cunt to mouth, but facing forwards.

Once more Henry began to lick, determined to make all three girls come for all that he had already taken his own orgasm. Doing so had always ensured good service in the past and he was keen to have all eight girls eager to please, rather than merely obedient. Lola certainly seemed grateful, playing with her breasts as he licked, her eyes closed in ecstasy. He had also been straddled, Ainikki now seated on his hips with her cunt spread over his middle, rubbing herself on his cock and balls.

Both girls came within moments of each other, crying out with pleasure before tumbling together in a sweaty heap on the pallet. Henry lay back, panting a little as Lola and Zokie cuddled up to his chest, while Ainikki had laid her head on his belly, idly toying with his cock. He could see very little, but Michelle and Maria still seemed to be tormenting Ginger, his cries of pain and pleasure mixing with smacks of the whip and cruel but still girlish laughter, while whatever Gorski was doing to his girls it was making one of them grunt and squeal like a pig.

Intrigued, he pulled himself up until he could put his back to the wall, allowing him to see the room properly. It was quite a view. One the far side of the room the two girls had Ginger on all fours, Michelle riding his back and alternately whipping him and pulling at his erection as if she were milking him, Maria kneeling to pull at his hair while she made him suckle at her chest. His buttocks were criss-crossed with red lines, but the state of his cock left no doubt about his reaction to their cruelty and a moment later he had come, spunking up in Michelle's hand as Maria pulled his face hard in between her massive breasts.

What Gorski was doing might have been less perverse but provided a yet more impressive view. Jacinta and the twins were lined up on a pallet, naked but for their peaked caps and heels, their bottoms lifted to present three wet cunts to the air and to Gorski's cock. He was in Jacinta, fucking her with long, deep strokes while she squealed and clutched at the bedding on which she was kneeling, only to suddenly withdraw and plunge himself up Assiatou's equally willing hole, to set her gasping and panting in turn while her sister looked on in open-mouthed expectation.

Ainikki had taken Henry's cock in her mouth once more, sucking gently while he cuddled up to Lola and Zokie. He could already feel himself beginning to stir and was sure he could make it a second time if he paced himself and the girls proved as rude and eager as before. With quick gestures he indicated that Lola and Zokie should get into kneeling positions and after a moment of hesitation they had obeyed, one to either side, their bottoms thrust out to allow him to stroke and smack at their bare cheeks or use his fingers to tease their pouted cunts and the tight dimples of their bumholes.

Across the room a little drama had developed. Ginger lay spent, his cock hanging limp down one thigh as he propped himself up on an elbow, watching as Maria and Michelle wrestled playfully together on the next pallet along. Each seem determined to subdue the other, but there was no real contest. Michelle was lithe and strong for such a small woman, but simply could not compete against Maria's strength and size. Soon the little French girl had been sat on and was having her bare bottom smacked to put her in her place before Maria rolled her over to use her face for a seat.

The spanking seemed to have done its job, as no sooner had Maria settled her full, dark buttocks across the pretty French girl's face than Michelle had stuck her tongue out to lick cunt for the girl who'd beaten her. Soon Maria's eyes were closed and her hands had gone to her breasts, kneading the heavy brown globes and squeezing at her nipples as Michelle's tongue flickered across his clitoris. Henry gave an approving nod for the girls' behaviour, while wondering if it might be fun to spank Maria in turn, or perhaps hold her down while Michelle did it, a thought that added to the rate at which his cock was stiffening in Ainikki's mouth.

It looked as if Maria was about to come when Michelle suddenly lurched to one side, unseating her mount. Maria sprawled on the floor, bottom up, and before she could recover herself Michelle had straddled her legs and was using one of the camel whips on her victim's bottom, laughing as the twisted leather thongs cracked down on the wriggling flesh. Three strokes had fallen, each one drawing a yelp of pain from Maria before she recovered herself enough to fight back, twisting her body violently to one side.

Michelle was unseated in turn and again the two were fighting on the floor, both desperate to subdue the other for punishment, and yet once again the outcome was inevitable.

Soon Maria was victorious, this time with the spitting, swearing Michelle laid across her lap, little pink bottom stuck high, one arm twisted behind her back, legs kicking in desperation as she was spanked once more. This time it was hard, quickly turning her pert little cheeks a rich pink, and before long she was begging Maria to stop and promising to be good.

At first Maria ignored Michelle's pleas, spanking until the French's girl's tiny bottom was red all over, then applying a half-dozen firm smacks of the camel whip before finally relenting. By then Michelle was shaking, her face wet with tears, but she made no protest as Maria sat back and spread her thighs, crawling obediently between them to once more apply her agile little tongue to the cunt of the woman who'd conquered her. The position left her bottom in the air, red cheeks well spread to show off her sopping cunt and her tight pink bottom hole, an invitation Henry found impossible to resist.

His cock was now hard in Ainikki's mouth and he pulled free, kissing her and promising he would come back before crossing the room to ease his cock in up Michelle's gaping hole. She took it willingly, sighing and whimpering into Maria's cunt as she licked and Henry's cock worked in her hole, plainly eager for a fucking. Henry had other ideas, working himself in and out until she was moaning in ecstasy and struggling to concentrate on her other task, then pulling out one last time to wipe his juice smeared cock between her bottom cheeks.

Michelle realised she was going to be sodomised and began to whimper, but she made no attempt to escape. Maria also saw and shared a grin with Henry as he pressed the head of his cock to the tiny pink hole of Michelle's anus, both watching as the little star first pushed in and then began to open, spreading slowly to the meat of Henry's helmet. Michelle continued to whimper and to lick at Maria's cunt, also gaping and panting as her buggering got under way, with Henry's cock forced slowly up her bottom hole, inch by inch until at last the wrinkled flesh of his scrotum was pressed to her empty cunt.

Ainikki had crawled close, and was looking up at Henry with her eyes full of excitement but also accusation. He shrugged and smiled, pushing himself deep up Michelle's bottom once more as he wished he had more than one cock and could come as often as he liked. Yet Michelle had already begun to masturbate, her fingers slapping at her cunt and clutching to Henry's balls as she licked Maria.

It was Maria who came first, crying out in ecstasy as Michelle fed from her cunt with ever more greed, to hit her own orgasm moments later. Henry felt Michelle's anus squeeze on his cock shaft, bringing him a wrenching sensation that would have been orgasm had he not come just minutes before and left him determined to make it again, jamming his cock in and out of Michelle's anus to make her scream as her orgasm reached a second peak.

He pulled free, meaning to jam his cock back up her gaping, slippery bottom hole one last time to bring himself to orgasm, only for Ainikki to grab his cock and take it deep in her mouth, sucking urgently and swallowing over and over before abruptly swinging around to present Henry with her own bottom, the slim, pale cheeks spread wide to offer him both anus and cunt. Michelle had come, collapsing sideways with her head still locked between Maria's thighs, and Henry lost no time in entering Ainikki, only not in the inviting pink wetness of her cunt but up her bottom. She was slick with juice, but cried out in protest as her ring spread to his cock head, then again as he jammed himself deeper.

'Remember what nanny used to say,' he told her, despite knowing full well she didn't understand. 'If you want to go to town, first Lady Pink then Mrs Brown, but never ever even think, first Mrs Brown then Lady Pink. Mark you, I had some damned peculiar nannies.'

Ainikki said something in Finnish, as much as sob as a word, but she stayed down, now playing with her cunt as Henry continued to bugger her. He was well in, and knew he could make it, with the bulk of his cock deep in up the soft, wet, warmth of her rectum and her anal ring stretched tight around the base of his shaft. As with Michelle, his balls were pressed to Ainikki's empty cunt, but instead of rubbing herself she had began to squirm, bumping her clitoris over the wrinkled skin of Henry's scrotum.

'That's the way to do it,' he sighed. 'Rub it on my balls. That's my girl, rub it on my balls … rub your cunt on my balls, and …'

He'd been holding himself as deep as he could get, allowing Ainikki plenty of friction between her clitoris and the skin of his scrotum, but as her wriggling grew frantic and she started to come her anus began to squeeze on his cock and he broke off with a cry. Unable to hold back, he began to thrust in an out of her gaping bumhole, pumping her full of spunk as they came together, both gasping and panting out their ecstasy, but Ainikki was also sobbing and shaking her head to make her long blonde hair swish from side to side as she gave in to the powerful sensations of being buggered.

Even when Henry finally pulled back to collapse on the pallet she wasn't done, turning to grab his still-hard cock and suck on it with near-crazed urgency as she continued to rub as her cunt, bringing herself to peak after peak, which died away only gradually. At last she let go, to kneel back, her head hanging in exhaustion and possibly shame, taking in long, slow breaths until she finally looked up again, peering shyly from beneath her fringe.

'Thank you,' Henry said, returning her smile. 'That was, er … remarkable. Thank you too, Michelle.'

Michelle, who had been watching Ainikki's buggering, cuddled up to Maria, as had Ginger, along with Gorski and the others, who'd finished their own games. Gorski handed Henry a bottle of beer, from which he took a long pull before passing it into Ainikki's eagerly extended hand. Detaching herself from Michelle, Maria got to her feet and padded across to the washstand at the far end of the room, followed by Ginger.

'Good idea,' Henry said, 'a quick wash and brush-up, and then we'd better be getting back to the airfield. But first we'd better get you girls something sensible to wear. We'd better go for those abaya thingamajigs, with the veils. That way nobody's going to ask any damn fool questions.'

79

He made for the stairs, quickly descending to check that the shop was clear before starting back up, only to meet Zokie halfway, once more in her scarlet uniform jacket but still with her bare cunt showing beneath the hem.

'Put the trousers on,' he said, only to be met by a look of blank incomprehension. 'What the Hell are trousers in Frog? Um ... *culottes ... met votre culottes sur ta cul*? Yes?'

She merely shrugged, so Henry took her by the hand, slapped her bottom and led her back upstairs. Michelle quickly took Zokie in hand, speaking in a pidgin French incomprehensible to Henry but which provoked a giggled response and a finger gesture in his direction which might or might not have been flattering. The other girls seemed to know what to do, pulling on their full uniforms, although the trousers were so tight over bare, feminine bottom cheeks that they looked only slightly less lewd dressed than they had bottomless. With all eight ready, Henry led the way back downstairs, calling for Sidqi as he came into the shop with the girls trooping along behind him, only to find himself face to face with Air Commodore Sir Pomeroy Pankhurst.

'Good evening, sir,' Henry managed, unable to think of anything better to say, let alone which would explain the eight girls in indecently tight-fitting World War One dress uniforms now clustered behind him.

'Good evening, Truscott,' Sir Pomeroy replied, looking doubtfully at the girls. 'And, ah ... who might these young ladies be?'

'They ... they're for the ... the cabaret concert,' Henry responded, extemporising frantically. 'We're putting on a show, Ginger Green and Sergeant Gorski and one or two others, before we head back to Blighty, you know the kind of thing.'

'Absolutely,' Sir Pomeroy answered him. 'What a splendid idea. Good for morale. A tonic for the troops and all that.'

'Precisely, sir,' Henry agreed, for once extremely glad that most of the girls spoke only French and weren't likely to say anything awkward, or at least not that the Air Commodore would understand.

'Yes, yes, a splendid idea,' Sir Pomeroy went on, 'but, ah ... shouldn't these girls have a chaperone? Somebody reliable, one of the WAAFs perhaps. Otherwise people will talk, you know, and that won't do at all.'

'I must admit that hadn't occurred to me,' Henry said.

'It wouldn't, of course,' Sir Pomeroy carried on. 'Decent young chap like you, why should it? Still, it would be for the best, don't you think? People talk, you know, get the wrong idea. I'll tell you what, I'll have a word with my daughter, Poppy. I take it you've met my daughter?'

'Er ... yes, we're acquainted,' Henry admitted, pushing away a sudden, unbidden picture of the Air Commodore's daughter's straining bottom hole moving back and forth on the shaft of his penis. 'Yes, we're definitely acquainted. Er ...'

'Poppy would be ideal,' Sir Pomeroy went on before Henry could think of a valid objection. 'She's a sensible girl and doesn't stand any nonsense, just the sort you need.'

'I'm sure she is, sir,' Henry responded weakly.

'Yes,' Sir Pomeroy continued, 'and speaking of which, and entirely between you and I, as gentlemen, I'd be grateful if you didn't mention where you met me to Poppy. Not that there's any reason I shouldn't be here, mark you. I'm after a new pair of boots, as it happens, but old Sidqi does have a bit of a reputation, don't you know?'

'Discretion is my watchword,' Henry assured him, deciding not to ask why Sir Pomeroy had decided he needed a new pair of boots at very nearly midnight.

Gorski brought the three hundredweight truck to a standstill at the end of a line of similar vehicles. He jumped down, followed by Henry and Ginger, and the three men set off towards the long, low huts that functioned as a barracks.

'So we have to run a cabaret concert,' Henry remarked, not for the first time.

'It could be worse,' Ginger pointed out. 'Now it doesn't matter if we're seen with the girls. We'll just have to cut Pinks in, I suppose.'

'I suppose so,' Henry admitted, 'if she's game. She a bit

unpredictable is young Pinks. Otherwise, we'll just have to sneak the pictures when we can.'

'She's bound to realise what's going on,' Ginger continued. 'She was there when we first came up with the idea, after all.'

'I remember,' Henry replied. 'Goodnight, Gorski.'

The sergeant had set off towards his own barracks, leaving Henry and Ginger to continue towards the officers' quarters. Neither spoke, each alone with his thoughts, until Ginger in turn went his own way, leaving Henry to walk the last couple of hundred yards on his own. The night was cool and quiet but for the noise of a lone cicada which seemed to have become confused about the seasons, it was also nearly black, with only the dull yellow lights on the Nissan huts to see by, so that when a figure detached itself from the shadows Henry jumped quickly back before recognising the petite figure and delicate features of Sally Green.

'Whatever are you doing here?' he asked.

'I heard you were back,' she said, stepping close. 'I wanted to see you.'

'I wanted to see you too,' Henry replied, taking her into her arms, 'but I had to go into Cairo.'

He kissed her and she responded with passion, opening her mouth beneath his and sliding one hand down between them to squeeze his cock. Henry steered her quickly into the shadows of the nearest hut, wondering what she expected of him and whether he was capable to giving it to her, as while his cock had responded to the gentle touch of her hand in the usual fashion it had also given a twinge of protest, while his balls ached. She lost no time in providing an answer, speaking as she eased his fly open and slid a hand inside.

'I want you to do it to me again,' she whispered. 'What you did before, only more.'

'Here?' Henry demanded. 'I know it's dark, but we're in the middle of the camp.'

'Not right here, silly,' she responded. 'In the ladies' bath house. It will be quite empty, and it's not locked.'

She had taken his hand as she spoke, to lead him off between the huts. Henry followed, somewhat bemused but determined to give of his best, to where the dark block of the ladies' bathhouse stood somewhat apart from the other buildings. Sally moved quickly forward into the wan yellow glow from the single light above the door, signalling to Henry as she pushed inside. He closed the door behind them, his nose wrinkling at the mingled scents of soap, perfume and less easily definable feminine aromas, bringing back memories of clandestine adventures from the days before the war.

'In here,' Sally whispered, pulling Henry behind her through the darkness, which was now absolute. 'Mind the door.'

Henry extended a hand, groping carefully through the darkness as they entered what was evidently a small room, warm, still and heavy with the smell of new washing. The door clicked to behind him and the light came on, revealing wooden racks piled high with fresh linen, a stack of huge wickerwork tubs and a single plain chair in front of an equally plain table. There were no windows for the light to betray their presence, only a ventilator set high in one wall. Sally was beside the door, her eyes glittering with excitement but also nervousness.

'You will play with me, won't you?' she asked. 'The way you said?'

'Yes, of course,' Henry promised, not entirely sure what she meant but eager to oblige.

'Strip me then,' she breathed, 'naked.'

As Henry stepped forward Sally had closed her eyes and stood limp as he began to unbutton her uniform jacket. Not at all sure what game he was supposed to be playing, he was more than happy to have her nude, and to follow her instructions, although as he peeled off her clothing it seemed that what she mainly wanted was for her own will to be ignored. She neither helped nor hindered, allowing him to remove her garments without a hint of embarrassment, but in gradually rising excitement, and while accidental touches to her flesh made her shiver and sigh, deliberate ones made her whimper.

He first stripped her to her underwear, removing her uniform and placing each article on the shelf beside them. She had very little on underneath, none of the thick, armour-like garments Poppy seemed to prefer, but a light cotton chemise and summer-weight knickers, with a delicate, lacy suspender belt to hold up her stockings. It all came off, her knickers last, to expose the gingery puff of her pubic hair and her pale, trim little bottom cheeks, which Henry kissed as he turned her about. His cock had began to respond, grudgingly, with a dull ache in both his shaft and balls as he got bigger.

She had put her hands on her head and her eyes were still closed, giving him complete and uncritical access to her naked body. He continued to kiss her, turning her slowly as his lips caressed the gentle curves of her bottom cheeks and the mound of her sex, her belly and breasts, all the while with her trembling growing stronger and her breathing deeper. Only when his mouth found her cunt and he had begun to lick at the little bump between her sex lips did she speak.

'Not yet. I want you to put me in a nappy.'

Henry looked up, surprised, but had the sense not to say anything. He remembered the state she'd been in when they'd first had sex, the position he'd put her in for her spanking and how she'd wanted to be treated. It was strange, but oddly appealing, and seemed little enough to ask, while it seemed a good guess that she'd want to be talked to while he did it.

'Yes,' he said. 'In your nappy you go, you naughty girl. You've done it again, haven't you? You've let a man take off all of your clothes and touch you in your private places, haven't you? Well you know what happens to naughty little girls, don't you?'

'They get spanked,' Sally whimpered.

'They get spanked,' Henry confirmed. 'Spanked on their bare bottoms, but in your case I think we'd better get your nappy on first, don't you?'

Sally responded with an urgent nod, her eyes still closed and her hands on top of her head but her body trembling so badly it was a wonder she could still stand. Henry left her as she was, searching the racks until he found what he wanted, a large white towel, easily big enough to make a convincing nappy around her slender hips.

'Come here,' he ordered, 'on the table with you.'

Her eyes finally came open, looking at him with a frightened, wondering expression, as if she'd never seen him before. She stepped towards the table, but on a sudden impulse he picked her up as she drew level with him, lifting her easily to lie her down on the flat surface. Taking hold of her ankles, he pulled her legs high, into the same rude, revealing position in which he had spanked and buggered her, her bottom and cunt spread to his gaze. Her eyes closed once more and her mouth opened wide, her hands clutched at the edges of the table and her shaking grew harder still, so that she seemed completely lost in ecstasy.

'Yes, Sally,' Henry went on, 'on the table with you and into your nappy. Then we'll see about your spanking, shall we?'

He'd lifted her by her feet as he spoke, allowing him to slip the towel underneath her bottom. She made no resistance at all, even when he spread her legs to pull the towel up between them. With no pins to hand, he tied off the corners of the towel at either hip, to leave her in a very effective nappy, her bottom and hips and cunt encased in soft, white towelling, so bulky that it made her petite body seem smaller still, adding to the effect.

'You do look sweet,' Henry told her, while, despite a touch of something akin to guilt for what they were doing, his cock had responded of its own accord, now stiff within his pants.

He pulled it free, stroking his erection as he drank in the sight of Sally lying on the table, naked but for the huge, puffy nappy, her legs rolled up to leave her deliberately vulnerable. The ache in his balls was stronger than ever and the skin of his cock felt sore, but that wasn't going to stop him taking his fill of her, even if it meant having to go without sex for a week.

'And now, Miss Sally,' he told her. 'I'm going to spank your naughty little bottom, and then I'm going to stick my cock right up that tight little bumhole of yours.'

'Oh, you are, are you?' a voice sounded from directly behind him and he spun around, to find Poppy standing in the open doorway, her arms folded across her chest, one foot tapping meaningfully on the concrete floor. 'Not while I'm

85

about, Flying Officer Truscott. Right, come here, you little pervert.'

She marched forward, pushing past Henry without so much as a glance to the side. Sally had realised what was happened and gave a squeak of alarm, but Poppy was already on her, grabbing one wrist to twist it hard up behind the now babbling girl's back.

'No, please, Pinks, no! I'm sorry! I'm sorry! I'm sorry!'

Her pleas were ignored and Henry watched in dumbstruck fascination as she was hauled down from the table and placed across the knee, with Poppy seated on the chair and her face set in fury and determination.

'Please, Pinks, no, not this!' Sally wailed. 'Not in my nappy!'

'That's the way you like it best, isn't it?' Poppy snapped back as she began to apply hard smacks to the wriggling seat of Sally's nappy. 'Being spanked in your nappies. Yes, it is, you dirty little pervert! Oh, this is no use at all! I don't imagine you can even feel it, and believe me, you ought to!'

As she spoke she had tugged the back of Sally's nappy down, exposing her bare pink bottom, which she began to spank with renewed fury, talking all the while and ignoring both Henry and her victim's frantic wriggling, desperate pleas and cries of pain.

'I give you what you need, Sally Green. I spank you, do you understand that, you perverted, dirty little brat!? I … spank … you … Nobody else, definitely not men, and definitely, definitely, definitely not Flying Officer Truscott! Is that clear!?'

'Yes!' Sally wailed at the top of her voice, now with her legs scissoring frantically in her lowered nappy as her soft little bottom cheeks bounced to the smacks. 'I'm sorry!'

'Not as sorry as you will be when I've finished with you,' Poppy retorted as she continued to spank. 'What did I tell you, after the last time? What did I tell you!?'

'Not … not to be dirty!' Sally managed, gasping the words out between squeals. 'Not to be dirty with Henry!'

'Yes,' Poppy went on, 'not to be dirty with Henry. And

what do I catch you doing? I catch you playing your filthy little games with him and all too willing to let him put his great dirty cock up your bottom hole, don't I? You slut! You dirty, perverted little slut! You ...'

She broke off, her mouth set in a hard line as she laid into Sally's jiggling, dancing bottom cheeks with all her force, her hand now smacking down on the same spot over and over again, the soft tuck of her victim's cheeks where they turned in around her sopping wet cunt and the tiny pink star of her anus. Sally was in tears, blubbering pathetically as she was spanked; moist, choking sounds punctuated by cries of pain, while she was struggling desperately across Poppy's knee with her hair flying, her legs kicking ever more frantically in her nappy and her fists beating in futile protest on the concrete floor. Then her reaction changed, suddenly, her screams taking on a new note that could only be ecstasy, her body jerking as he muscles began to spasm.

To Henry's astonishment he realised that she was coming, purely in response to the smacks being applied to her naked bottom, but then so had he, a dribble of spunk now running down his fingers from the tip of his cock, although he'd barely been aware that he was masturbating as he watched Sally being punished.

Chapter Six

'RATHER AN AWKWARD SITUATION, I'm sure you'll agree,' Henry remarked to Gorski, who alone of his crew he'd felt able to confide in, even then leaving out the most bizarre details.

The big Pole responded with a thoughtful nod and Henry went on.

'They're obviously having an affair, and a damned peculiar one at that. I mean to say, I always knew Poppy was a bossy little bitch, but really! And Sally seems to like it. In fact, judging by what Poppy said afterwards the only reason Sally showed any interest in me was so that she'd get punished, which is hardly flattering. Not that I believe it, as it goes, because she didn't get caught on purpose, or I don't think she did. Who knows? Women, eh?'

'English women,' Gorki corrected him.

'Perhaps,' Henry admitted, 'although Michelle and Maria are no different.'

'They are professional girls.'

'Maria's not. She's a cook, although goodness knows I don't suppose she learnt to pleasure a man's cock like that in the kitchens at Fort What'sit. Michelle's not a whore either, not really, or at least she didn't start out that way, although I don't suppose many do. Then there's Ainikki, who's as dirty as they come, and as far as I can make out she was attached to some sort of diplomatic mission during the war, at first anyway.'

'Still, they are trained, I think.'

'And Poppy and Sally are just plain perverted? I don't buy it. I think it's more a case of most girls being a bit perverted underneath, but the respectable ones don't get so much opportunity to express it, and bear in mind that if you don't want to admit to yourself what you really like, it must be ever so much easier to do it because you're being paid.'

'Perhaps,' Gorski admitted and Henry found himself smiling, having for once managed to get his friend to express doubt rather than a clear and exact opinion.

'One way or another, it's rather an awkward situation,' Henry repeated, 'but all for the best. I always thought Pinks was a bit of an invert, and now I know for sure, so when it comes to photographing the girls, and this cabaret concert business, she's really no better than we are, worse in fact, because while their airships more or less take it for granted that we're going to roger every bint we can lay our hands on, they expect the girls to be models of decorum. God knows why, but there it is, and is applies double to young Pinks with Daddy in the driving seat. We'll strike a deal with her.'

They were approaching the camp reading room, where he had agreed to meet with Poppy to discuss the concert. Henry had mentioned the situation the night before, in a vain attempt to change the subject while Poppy gave a tear-stained Sally Green a serious dressing down to add to her spanking. Poppy had merely nodded and said she would speak to her father in the morning, leaving Henry with little choice but to make a polite withdrawal, while Sally had been led away by one ear, still in the nude and begging to be allowed to at least put her knickers back on as she was marched back towards the huts.

Poppy was already in the reading room, seated behind a desk as if the place was her office, with a pile of papers neatly stacked in front of her. She looked up as Henry and Gorski entered, her expression cool and ever so slightly smug, and while she did rise to her feet and salute she somehow managed to make the gesture more insolent than respectful. Henry returned her salute and went to lean against the window, determined not to become part of what he suspected was a clever mind-game, making him sit in front of her as if she were the senior officer.

'Cabaret concert,' he stated. 'Have you spoken to Daddy?'

'I have … sir,' she responded. 'These are the orders … sir.

You are to be responsible for the overall organisation, the programme of entertainment, a venue, suitable refreshments and so forth, assisted by Pilot Officer Green and Sergeant Gorski. I am to take responsibility for the organisation of the cabaret itself, and to look after the moral welfare of the girls.'

'Spank 'em regularly, you mean?' Henry joked.

'I might well use physical discipline,' Poppy responded without so much as a blink, 'should it prove necessary. This is not an Air Force matter, after all.'

'That didn't seem to stop you with Sally,' Henry responded, 'but never mind that. You're not going to make too much fuss over this moral welfare business, are you? I mean to say, the girls are quite safe with us, and ...'

'Safe?' she broke in. 'No girl is safe with you, Henry Truscott, and even if they were, look at your crew! Ginger Green and Sergeant Gorski are relatively normal, I suppose, but a street trader from the Campbell Bunk[5], a blatant spiv and an ape of some sort who's presumably a mascot, but ...'

'Do you mean the Egg?' Henry interrupted. 'I assure you he's human, and while Bunker and Slick may not be exactly the cream of society, they're my crew.'

'He doesn't look human,' Poppy retorted, 'and my father expects me to take this task seriously, so no, you're not getting anywhere near them. For one thing I'm going to have them moved out of that doss house you'd put them in to more suitable accommodation.'

'Do calm down, old girl,' Henry went on. 'As you've no doubt realised, they're the girls we're planning to photograph for that wheeze we were discussing the other night, along with whatever Fat Babu can provide, so we need to be able to see them and to take them out into the desert now and again, or down along the river or wherever it might be. We'll cut you in.'

'Are you trying to bribe me, Flying Officer Truscott?' Poppy asked, raising her eyebrows.

'Not at all,' Henry assured her, 'but since you're on the team you might as well benefit. You can pose yourself, if you ...'

He broke off in response to an icy glare, and as she turned to stack the papers on her desk her nose was tilted into the air.

'There is something to be said for the idea, I suppose,' she admitted after a pause, 'but why should I involve you at all, let alone your crew? I can hire a photographer easily enough, and the necessary muscle with no difficulty at all, while if I have any nonsense from you all I have to do is …'

'Tell Daddy?' Henry finished for her. 'Don't play me for a fool, Pinks. You and I know far too much about each other for that sort of behaviour. Besides, I thought we were friends?'

She responded with a haughty sniff and spent a moment pretending to examine the papers she was holding before speaking again.

'Fifty per cent.'

'Fifty per cent!?' Henry echoed. 'There are six of us, seven including you, and you have to consider our overheads, not least paying the girls. Ten per cent, after overheads.'

'I think you'll find that your little scheme won't work at all without me,' she said, 'especially if you want pictures of Sally Green. Forty per cent.'

'Be reasonable, old thing,' Henry insisted. 'Fifteen per cent, and that's a fair share.'

Poppy considered for a moment before replying.

'Very well, fifteen per cent, but the cabaret is to be called Poppy's Pin-Ups and I take the credit, and top billing on the posters. Clear?'

'Roger,' Henry agreed.

'Georgina Hayes, ATS, private,' the smart young woman stated as she stepped out on to the improvised stage on which the cabaret concert was to be held.

She was of medium height, pretty, with luxurious brown hair and a splash of freckles across a snub nose, while her uniform hinted at a well-proportioned and fairly generous figure.

'Thank you, Georgina,' Henry answered her, glancing at his notes. 'And you know Sally Green? I take it she explained what's expected of you?'

'Yes, sir,' Georgina replied and promptly began to undo the buttons of her uniform jacket, revealing first the light cotton of a chemise, then a full-cut bra and finally two large, rounded breasts tipped by deep pink nipples.

Poppy spoke up.

'Very good, so far.'

'Yes, ma'am, Georgina responded, now blushing slightly as she turned around to push out her bottom.

Henry made himself comfortable as Georgina tugged up the khaki shirt of her uniform and found himself swallowing involuntarily at the revelation of what was beneath. She had caught up her shirt tail along with her skirt, which suggested practice at displaying her rear view. It also revealed a slice of her girdle and the full, taut length of the suspender straps that held up the American nylons that encased her long, shapely legs. Those legs alone would have been enough to sway his decision, but the verdict was put beyond all possible doubt by a yet more alluring detail. She had no knickers on, leaving the perfectly rounded peach of her bottom stark naked, while the gap between her thighs revealed a hint of what lay between. He swallowed a second time, and was about to state his approval when Poppy spoke up.

'You'll do. Next!'

'We might have let her …,' Henry began.

'Control yourself,' Poppy told him.

'Easier said than done,' he muttered and adjusted his cock as another girl stepped out on to the stage.

She was a great deal less sure of herself and clearly didn't know what was really going on, but she also had a shy appeal which Henry found attractive. He leant close to Poppy, whispering into her ear.

'She's pretty. Perhaps I could talk her around?'

'You'll do nothing of the sort, Henry Truscott,' Poppy answered him quietly, then raised her voice to address the girl. 'We'll get back to you. Next!'

Henry drew a sigh as yet another girl stepped out on to the stage. Poppy's involvement had proved both a blessing and curse. As the daughter of an Air Commodore she was above suspicion, while in practice she was rather less moral than the rest of the team, with the possible exception of the Egg, happily instructing the girls to strip and pose for Bunker's camera, including Sally Green. She had shown extraordinary skill at organisation, and at taking full advantage of the Air Force bureaucracy, so that not only were the girls now housed at the expense of the RAF but she controlled a fund for the cabaret concert. On the other hand she was extremely bossy, dishing out orders and making decisions without thought for rank or any other consideration, while she had taken her duties as chaperone extremely seriously, especially where Henry was concerned. In fact, he considered, she seemed to be taking a deliberate pleasure in allowing him a taste of what might be on offer but then denying him a chance at satisfaction.

She had also insisted that they involve more British girls, arguing that there would be greater demand for photographs of apparently respectable girls stripping out of their uniforms than for ones of girls who made their living by taking their clothes off. Henry had been unable to deny the logic of this, nor of Poppy's suggestion of using an audition for the cabaret concert as a cover to make their selection. Now, with Georgina Hayes and three other girls selected, each of who had at the least provided a peep of her underwear, he was finding it increasingly difficult to concentrate, his head boiling with lust and frustration and his cock aching to be touched as girl after girl paraded herself on the stage. When the auditions were finally over he felt more relief than anything, but also found himself wondering if Poppy herself might not have been similarly affected.

'That went well, I thought,' he ventured, 'but it's thirsty work, don't you think? Can I tempt you to a drink?'

'I've no time for any of your nonsense, Henry Truscott,' she answered, rising to stack the papers on her desk in a brisk, efficient manner. 'I have to talk to the four new girls, then, two ack emma, Maria, Zokie and the twins to Menkaure's pyramid.'

'Perhaps I could help?' Henry offered.

'Yes,' she told him. 'You can help Slick Delaney and your

pet monkey put together the sets of photographs and make sure they actually get some work done.'

She moved off towards the back of the stage where the four girls they'd chosen were waiting. Henry was left standing, his cock uncomfortably hard and his frustration now too strong to be denied. The prospect of an afternoon spent sorting out pictures of naked and half-naked girls was unbearable, as he was sure Poppy knew only too well. It was also the ideal job for the Egg, who thrived on anything rude, while Slick as the salesman was technically in charge of handling the finished prints.

Henry needed relief, and with four of the girls on location all afternoon and the rest under the watchful eye of Hills Hennigan, whom Poppy had roped in as her assistant, his options were somewhat restricted. If he simply defied her it was sure to cause trouble, but one possibility remained, which he'd been intending to explore from the first but had yet to get around to, the delectable Jamila. A trip to the Berkha was clearly in order. Hobbling slightly due to the stiffness of his cock, he set off for the motor pool.

Half-an-hour later he was dropped off at the end of the Wagh el Birkhet itself. The street was as lively and colourful as ever, full of uniformed troops and Egyptians in local dress, with girls hanging out of the windows to solicit passers-by and the hot, still air full of the scents of perfume and spice, sharp and sweet in contrast to the heavier background reek of dung and close-packed humanity. Entering Fat Babu's, Henry glanced cautiously from side to side, sure that Captain Smith would not have forgotten the incident of the previous week.

'Officer Truscott!' Babu greeted him. 'You have been away? I have many fine girls for you, breasts like pomegranates, bottoms like ripe …'

'We're all right for girls at the moment,' Henry replied, 'but keep them on stand-by just in case. For now I'm after young Jamila from down the road, but I want to avoid the Gorilla.'

'You are wise,' Babu replied. 'Captain Smith, he says … he says he will fry your testicles in oil and make you eat them.'

Henry winced.

'Ahmed al-Ashal also wishes to kill you,' Babu went on.

'What the hell for?'

'For Jamila.'

'What!? When he'd sold her virginity to the Gorilla, the blasted hypocrite! Not that she was a virgin anyway, but I suppose that's beside the point. Honestly, the fuss people make over a rogered tart!'

'This is true, Officer Truscott, but Captain Smith, he was to pay fifty pounds. Now he will not pay.'

Henry gave a sour grunt and glanced at the door before speaking again.

'Is he about, the Gorilla?'

'I do not believe so, but the lovely Jamila, she is not permitted to leave her room.'

'Ah-ha,' Henry said. 'Do you mind if I use your upstairs for a while?'

'You are always most welcome. At the usual rate.'

'Set it against what you owe us for the fezzes,' Henry told him, ignoring Babu's automatic protest as he made for the stairs.

A moment later he was letting himself out on to the flat rooftops behind the houses. The air seemed hotter and stiller even than it had in the street, but the noise and bustle was gone, with a thin tabby cat lazing in the shade the only immediate sign of life. Henry moved cautiously over the roofs, towards the window of Jamila's room, only to stop abruptly as he caught the sound of voices, first an angry, bass rumble he recognised as the Gorilla himself, speaking in pidgin English, then a reply, high-pitched and frightened, in Arabic. He swore softly under his breath, made to move back towards the window of Babu's, only to stop once more at the sound of a meaty thwack followed by a scream of pain.

'Oh hell!' he muttered, starting towards Jamila's window once more and speaking as he reached it. 'Look here, Smith, that's just not on, don't …'

Henry's voice was drowned by a second thwack of leather on flesh and the answering scream. He stopped. Captain Smith was standing with his back to the window, stripped to the waist, his massive, thickly haired shoulders bunched with muscle as he flexed a hippopotamus hide sjambok for another strike at the cowering Jamila. On a wall between two roofs was a line of pots, each with a tangle of herbs growing in it. Henry snatched up the nearest one, stepped forward and brought it down on the back of Captain Smith's head with all his force.

Smith had began to turn an instant before the pot hit him, and it burst on his temple, scattering earth and shards of pottery into the room. For one terrible instant the two of them were eye to eye, Smith's bright with a mad glitter of recognition, before he collapsed to the floor, striking his head on the corner of Jamila's pallet as he went down. She was curled into one corner, naked, with two livid welts marking one smooth hip, and looked up from wide, frightened eyes.

Henry extended a hand and she took it, allowing herself to be drawn through the window and supported on his arm as he made for Babu's once more. His emotions were confused, anger and guilt warring with a fierce urge to take her then and there on the rooftops. He forced his need away, but as he helped her in at the window he found she wouldn't let go, clinging hard to his body, shivering and babbling in Arabic.

'Oh hell,' he swore once more. 'Forgive me ...'

Even as he spoke he'd freed his cock from his trousers, and as he lifted Jamila under her bottom he slid into her with ease. She made no protest, clinging to him with even greater urgency as he pushed himself up inside her, faster and faster, the long hours of gradually rising frustration and her urgent, animal reaction coming together to bring him to orgasm in moments. He cried out as he came inside her, his teeth gritted and his fingers locked in her flesh, just as hers were in his.

'Sorry, had to,' he gasped as he withdrew, but she continued to cling to him, whimpering softly with tears running down her face.

Henry manhandled her from the room, finally managing to loosen her grip in the corridor before rushing up to the next floor to find a blanket, which he draped around her as he led her down to the bar. Babu stood as before.

'Not a word to anybody,' Henry said, 'especially the

Gorilla.'

He scooped some notes from his pocket and slapped them down on the counter before steering Jamila to the door and into the street. She made no effort to resist, allowing him to lead her into an alley and away without objection. He had soon secured a cab, helping her in and giving instructions to the driver before joining her and only then allowing himself to relax.

'I thought you were sorting out pictures?' Poppy demanded as Henry drew close.

'I had better things to do,' he replied. 'This is Jamila, who'll need to be looked after for a while. She only speaks Arabic, although I think she understands a bit of pidgin.'

Poppy made to speak but Henry cut her off.

'She's had a bit of a rough time, with Captain Smith. You know, ghastly fellow, manners of a baboon. She's damn fine-looking as well, as I'm sure you'll agree?''

Poppy cast a critical eye over Jamila, who stood placidly to one side, still wrapped in the blanket Henry had taken from Babu's.

'So I see,' she said, 'but we can't simply take on every waif and stray you happen to take pity on. We're supposed to be making money.'

Henry tugged Jamila's blanket open to show the livid welts on her hip. Poppy winced and nodded, then put an arm around Jamila's shoulders and led her towards the truck they'd been allocated for support, leaving Henry to move towards where Bunker was taking pictures. It was an impressive sight, Maria, Assiatou, Khadjia and Zokie, all four stark naked and perched on camels, with Menkaure's pyramid and the great Giza necropolis as a background.

'This will be popular,' he said as he approached.

'Back home, sure to be,' Bunker responded. 'Out here, not so much. The best seller's little Sally Green undressing for her bath, by a mile.'

'Pretty girl, Sally,' Henry replied, ignoring a sudden stab of jealousy, 'but so are the others.'

'Air Force girl, that's why,' Bunker explained. 'The boys

love to see one of their own stripped down.'

'Poppy was saying the same thing,' Henry responded. 'Not that she's going to join in, unfortunately. We'd make a fortune with her, but you wait until you see Georgina Hayes. She's an absolute cracker, and there's three more besides.'

'And how about Hills?' Bunker said. 'She's bigger than Maria, up front.'

'Another one who won't take her clothes off,' Henry sighed, 'although we might have had her at poker the other night, and yes, that's one pair of melons I'd like to see, and to get my hands on for that matter.'

Bunker made a rude gesture in agreement and went back to his camera, leaving Henry with a picture in his mind of Hills Hennigan's straining jacket front and wondering if her breasts really were bigger than the bouncing brown globes Maria was displaying so nicely as she rode her camel. The urgent, instinctive fuck with Jamila had relieved his outer tension, but no more, leaving him with a strong core of desire stoked by the abundance of female beauty all around him.

He considered the possibility of getting one of the girls alone once Bunker had finished photographing the camel scene. It had to be practical, especially as Bunker was sure to oblige by arranging another set out among the tombs or among a group of palm trees, which would provide ample cover to give Maria a good, slow rogering, or perhaps Zokie, or the twins, both together as he'd enjoyed them in the brothel at Dakar.

Strangely, none of these options really appealed, while his mind kept coming back to Poppy, who had made it very clear that she was unobtainable, and to Hills Hennigan, with her abundant bust. It had to be admitted that there was something in what both Poppy and Bunker had said, that too casual a display of a girl's charms diluted her appeal, whereas there was an added thrill to teasing a shy, reluctant girl out of her uniform, especially if he could then make as thorough a pig of himself with her as he would have done had he been paying for his pleasure.

'Where are Hills and the others?' he asked as Bunker once

more emerged from beneath the black cloth he'd rigged up to improve his view through the big aviation camera.

'Give us a mo', Skipper,' Bunker replied, then called out. 'Nice one, Maria! Now let's have some arse. Ride 'em around behind me, then come past, nice and slow, only up in the saddle like you was racing. Bums well out, yeah? Sorry, Skipper. They're rehearsing.'

Maria signalled her understanding and gestured to the other girls, bringing the four camels into a line and swinging them around to trot past where Henry and the photographer stood. As she drew level with the camera, Maria lifted herself in the saddle, displaying her full, dark bottom to perfect advantage, thrust well out with her thighs spread across the beast's hump to show off both her cunt and her anus.

Unfortunately the other girls hadn't fully understood the instructions and the manoeuvre had to be repeated four times before Bunker was satisfied with the results. By then Henry's cock was a rigid bar in his trousers and he no longer cared for such subtle distinctions as whether a girl was readily available or not.

'How do you cope?' he asked Bunker.

'When you're behind the camera,' Bunker explained, 'it's like a job of work. Yeah, it gets to me, in the end, and I always fuck one when we're done, two or three, sometimes, if they want their share.'

'I thought Poppy had put a stop to that sort of thing?' Henry asked.

'Only for you, Skipper, only for you,' Bunker answered. 'Me an' the lads, she knows what we need and how to keep us sweet.'

'The little bitch!' Henry exclaimed.

'I reckon it's like Gorski says,' Bunker told him. 'She's sweet on you, an' she don't like to see you with other bints.'

Henry merely grunted, his frustration now at boiling point. Glancing back towards the truck, he found that Poppy was seated on a shooting stick. In one hand she held a clipboard, on which she was making marks with an air of carefully deliberation. Jamila was nowhere to be seen and so presumably inside the truck. Walking over, Henry greeted her with a bright smile.

'All seems to be going well, then?'

'Very well,' Poppy agreed, 'especially sales to the army.'

'Yes, well,' Henry replied, 'I suppose it makes sense that army boys will be keen to see Air Force girls stripped down, and *vice versa*, I shouldn't wonder.'

'Very possibly,' Poppy stated, still looking at her clipboard.

'I thought a celebratory drink might be in order?' he suggested. 'Perhaps at the Malqate Palace? Just you and I, of course.'

'What,' she answered him, 'so that you can get me drunk and take advantage of me?'

'Not unless you want me to,' Henry laughed.

'You really don't understand me at all, do you?' she told him, glancing up, but only for a second.

'Frankly, no,' Henry retorted. 'I mean, damn it, Pinks, you were keen enough at Babu's! You came back for more, after all, and I treated you well, didn't I?'

'Treated me well!?' she snapped back. 'You ... you had me strip in front of your friends, you spanked me, and you stuck your thing up my bottom!'

'You enjoyed every moment of it,' Henry answered, 'and besides, we've had this out before. Now come along, Pinks ...'

'I think better not,' she interrupted. 'I'm not at all sure you're the man I thought you were.'

'What's that supposed to mean?'

'Merely that the man I thought you were would know what to do.'

'Know what to do? I know every well what to do, as I would hope I'd demonstrated!'

'Perhaps you have, perhaps not.'

'I have absolutely no idea what you are talking about!' Henry said. 'Now are coming for that drink or not?'

'I think not.'

Henry threw up his hands in despair and walked away, back towards the camp with his mind seething with frustrated lust and confusion. In a hollow just beyond Poppy's range of vision

100

Bunker was still taking photographs and appeared to have abandoned all restraint in his choice of subject. He now had the four girls lined up on their knees in the sand, each with her bottom pushed out behind and her breasts lolling forward as she sucked and wanked on a big, dun coloured penis.

'Make the dirty buggers pay for that!' Henry called out in an attempt at a jocularity he didn't feel.

Bunker responded with an insulting gesture and one of the camel herders with a rude one, but the girls continued to suck, Maria acknowledging him with a wave but without pulling back from the cock in her mouth. Henry paused, drinking in the obscene sight in the hope that it would calm his emotions, but succeeding only in stoking his lust. After a moment Zokie had her mouth filled with what looked like a good pint's worth of spunk, which exploded from around her lips and out of her nose to leave her gagging onto the sand as the huge cock in her mouth finally slipped free, but despite a twinge of disgust and sympathy Henry found himself wanting to give her the same treatment.

With the other three girls still sucking cock and Bunker taking pictures it was clearly unwise, especially with Poppy so near, and he walked on, between the smaller tombs and past the great bulk of Menkaure's pyramid. The heat was beginning to drain from the day, but by the time he managed to pick up a cab at the edge of the city he was desperately thirsty. A beer in the officers' mess helped, but he collected two more before making for the small hanger in which the cabaret was being rehearsed. Gorski was on the door to ward off casual sightseers, and tipped Henry an easy salute as he approached.

'All well, Skipper?'

'Not entirely,' Henry admitted. 'Pinks is being her usual awkward self. Bunker's doing well though. He's got the girls in the nude, riding camels and generally being filthy dirty, really getting the goods. How's the cabaret shaping up?'

'See for yourself.'

Henry went inside, his eyes taking a moment to adjust to the dim light. The door led into a cubicle normally used as an office, with another door leading into the body of the hanger, along with a single, long window. Hills Hennigan was seated at the office desk with her feet up, reading a long out of date copy of Punch.

'Don't mind me,' Henry said as Hills quickly removed her feet from the table. 'Care for a beer? They're cold.'

She hesitated, but then accepted the beer. Beyond the window Michelle could be seen standing in front of a line of eight girls. All were in the scarlet dress jackets they'd bought in the market, but with frilly knickers and stockings in the same brilliant colour rather than nothing but their shoes. There was a notably gap between the four service girls on the left and the four Dakar working girls on the right, while Michelle seemed distinctly exasperated by their efforts at following her movements.

'Best leave them to it, I think,' Henry remarked.

'My thoughts exactly,' Hennigan agreed. 'Michelle Boudin seems to know what she's doing.'

'I always used to assume that French girls learn that sort of thing more or less from the cradle,' Henry remarked. 'You're not tempted to join them then?'

'Too short. Too fat,' Hills replied.

'Nonsense,' Henry chided. 'You're very well proportioned.'

She threw him a sarcastic look and took a swallow of her beer.

'Seriously,' Henry insisted. 'Bunker was saying what a shame it is you won't pose for him. Mark you, considering what he was up to just now, perhaps it's just as well, really.'

'What?' she demanded.

'He had the girls lined up to, er … provide a spot of fellatio, Cairo style, not to put too fine a point on it. He said it was a shame you didn't lose at poker the other night too, and I have to agree.'

She didn't answer, and Henry hastened to push what he hoped was an advantage. Her response was cautious, but gradually became coy as he did his best to flatter her, while as they talked she seemed to be having increasing difficulty keeping her eyes from the front of his trousers. He had been at least half stiff most of the day, and watching the girls with the camels had left him with an aching erection that had barely reduced since, but the opportunity was too good to pass up.

'I'm sorry about this,' he said, hastily adjusting himself, 'but you know how it is, talking to an attractive girl when you're all keyed- up.'

'I don't mind,' she told him, and for a moment her tongue had poked out to moisten her lips.

'No?' Henry asked. 'In that case ... I mean to say, don't take this the wrong way, but would you like to ...?'

He left the question unfinished, now fairly sure she was willing but not sure how far he could push it, especially with other people about.

'What about Pinks?' she asked.

'Pinks?' Henry queried. 'What's she got to do with anything?'

'I thought ...,' she began and then broke off, now biting her lip.

'How about it?' he asked, now struggling to hold himself back. 'Do I get the green?'

'But Pinks ...'

'Never mind Poppy,' he said as his frustration finally boiled over. 'Just undo your jacket, please?'

'That's what you want, is it?' she said, her voice no longer uncertain. 'It always is with you men. Oh all right, but it's private.'

Henry was in no mood to argue over details, but watched in fascination as she took a hasty glance into the interior of the hanger and then began to undo her jacket. Each button was under considerable stress, and came open to reveal a hint of white cotton chemise and the plump bulge of her breasts beneath. He put his hand to his cock, squeezing it through his trousers, and when she made no objection he began to massage his already straining erection. She didn't comment, but licked her lips once more and continued to undo her jacket, opening all but the lowest buttons before pulling the side apart to leave her breasts bulging out of the gap.

'More?' she asked.

'Oh yes, everything,' he told her and she smiled.

Henry continued to play with his cock through his trousers as she tugged down her chemise and unfastened her bra, pulling it low to leave her breasts fully exposed, two fat pink globes of girl flesh topped by straining nipples and squashed together by her half-open jacket to make a deep and enticing cleavage. She took hold of them, one in each hand, her abundant flesh spilling out around her fingers as she lifted them fully clear of her uniform while looking up into Henry's eyes as if seeking approval.

'Superb,' he managed, 'magnificent, colossal!'

'Get your thing out then, and you can … you know, over them.'

Henry wasted no time in pulling his cock free from the confines of his clothing. She gave an excited giggle as she saw how hard he was and held her breasts up higher still as he stepped forward. With his eyes fixed on the display she was making of her chest he began to masturbate, over her at first, then closer, so that his dangling balls were rubbing in her cleavage. Still she made no objection, and after a moment pulled them apart to offer a slide for his erection.

'Do it between them, if you like,' she said, her voice now hoarse.

'Yes, please,' he answered, pushing his cock down to fuck in the warm, soft slit between her huge breasts.

It was a wonderful sensation, not only the feel of her smooth, female flesh against his cock and balls but the sheer relief of being able to take out his frustrations between her breasts. His sense of gratitude was overwhelming as he pushed up and down, bringing with it guilt for using her in what he realised was a thoroughly cavalier fashion. Not that she seemed to mind, alternately giggling and sighing gently as he fucked in her cleavage, but when he felt the first stirrings of orgasm he drew back.

'I could do it, so easily,' he said, 'but isn't there anything you want?'

'I'll tell you,' she breathed. 'Go on, do it … do it all over me.'

He pushed his cock back between her breasts, no longer

guilty as he began to fuck them, his cock now popping up and down between the fat, pink pillows, faster, and faster still until he finally let go, sending a jet of thick, white spunk up into the air to splash down on her breasts, a second into her face and a third into her open mouth. She made a face, but swallowed, and she was smiling as Henry stepped back to offer her a handkerchief.

'And in return?' he offered, intent on keeping his word and perfectly happy to lick her, which seemed to be what she was hinting at.

'Lick up your mess,' she sighed.

'My ...,' Henry queried. 'Oh, I see ...'

'You said you would,' she insisted as she began to tug up her uniform skirt, 'and it is yours.'

'That's true,' Henry admitted, 'but er ... are you sure you wouldn't like a nice lick instead?'

'You can do that too,' she said, spreading her thighs as she made herself comfortable. 'When you've cleaned me up. Come on, Henry. I know you let the girls sit on your face.'

She had begun to masturbate, pulling the split seam of her old-fashioned drawers wide to spread out her cunt, with one finger already busy with the bud of her clitoris. Henry hesitated a moment more, then squatted down, very glad that he'd relieved himself inside Jamila earlier, although Sarah Hennigan's breasts were nevertheless quite liberally splashed with his come.

He kissed her first, wincing at the salty, male taste in her mouth and thinking of all the times he'd made girls swallow as he in turn gulped down his first mouthful. Yet she was passionate in response, kissing eagerly and rubbing at her cunt, then taking hold of the back of his head to ease him further down. Henry did his best to comply, lapping up the spunk with the tip of his tongue and swallowing it down, although he was unable to stop himself from grimacing in disgust.

Sarah watched, rubbing herself with rising urgency as he cleaned first her cleavage, then one plump breast and the other, finishing with her straining nipples. At that she came, her fingers locked tight in his hair as she panted out her ecstasy, and at the last moment pulling his head hard in between her breasts. For a long moment Henry found himself unable to breath, while he also realised that he had missed quite a bit of the spunk in her cleavage as his face was rubbed into it, but he made no effort to pull back until she finally relaxed her grip with a long, heartfelt sigh.

'I've always wanted to make a man do that. Men always want to do it on my breasts, and they usually make me swallow, but I've always liked the idea of getting my own back.'

'Well, yes, I can see that you might,' Henry admitted, reaching for his unfinished bottle of beer.

'Do you intend to seduce every single one of my colleagues?' Poppy demanded.

Henry had been expecting the question, or something similar, having been fairly sure that Sarah Hennigan would admit to what they had done. Just as with Sally Green, Poppy seemed to exert a strong influence on her subordinates.

'Not every single one, no,' he answered her, 'but I don't really see that it's any of your business. Well, Sally, maybe, as the two of you seem to have an understanding, highly peculiar though it may be, but Hills is a big girl and she can do as she pleases.'

'You're nothing but a satyr, Henry Truscott,' she told him. 'A lascivious, dirty-minded old satyr, and a perverted one at that.'

'I resent that,' Henry responded. 'I'll be thirty on my next birthday, I'll have you know, and as for being perverted, well, I expect you've heard about little girls who throw stones in glass houses, eh?'

Her response was an angry snort, but she had settled herself into the seat next to him, beside the central aisle, and clearly intended to stay there during the performance, which was due to start within a few minutes. They had chosen the maintenance hanger as the only building large enough to accommodate all those who wanted to attend, so that while the makeshift stage was set on a wide area of clear floor with seating to the front and a curtained-off area behind, to one side were gantries, an assortment of machinery and several huge aircraft wheels, and to the other the ragged fuselage of a Lancaster which was being cannibalised for spare parts. Henry, Poppy and the others who'd worked with them occupied the second row, with the first reserved for the most senior officers, including Poppy's father, while Michelle and to a lesser extent Maria were in charge behind the scenes. The stage was bare save for a somewhat battered grand piano.

The hanger was rapidly filling up, which gave Henry a great deal of pride and satisfaction but also made him wish he'd found some method of directing what was being charged for admittance to himself and his crew rather than the benevolent fund. Nevertheless, it was satisfying to see so many of his fellow airmen eager to watch what was ultimately his creation, for all his lack of input into the details, and to know that every single male present envied him his close contact with the girls involved.

Among the last to arrive were the senior officers, with Sir Pomeroy Pankhurst seating himself directly in front of Poppy and turning to talk to her, while beyond him on the far side of the aisle was the Air Vice Marshal himself. A short, stout man with a pink face and very unmilitary tweeds in a loud check came to sit in front of Henry, to his relief, as the man's lack of height allowed an unobstructed view of the stage. As the last few took their seats the lights went dim. Poppy rose, walking quickly to the stage and climbing up, to face the audience. A single spotlight illuminated her as she announced the show, and the title of the cabaret troop, making Henry wish he'd insisted on keeping rather more of the glory for himself, but it was plainly too late to do anything about it.

The moment Poppy had returned to her seat more spotlights came on, illuminating first Georgina Hayes and then all fourteen girls as they trooped out on to the stage, every single one in a smart scarlet Great War dress uniform jacket accompanied by frilly knickers and stockings. They were led by Georgina as the lieutenant, with Maria now promoted to sergeant and Michelle and Lola as lance corporals, each taking her role as the remaining girls were put through parade paces, giving the audience an opportunity to appreciate the view from every possible angle. Jamila was last in the line and always slightly out of step, drawing laughter from the crowd in addition to applause and wolf whistles, also lewd comments, all of which went quiet as Georgina stepped to the front of the stage. Only when the music started did Henry realise that one of the army girls had seated herself at the piano, and with that Georgina began to sing *Mademoiselle from Armentières* with other members of her troop joining in with each verse until all fourteen were singing.

As the song died away the applause began once more and Henry noted an elderly colonel wiping a tear from his eye. The girls left the stage, all but Georgina, who stayed to thank the audience, the girls and Poppy in particular, again provoking a touch of discontent for Henry, who wasn't mentioned. Georgina then saluted, turned smartly about on her heels and walked from the stage, the sight of her bottom wiggling in her frilly scarlet knickers again provoking whistles and comments from the audience. Sir Pomeroy Pankhurst turned in his chair to speak to Poppy.

'All rather vulgar, my dear, but then again that is what the troops like, and always has been. Good show.'

Poppy smiled her appreciation for her father's comments and then put her finger to her lips as a group of girls came out on stage for the next number. This was *Run Rabbit Run* performed by Maria in abbreviated tweeds with most of her chest bare and the rear cut out of her trousers to show off her frilly knickers, while Michelle, Lola and Jacinta were the rabbits, complete with skin-toned bathing costumes, long bunny ears and fluffy tails sticking out above their bottoms. Henry found himself enjoying both the view and the song, and yet more so with the following piece, *A Bicycle Built for Two*, with the twins pretending to be man and wife, Khadija in a tail coat and top hat, Assiatou in a pair of ancient bloomers that kept coming down as they cycled around the stage, displaying her naked bottom to the cheering, clapping crowd.

'That's better,' Henry remarked to Bunker on his right as

the song closed. 'Nothing like a bit of accidentally exposed flesh to get the boys going.'

'It was carefully staged,' Poppy remarked in an undertone. 'Nothing tonight has been left to chance.'

'Good show then,' Henry conceded. 'What's next?'

'You'll see,' she responded as Michelle stepped out on to the stage.

To Henry's delight Michelle began a comic strip, pretending that she had a flea in her costume[6], which forced her not only to remove her clothing a piece at a time but to adopt a series of poses that were at once rude and ridiculous, most of them with her bottom stuck well out. As she exposed more and more flesh Henry could feel his pulse quickening, but to his disappointment she discovered the imaginary flea in one of her stockings, while she was still in a pair of old-fashioned combinations, allowing her to leave the stage with at least some dignity intact.

'More tease than strip, I'm afraid,' he whispered to Bunker. 'Not bad though.'

'Not Michelle's choice,' Bunker replied. 'She'd 'ave gone starkers an' pretended it had crawled up her fanny.'

The piano had started once more and Henry turned his attention back to the stage, where Sally and the two other WAAF girls had come out in full and correct uniform to perform *Coming in on a Wing and a Prayer*. A raucous version of *Roll out the Barrel* performed by six of the girls in just their underwear followed, then a double striptease from the twins, with each feigning shock as the other removed her clothes but always keen to outdo her sister. Again they kept their knickers and bras, to Henry's disappointment, although it was plain that the sort of exhibition he'd have preferred would have been barred by the senior officers.

One act followed another, popular songs mixed with comic routines and partial stripteases, all arousing but never fully satisfying. Henry watching with a mixture of approval and frustration, which reached its peak with the final act, with all fourteen girls dancing the cancan while clad in full male evening dress from the waist up and nothing but stockings and lacy Victorian style drawers below. As the girls kicked high and twirled to flip up the tails of their coats and show off their bottoms the splits in their knickers provided brief and enticing glimpses of bare, rounded flesh and the all too brief display of Lola's cunt, but no more.

Whatever Henry's reservations, the audience clearly approved, clapping, whistling, stamping their feet and yelling for more, a request that Michelle obliged with another and yet more vigorous cancan and further teasing exposure of bare female flesh, which left Henry with an aching erection and an urgent need for sex but also a strong sense of having been denied his full measure of display. Nevertheless, there was no disputing Poppy's success and the moment the applause had died down he turned to congratulate her.

'That rang the bell for the boys. A bit tame, perhaps, for my own tastes, but still, jolly good stuff.'

'We know all about your tastes,' she responded, then glanced quickly around to make sure nobody was going to hear before going on in a whisper. 'I suppose you'd have had them lined up and spanked one by one?'

'Something on those lines,' Henry admitted. 'In fact, what a picture, but I'd happily trade it to have you across my knee again.'

'You're a disgrace to you uniform, Henry Truscott,' she answered, but to his astonishment there was no bitterness in her voice and she had looked down as she spoke.

Henry found himself involuntarily moistening his lips, and with his pulse beating faster than in response to any of the cabaret acts, but Sir Pomeroy had turned to speak to Poppy, cutting off any possibility of taking the situation further. More frustrated than ever, he was forced to make polite conversation, with people of every rank and from every service keen to congratulate Poppy on her triumph, making it impossible to speak to her privately. Few took more than passing notice of Henry, while Bunker, Slick and the others had gone off to sell pictures to the now dispersing audience, so that he quickly found himself at a loose end.

A squad of military police had been on hand to keep an eye

on the behaviour of the audience and some of their number had now positioned themselves to either side of the stage, preventing anyone from going behind to join the girls. Fortunately the Corporal knew Henry and about his involvement, so allowed him through to where all fourteen were laughing and chattering together over the success of their venture. Henry was quickly surrounded, and found his spirits rising as he was greeted with kisses, hugs, and, by the Dakar girls, rather more.

Ainikki was especially bold, squeezing his cock through his trousers, which would have been too much had it not been for the press of girls eager for his attention, who included Sally, Georgina and their fellow servicewomen. Jamila came close, to hug him, kiss him full on the lips and pour out what seemed to be thanks in a mixture of Arabic and pidgin English, then Maria, with her huge breasts straining at the fabric of the gent's dress shirt she was still wearing from the cancan performance, and Michelle, to tell him that she'd have preferred to strip naked and ask if he'd like a private performance at a later date. Then there was Georgina, leaning close to whisper that she'd do the same if he wanted, and with that he could hold back no more.

'Frightfully sorry,' he gasped, 'but you're going to have to help me with this.'

He'd freed his cock as he spoke, to tug furiously on the shaft as he let his free hand slip into the rear slit of Michelle's Victorian drawers, to squeeze one petite bottom cheek. The other girls responded with giggles and shrieks of shock or pleasure or both, most crowding close. Maria had quickly taken hold of his cock, allowing him to use both hands to grope at nubile bottoms. Girls were kissing him, touching him, craning close to see his cock, giggling and calling out to each other in delight for his excitement, their warm, soft flesh pressed to his body. Ainikki's hand found his balls, Jamila's breasts popped free of her shirt as she pressed close to him and he came, a fountain of spunk erupting from his cock just as Maria went down on her knees to take him in her mouth, catching her full in the face to the delight of the others and of Henry himself, who finished by sticking his erection as far down her throat as it would go.

Chapter Seven

SLICK DELANEY UPENDED A sack onto the navigator's table in Jazzy Jess, spilling out a glittering cascade of coins, with not a few notes mixed in, the take from sales of pictures after the cabaret concert.

'Good God, now that's a sight for sore eyes!' Henry exclaimed. 'How much is there?'

'I've not counted it yet, Skipper,' Slick told him, 'but it tops a hundred quid, easy, and there'll be more where that came from.'

'They all wanted signed pictures,' the Egg put in, 'of Michelle and Georgina mostly, but if we had a group shot signed by all the girls we'd make a bleedin' fortune.'

'See to it, Bunker,' Henry instructed, 'and individual shots of all the girls posing, not too smutty. That way we can keep the dirty stuff back for higher prices.'

'That's the way to do it,' Slick agreed as he began to sort the money into piles, 'but they're good, ain't they? We'd never have got this much without the show.'

'That's very true,' Henry agreed, 'and no sign of the Gorilla?'

'Not that I saw,' the Egg confirmed. 'Probably still in the infirmary.'

'Where he'll stay until we're gone, with any luck,' Henry responded. 'It's a damn nuisance, having to look over my shoulder all the time.'

'Stick with us,' the Egg advised. 'Oh, an' we got noticed, an' all, the cabaret did. There was some fellow called Pettigrew there, a London impresario, so I hear.'

'Short, fat fellow, red face?' Henry queried. 'He was sitting in front of us, wasn't he, Bunker?'

'Yeah, I reckon,' Bunker agreed. 'I remember they had him down the Empire before the war. Forty show girls he had on stage, and they said that when he did the show in Paris they was in the nude. Weeks I spent totting, all round North London, until I could afford tickets for that, an' then the bastards wouldn't let me in.'

'Why not?' Slick asked. 'On account of you being from the Bunk?'

'Nah, not that. They said I was too young. I was bleedin' twelve, nearly.'

Both Slick and the Egg made solemn expressions of sympathy for their comrade's plight, while Henry shook his head in wonder, recalling his own relative innocence.

'Pettigrew Presents, it was called,' Bunker went on wistfully. 'Forty show girls.'

He smacked his lips at the memory, then sat down to help Slick count the money.

'We have fourteen,' Henry pointed out, 'which isn't bad going at all, but what we don't have is a great deal of time. Three days to relief, and I want you to spend every minute of them selling, except for you, Bunker. We've still time to get some more pictures, the group shot for a start and then anything we won't be able to get back home, so maybe you should go out to the pyramids again, or down to the Nile. Once we're back home things change, and we don't know who we're going to have.'

'Or where we're going to be,' Bunker pointed out.

'That I do know,' Henry told him. 'We're at Fairlop, and we're staying there at least until demob's finished.'

'What about the girls?'

'That depends. Some want to stay here. Some want to come with us, but there's the problem of getting them over. Sally's up for demob, Georgina too, and I dare say Poppy can wangle them a ride. Otherwise, we'll just have to do the best we can.'

'A/CDRE wants you, Skipper,' Gorski announced, poking his head in at the door of the Lancaster.

114

'Hell!' Henry swore. 'Look, if I'm up for a black, make sure the money and the pictures are safe. In fact, hide them now.'

He left the plane, walking across to the command buildings and into the office of Air Commodore Sir Pomeroy Pankhurst, who was seated behind his desk and to Henry's relief seemed to be in a good mood.

'Ah, Truscott, splendid show last night. Poppy was just the girl for the job, don't you think?'

'Yes, sir, absolutely,' Henry agreed, 'and the girls of course, little Michelle in particular.'

'Ah, yes, but she's a professional.'

Henry swallowed hard, despite being unable to reconcile Sir Pomeroy's cheerful tone with the expected reaction to the discovery that Michelle was a prostitute.

'She did her bit, yes,' Sir Pomeroy went on, 'but I mean to say, a woman who's been on the Paris stage isn't going to make a fuss over a little Air Force concert, is she? Whereas my Poppy's never put together anything more demanding than a school play.'

'That's true, sir,' Henry admitted with considerable relief, although he wasn't sure if Michelle had even been to Paris, let alone on stage. 'You wanted to talk to me, sir?'

'Ah, yes. Just a couple of points. You're a Devon man, aren't you?'

'Yes, sir.'

'There's a high ranking USAF officer who'd like to be set down at Plasterdown Camp[7], near Tavistock. D'you know it?'

'It's about five miles from my house, sir, but this officer. It's not a Colonel Millard Jackson by any chance?'

'No,' Sir Pomeroy confirmed. 'Some fellow named McLellan, and he's a General. Well, it's your mission if you want it, and feel free to take a day or two's leave before you report for duty at Fairlop. Now, the other matter. The rumour mill has it that your man Sloper has been taking one or two pictures of your cabaret concert girls. Is that so?'

'Yes, sir,' Henry answered weakly, his stomach sinking but buoyed by a faint hope in that the Air Commodore's tone of voice suggested more embarrassment than disapproval.

'I see,' Sir Pomeroy went on, 'and that being the case, I was wondering if you might be able to do me a small favour? I am something of an amateur of the artistic nude myself, you know ... a discerning collector, one might say, and certain subjects are harder to find than others. I'm especially keen to get hold of some pictures of girls, um ... tied up, you know the sort of thing, damsels in distress and all that. Purely artistic, you understand, and not a word to my daughter, of course. Girls are apt to put the wrong construction on that sort of thing, and you know what Poppy's like.'

'Absolutely,' Henry agreed, 'and er ... speaking of small favours, sir. One or two of the girls are er ... rather keen to visit England, so I was wondering ...'

'Say no more,' Sir Pomeroy interrupted. 'Matters are already in hand. Some of the girls want to stay here, or go home, so you'll be dropping young Lola Céret off at Toulouse when you refuel.'

'Er ... right ho, thank you, sir,' Henry answered, taken aback. 'May I ask who is coming and who's staying?'

'Let me see. Ah ... yes, Green and Hayes are due for demobilisation, so they're going. Miss Esposito has accepted a place working in the canteen, so she isn't, and nor are the twins, or Lola Céret, but Michelle Boudin is, of course, and the other four. Poppy has arranged everything.'

'So I see,' Henry responded. 'Well, if that's all, sir, I'd better see to your request.'

'Good man, Truscott.'

Henry left the office, giving Hills Hennigan a playful pat on the head as he went but unable to stop and talk with her in case the Air Commodore overheard. Poppy has surpassed herself in organising transport for the girls, but Henry was left with a feeling that he had somehow been usurped and was keen to find out more. Yet finding her wasn't necessarily going to be easy, while Sir Pomeroy's request held so many advantages that it needed to be dealt with promptly, certainly before Bunker left the camp. Hurrying back to the Lancaster, he discovered that he was only just in time, meeting Bunker as he climbed down from the door, his camera equipment in his hands.

'Whatever you were planning, drop it,' he instructed. 'I have a special request, a spot of bondage, artistically done. A girl staked out in chains for the local monster, that sort of thing.'

'Monster?' Bunker queried. 'Don't know about that, Skipper. All we've got is camels, or crocodiles, maybe, but they're dangerous buggers, them.'

'We don't actually need a monster,' Henry told him, 'just a girl and some chains.'

'Chains I can do,' Bunker assured him as they set off for the girls' quarters. 'How about one of the bints spread out on a big stone block, like she's going to be sacrificed? Maybe on top of one of them little pyramids? Tricky angle, mind you …'

He went quiet, pondering the possibilities for chaining girls into artistic poses and how to photograph them. Henry was also deep in thought, wondering which of the girls it would be the most fun to take out on location and what possibilities might be offered once she was chained up. Maria, Zokie and Lola were tempting as it might be his last chance with them, also the twins, but when they reached the hut it was empty but for Georgina Hayes, who was sitting on her bunk industriously polishing shoes.

'Where's everybody else?' Henry asked.

'Corporal Pankhurst has taken them into Cairo for a celebration lunch, sir,' Georgina answered him. 'Except for me. I'm on fatigues.'

'On fatigues? Why? And for that matter, since when has a WAAF corporal had the authority to put an ATS girl on fatigues?'

'I … I was cheeky.'

'Cheeky? Where does she think she is, St. Cyprian's[8]? Mark you, knowing Pinks you're lucky you didn't get a spanking.'

'I did,' Georgina replied, very voice barely audible.

'Oh dear, I am sorry,' he replied, trying to mean it as he imagined how she'd have looked bare and kicking over Poppy's knee. 'Not in front of the others, I hope?'

'Yes, all of them,' Georgina said weakly, 'and she had

117

Maria hold my legs.'

Her voice had taken on an edge of self-pity and her lower lip had began to tremble. Henry stepped forward to put his arm around her, giving her what he hoped she would interpret as a brotherly squeeze. She began to snivel, at which his cock started to grow hard and he found himself obliged to pull away before she noticed, speaking in a hearty voice as he rejoined Bunker.

'Oh well, never mind. No real harm done, I don't suppose, but you're not to bother about her silly fatigues. Bunker and I need you for some more pictures.'

'But Corporal Pankhurst ...'

'Damn Pinks Pankhurst. If she says anything, refer her to me, and you can tell her that if she gives you another spanking she'll get the same treatment from me, bare-bottom. Clear?'

Georgina smiled in response and finally put down the shoe she'd been polishing. Her nose had begun to run and Henry passed her his handkerchief.

'Girls who get spankies often need hankies,' he said. 'My sister Stephanie had to write that out a hundred times after an incident involving one of my aunts, I forget which.'

As she accepted the handkerchief another smile brightened Georgina's face and Henry gave her hair a friendly ruffle. Bunker had been watching with a faintly shifty expression on his face and winked at Henry when Georgina turned her back to wipe her nose.

'I've heard that one,' he said, 'only down the Bunk it goes "girls who get spankies often give wankies". They do an' all.'

'It's the way the smacks heat their cunts,' Henry remarked quietly, 'that and being made to go bare-bottom, I expect, but today I'm hoping for rather more. All we need is some gauze, a few yards of good chain and a ruined temple.'

Georgina lay spread over the fallen column, all four limbs securely fastened with chain, her head hanging down at one end as if in forlorn resignation, her bottom lifted at the other in a position so tempting than any monster coming across her would have had difficulty deciding whether to eat her or fuck her. Henry had no such doubts. His cock had been painfully stiff for some time, while the wet, slightly open mouth of her cunt not only betrayed her arousal but the fact that she was no virgin.

The temple was a site they'd often seen from the air, in a lonely spot of desert somewhat south of the Giza necropolis. Henry had no idea who had built it, although the litter of fallen columns and broken slabs spoke more of Greece than of Egypt, but there was no denying that it was the perfect place to photograph naked girls chained to rocks. They had started with one of the few columns that remained standing, fixing Georgina to it with her arms pulled back and her wrists wrapped in chain. She been naked from the start, and the length of gauze they'd purchased on the way out of Cairo was completely transparent, doing more to accentuate her curves than to conceal.

Once Bunker was satisfied with her poses chained with her back to the pillar they had turned her around, circling her waist with the chain and fixing her arms into it so that she had little choice but to show off her bottom as she pretended to struggle. They'd then tried a stone block, with Georgina spread out on her back as if in preparation for sacrifice, a set of purely artistic poses set against a frieze of men in chariots, and lastly the fallen columns and a pose that might or might not have been artistic but was definitely provocative.

Bunker had been the consummate professional throughout, concentrating on his equipment and Georgina's poses, always keen to get the best out of her body, with shots that seemed to display or accentuate her breasts, bottom and cunt as if by accident, but never so much as adjusting his cock. Henry had been less reserved, making no secret of the pleasure he was taking in watching her pose or attempting to hide the outline of his erection within his trousers. Georgina in turn was plainly willing, smiling and showing off as she got into her poses, so that Henry was sure a polite request would be all that was needed for full access to her body.

'All done, Skipper,' Bunker said. 'No more film.'

'I'm sure those will hit the spot,' he answered. 'Splendid

show, Georgina, and now ...'

He squatted down by her head, to lift her chin beneath one finger, leaving her soft brown eyes peering out from beneath a fringe of dishevelled hair.

'May I?' he asked, his fingers already fiddling with his fly.

'I'm in chains,' she breathed. 'You can do as you like with me.'

'True, but it's always polite to ask,' Henry told her.

'Anything you like,' she repeated, 'really ... anything. I can't stop you.'

'Message received,' he answered and rose to slide his erection into her mouth.

Georgina began to suck, willing and eager, her head bobbing up and down on Henry's cock as he tugged at the base of his shaft to masturbate into her mouth. It would have been easy to come, but he pulled out before it was too late, once more sinking down to talk to her.

'Good girl. And now, perhaps, for your pretty cunt?'

'Just don't ... don't do it in me, you know, your stuff,' Georgina answered.

'I'll look after you,' Henry promised, 'and will you look after Bunker too?'

Georgina nodded, blushing, and Henry rose to push his cock into her mouth once again, allowing her to suck briefly before withdrawing and walking around behind her.

'You're on, Bunker,' he said. 'In her mouth.'

Bunker lost no time, whipping a long, skinny cock from the recesses of his uniform trousers and feeding it into Georgina's mouth, even as Henry began to rub his erection between the cheeks of her bottom. She was well spread, her thighs cocked wide across the smooth white rock, her cunt agape and completely vulnerable, the soft, pink dimple of her anus on open show, both holes tempting penetration.

'What a good girl you are,' he said happily and gave her bottom a slap. 'Imagine it, eh? Two men, one in you at each end, and there's nothing you can do about it. So, up goes Willy!'

He'd been rutting in her slit as he spoke, and with the final

120

words pushed his cock in up the wet, easy hole of her cunt. She was tight, but there was no hymen to slow him down and as he began to fuck her he was wondering what lucky man had taken her virginity and who else had had her. Again he slapped her bottom, making the soft flesh ripple and bounce, and again, spanking her as he fucked in her hole and speaking at the same time.

'Come to think of it, you're not a good girl at all. You're a bad girl, aren't you, Georgina? Some lucky man's been in you already, hasn't he, maybe more than one, and look at you now, chained to a rock, a cock in your mouth and a cock in your cunt. Such a bad girl, and bad girls need spanking.'

Georgina had begun to make odd gulping noises on Bunker's cock, which might have been excitement or might have been shame, but Henry continued to spank and continued to fuck until his need for orgasm had risen to the point at which he had to stop or risk doing it inside her. He pulled his cock free, once more sliding it up between her now bright red bottom cheeks to rut in her slit.

Bunker was doing well, fully erect and pushed deep into her mouth. She was doing her best to accommodate the length of his cock, but not altogether succeeding, with a beard of spittle hanging from her chin and mucus squeezing from her nose, to which he seemed oblivious, holding her by the hair as he fucked in her throat.

Henry paused in his rubbing, knowing that with a few more pushes he would simply spunk up her back, but her well spread and well spanked bottom was too much to resist, especially with the sweaty little ring of her anus squeezing and pulsing against his balls.

'Sorry, darling, but it's the bumhole ballet for you,' he said. 'I hope you've done this before?'

Georgina was busy gagging on Bunker's cock and didn't answer, but she made no effort to wriggle away as pushed his cock back in up her cunt to dig out the juice he needed to lubricate her anus, nor when he pressed his knob to the tiny pink hole. She was tight, her ring spreading only reluctantly to the pressure, and he was obliged to dip his cock back in the slippery honey pot of her cunt several times before he was rewarded by seeing his head disappear in up her bottom hole.

'That's the way,' he sighed. 'Now up we go, nice and easy, all the way inside where it's hot and wet, and your little hole is so tight ...'

He broke off with a groan as he began to bugger her in earnest, now so deep in that with every push his balls squashed to the wetness of her cunt. She was in a fine state, juice squeezing from both ends as they rocked her back and forth on their cocks. They shared a grin as Henry took hold of her hips and Bunker got a grip under her arms, both pushing themselves as deep as they could get.

'A little more,' Henry grunted. 'Just a little more, darling and I'll be there ...God I've wanted to fuck your bottom since the moment you pulled your skirt up and I saw you were bare underneath, Georgina, you darling little tart!'

He finished with a grunt and he'd come, deep in her rectum, holding himself in even as Bunker finished with a last, strong push to jam his erection as far in as it would go, to spunk up in her throat. Georgina was promptly sick, spunk and mucus and more exploding from her mouth and nose, all over Bunker's balls and the front of his trousers. He didn't even notice, holding himself deep as he ejaculated down her neck and she struggled to cope with what was coming out and the erect penis in her bottom hole at the same time.

Henry also held himself deep until he was fully finished, pushing in and out of Georgina's straining bottom hole with short, hard thrusts until he had drained the full contents of his balls into her rectum. Only then did he withdraw, slowly, to leave her oozing mess down over the lips of her cunt and onto the hot stone beneath her, quickly at first, then in a series of bubbling farts as her anus slowly closed. Bunker had already pulled from her mouth, finally realising the state his trousers were in.

'Aw, look what you've been and done!' he exclaimed.

'Then ... then you shouldn't be so ... so rough with me,' she answered, still panting for breath, 'but it was nice. Thank you, boys.'

Henry laughed and slapped her bottom, although privately relieved that she'd taken it so well, as from the moment he'd entered her cunt he'd been thinking only of his pleasure, while Bunker clearly felt if he was going to have his long, skinny cock sucked then it ought to be all the way in. Blowing out his breath, Henry picked up the piece of discarded muslin to wipe his cock, then ducked down to unfasten the chains securing Georgina to the fallen column.

'First me, then Sally, and now poor Georgina!' Poppy stormed. 'Can't you even see a girl without wanting to stick your disgusting thingy up her bottom?'

'Frankly, no,' Henry admitted. 'Not that it's any of your business, and besides, you're a fine one to talk when you don't seem to be able to see a girl without wanting to spank her bottom.'

'I ... I have never heard ... I ... you're an unspeakable pig, Henry Truscott!'

'Perhaps, but a rather happy pig. Come along, Pinks, it's all good fun, you know, one up the bum and no harm done, all that sort of thing, and you jolly well enjoyed your own treatment. So did Georgina, for that matter, and speaking of Georgina, I made her a little promise, that if you spank her again you'll get the same treatment yourself, bare bottom.'

Poppy, who had been pink in the face even when she first accosted Henry on the open concrete of the airfield, now began to blush a rich red, and while her mouth had come wide she seemed unable to produce any sound beyond a queer gulping nose, rather as Georgina had done while sucking Bunker's cock. Henry waited for her to regain her composure, struggling to keep a serious expression on his face, but was finally obliged to act when a Short Stirling turned towards them on its way to the main runway.

'I think this chap wants to take off,' he pointed out, slipping his arm into Poppy's to steer her out of the way.

For a moment she let him lead, only to shake his arm off the moment they'd left the concrete. Henry threw a casual salute to the pilot of the Short Stirling, waiting until the heavy drone of the engines had died a little before speaking again. Poppy had also waited, with her arms folded across her chest and her face set in an angry scowl, but showing no inclination to leave.

'You shouldn't make threats you can't keep,' she said, her nose pointed firmly into the air.

'I'm a man of my word,' Henry assured her. 'And besides, wouldn't you enjoy it, rather? Come on, come clean. There's no need to be coy with me.'

Poppy gave a scornful sniff and tilted her nose up at a yet steeper angle.

'Come on, old girl, let's be rational about this,' Henry continued. 'Never mind the spanking ... for the moment. You're up for demob and we'll both be in London regularly once I've delivered this Yank bigwig to Devon. Perhaps we could step out now and again?'

'What a delightful prospect,' she replied, 'sharing you with Sally, and Hills, and Georgina, and no doubt a couple of dozen assorted tarts into the bargain!'

Her voice had risen in volume as she spoke, but Henry merely shrugged as he carried on.

'I can explain all that. It's really just a matter of opportunity ...'

'Yes, you stick your dirty big thing up girls' bottoms at every opportunity you can get.'

'No ... well, yes, perhaps, but that's not what I meant. Let me explain. When we were flying out of East Kirby we never knew if we'd be coming back one day to the next, so we took what we could get, money no object, if we had it, and believe me, the last thing you wanted to do was find a special girl, because that made it all ten times worse, and it would be worse still to leave her pregnant. So I'd always pop it up a girl's bottom if she was game, and that way she needn't worry about not being a virgin any more, and you'll have to admit I was kind to you about that. Anyway, I suppose I've rather got into the habit of it, that's all.'

They had begun to walk back towards the buildings and Poppy didn't answer so Henry continued.

'Let me tell you about the Vicar. David Hobbs was his real

name, a Londoner, from a quiet suburb. He'd been training for the clergy, but he signed up in 'thirty-nine and ended up as our mid-upper gunner. He was a quiet, boy, used to pray a lot, not only for us, but for the Jerries. He didn't believe in fornication, either, and used to chide us for our behaviour, always very gently. We took no notice, but we didn't mind. He was a bit of a lucky mascot for us, you see, and everybody used to say that the reason we were so damn lucky was because we had the Vicar with us. That was until our thirtieth mission, the very last. Coming back was … unreal. Hardly anybody spoke. The Egg had got an Me 262, the jet job, which was quite something, let me tell you, and we knew we had a line of bullet holes through the fuselage, but what we didn't know, not until we'd touched down, was that one had gone clean through the Vicar's head. So I'm sorry if my behaviour is a little boisterous at times, but perhaps that will give you an idea why.'

Poppy didn't answer, and a moment later reached out as if to take his hand, only to think better of it and pull away, then turn her steps towards the command buildings while Henry made for Jazzy Jess.

The next three days were hectic, with all the tasks attendant on stepping aside for the relief squadron to be seen to and, despite a touch of guilt for Poppy, last chances to be taken with the cabaret girls, both for photographs and pure indulgence. Henry concentrated on those who'd be staying in Egypt, first catching Maria as she cleaned up in the canteen after hours. She was as eager as he was, keen both for sex and to thank him for what she saw as her rescue from the remote outpost of Ascension Island.

Henry took full advantage, allowing her to employ all her skill on his cock and balls as she sucked him erect before fucking first her breasts, then her cunt and finally her bottom hole, well lubricated with olive oil from the canteen stock. By then she was bent over the great, scared chopping block, stark naked, her full, dark breasts squashed out on the wooden top and her meaty bottom lifted to accept his cock as he pushed himself in and out of the dark little hole between her cheeks.

She was playing with her cunt as he buggered her, and they came together, the contractions of Maria's anus milking his spunk up her bottom to provide a long, glorious orgasm and the perfect farewell.

The twins were harder to track down, as they'd disappeared into the seedy underbelly of Cairo life without explaining to anybody what they were up too. It was only by chance that Henry heard of a new brothel in the Berkha, said to be run by two beautiful black girls who would perform together on request. It seemed the ideal way to spend his final evening in Egypt, and he took care to leave the airfield as soon as was conveniently practical, intent on starting early and so avoiding the rush at what seemed likely to be a highly popular venue.

It was still light when he arrived in the Berkha, to find the address he'd been given in an alley not far from Babu's establishment. Assiatou and Khadija greeted him cordially, agreeing to his request without hesitation and even allowing him a reduced rate. Leaving one of the three girls they'd taken on to mind the door, they took Henry upstairs to a room more comfortably furnished by far than those Henry was used to in the Berkha brothels, with hangings on all four walls and a wide pallet spread with fleeces on the floor.

'Very nice,' Henry remarked.

'Money,' Assiatou explained, rubbing her fingers together. 'Dirty picture money.'

'I see,' Henry answered, 'and very wisely invested too, if I may say so. I expect you two will make a fortune, but watch out for pimps. They'll have the fillings out of your teeth if they can, so to speak … No, seriously. Pimps. Bad men. Make girls work hard. No money.'

Khadija gave a solemn nod and pulled aside the wrap she wore around her hips to reveal a British commando dagger, unusual only in that the handle had been decorated with tiny lapis lazuli beads.

'Ah, I see,' Henry, 'and where did you get that?'

'Man Slick,' she explained. 'One dagger. One fuck.'

'Not a bad deal, as it goes,' he told her, 'but then Slick's an old softie at heart. Now, if you'd care to remove your weapons, and then your clothes, we can get down to business. Nice and slow, mind you.'

'Half price. Bums in face,' Assiatou reminded him.

'Absolutely,' Henry agreed, 'bums in face. Yes, why not.'

He made himself comfortable on the pallet, opening his trousers as he lay back to pull out his cock. Assiatou got down beside him, to take him in hand, rolling his foreskin slowly back and forth as her sister began to strip, dancing with slow, sinuous movements as she teased with her wrap. She had nothing on underneath, showing off her firm, dark breasts and neatly turned little bottom, quite naked, before finally dropping the wrap to the floor and taking her sister's place.

Khadija's took Henry's cock in her mouth as Assiatou in turn began to strip and he was soon hard, his fingers exploring her bottom and the silky slit between her thighs as he fucked her full lips. She had already begun to get wet, and lost no time in straddling Henry's head as her sister, now nude, joined them on the pallet. Henry gave a pleased sigh as Khadija poised herself over his face, her firm little bottom slightly parted to show off her jet black cunt lips and the pink of her slit as well as the dark, velvet-smooth pucker of her anus.

'Perfect,' he sighed. 'I'll miss you two. Sit yourself down then.'

She responded, slowly lowering her bottom into his face and giving a little wriggle of encouragement that also spread her cheeks properly, anus to mouth. Henry began to lick, lapping at her soft anal flesh and then poking his tongue in up the tight little hole, lost in ecstasy even as Assiatou straddled his hips to guide his cock up into her cunt. The girls began to kiss as they rode him, giggling and playing with each other's breasts as he did his best to pleasure both of them at once and to hold off from coming in Assiatou's cunt before he'd had his money's worth.

They were also talking, in their own language, and swapped suddenly, Khadija easing his cock in up her hole while Assiatou put her bottom in his face, again with her anus to his mouth. Once more Henry began to lick, but Khadija had begun to play a trick, squeezing her cunt on his erection as she drew herself slowly up and down, a sensation that made it impossible to hold back. He came, deep inside her, with his tongue pushed as far up her sister's bottom hole as it would go, lost in the ecstasy of the moment, so that he barely heard their delighted giggles as they realised what they'd made him do.

'Us too. Lick good,' Assiatou demanded, wriggling her bottom in Henry's face.

He did his best to oblige, licking her bottom hole as she played with herself and then her cunt as she moved back to rub it against his mouth and nose. His cock was still up Khadija, deflating only slowly, and she had began to rub herself on him, both girls kissing and snatching at each other's breasts as they rode him to mutual orgasm, dismounting only when both were thoroughly satisfied.

'Frankly,' Henry gasped as Assiatou finally lifted her bottom from his face, 'I'm not sure who should be paying who here, but never mind. That was very good.'

'Very good,' Khadija agreed. 'Bums in face. Good fuck.'

'Good fuck,' Henry agreed. 'I'll have a bottle of beer, if I may, and perhaps another fuck later. Yes?'

'Beer now. Fuck later?' Assiatou queried.

Henry gave her a thumbs-up and relaxed back onto the pallet. With the whole evening ahead of him it seemed sensible to pace himself, enjoying a refreshing beer and waiting until he was ready to tackle the girls a second time, perhaps inserting his cock up their neatly turned little bottoms instead of his tongue, just for a change. It was an appealing thought, and with the bottle of beer in hand and the girls downstairs he'd begun to massage his balls and stroke the shaft of his cock in preparation for another bout, only to stop short as he recognised the voice of the customer the twins were talking to, a bass rumble he knew only too well.

'Virgin,' Captain Smith was saying. 'You find virgin. I pay well.'

'Damn!' Henry swore, hastily returning his cock to his underpants. 'Of all the bad luck.'

He moved to the window, opening the shutters to find a sheer drop on to the flat paving stones of another alley with the

128

blank wall of a neighbouring house just feet away in front of him. Again he moved back to listen to the conversation, hoping that as neither of the twins were virgins and the other three girls were highly unlikely to be, the Gorilla would eventually go away.

'A virgin,' Smith was trying to explain. 'A girl who's never been fucked.'

'You want girl who never fuck?' Assiatou queried, evidently puzzled. 'Why?'

'Here we have girl who fuck,' Khadija put in. 'Plenty girl. Plenty fuck. I fuck good. My sister, she fuck good. You fuck both, maybe?'

'I want a virgin,' Smith repeated, now speaking in a loud, slow voice. 'A virgin. A girl who has never been fucked.'

'We brothel,' Assiatou responded. 'Here girls fuck, always.'

'You pay. We fuck,' Khadija added helpfully.

'I know,' Smith began once more, now speaking more deliberately still. 'I want to fuck a girl who has never been fucked before.'

There was a moment of silence, then Assiatou's voice came once more.

'We not understand. Upstairs is Flying Officer Henry Truscott. He English. He understand.'

'Truscott?' Smith demanded. 'Truscott's upstairs?'

'Yes,' Assiatou replied. 'He good man. He fuck us both good.'

'And I'm going to fuck him good,' Smith replied.

'No, no, he not for fuck,' Khadija answered in sudden alarm, although her sister took a more practical attitude.

'You still pay, Monsieur!'

Henry was back at the window, considering a drop that would almost certainly mean a broken ankle and before he could make up his mind whether or not to take the risk the Gorilla was on him, hurling back the door with a crash.

'Ah, Captain Smith,' Henry managed, backing against the window frame. 'What a pleasant surprise.'

'Yes, isn't it?' Smith growled. 'And now, you sneaking, low down little cunt thief, I intend to tear off your balls and make you eat them, that's after I've given you the thrashing of your wretched life!'

He was holding his sjambok, but paused to roll up his sleeves, evidently relishing the moment and allowing Henry to plead his case.

'She wasn't a virgin at all, you know. Jamila, that is. I mean to say, really, old chap, I've never known a more willing tumble. That Ahmed al-what'sisname fellow was pulling a fast one on you, so it's really just as well I ...'

The sjambok lashed out, catching Henry's hip to lay a line of fire across his flesh and knock him to one side. He tried to lash out with his foot as he went down, but missed, leaving the Gorilla standing above him, the sjambok raised for another blow.

'First you,' Smith grated, 'to within an inch of your life, then maybe those two nigger whores downstairs, just for practice, then that incontinent little slut Jamila, so you'd better tell me where you've hidden her.'

'Certainly not!' Henry answered, and rolled, snatching for the empty beer bottle in the faint hope of being able to use it as a weapon.

The sjambok came down again, missing by inches even as Henry brought the bottle up, as hard as he could against Smith's knee, provoking a roar of pain and another vicious slash with the sjambok, again missing by inches. Again the whip came up, Smith's face contorted with fury, only to freeze as a blade of blackened steel was touched to his neck and another pricked at the level of his kidneys.

'Good girls ... wonderful girls ...,' Henry panted as he pulled himself to his feet.

Smith's face was working in fury, but he dared not move, and in a moment Henry had relieved him of his revolver, levelling it at his face as he spoke to Assiatou and Khadija.

'Tie him. Good knots.'

'You'll regret this, Truscott,' Smith snarled as Khadija disappeared, leaving her sister with her commando knife still at Smith's throat.

'Yes, well, that is a bit of a problem,' Henry admitted. 'If I

130

had any sense you'd be floating down the Nile in an hour's time, with your throat cut, but you know I won't do that. What if I ask your word that you'll back off?'

'Never!'

'No, I didn't think so, but Jamila really wasn't a virgin, you know. In fact, she strikes me as quite experienced, and did from the first, so ...'

Smith's fingers had begun to clench in fury, so Henry broke off, realising that explanation was futile. Khadija had returned, holding a great bundle of cord which had presumably been purchased for tying up clients with specialised tastes, and quickly set to work lashing Smith's wrists behind his back. Henry held the revolver level between Smith's eyes until he was certain his captive was completely helpless.

'Now what?' he said, more to himself than to the girls.

Chapter Eight

'RANGOON, YOU'RE SURE?' HENRY queried as he watched the Lancaster Lazy Ace rev her engines.

'Via Muscat,' Hills Hennigan confirmed, 'and you owe me an awfully big favour, Henry.'

'Anything,' Henry replied. 'You too, Gorski, but by God he was a weight, wasn't he? Fourteen stone if he's an ounce.'

'Sixteen, maybe,' Gorski suggested. 'A big man. He will not be comfortable.'

'Good,' Henry responded. 'It's a damn nuisance though, because I don't suppose for a minute he'll have the decency to stay in Burma. The girls were for killing him, you know, then sticking him in an old tomb, but it's really not done, and besides, some nosey parker of an Egyptologist would be sure to dig him up again.'

The Lazy Ace had begun to pull forward from the rank, trundling slowly out across the concrete. In the bomb bay was Captain Smith, securely trussed to the grid to make sure he couldn't fall out, or escape. He was also well gagged, with a pair of Hills Hennigan's regulation issue winter weight knickers stuffed into his mouth and tied off behind his head, but Henry still found himself biting his lip until the plane at last rose into the air, which ensured that Smith would not be discovered until the plane reached Muscat at the earliest.

'Good riddance,' he remarked. 'Now then, chaps, our turn soon, so where the hell is everybody?'

His question was answered immediately, as Bunker, Slick and the Egg were already walking towards them, in company with the crews of other Lancasters, also Lola.

'I'd better get back,' Hills said. 'Goodbye, Gorski. Goodbye, Henry. I'll see you both at Fairlop.'

'Have a good flight,' Henry replied and bent to kiss her, 'and thanks again, we'd have been stuck without you.'

'Good as gold, that girl,' Henry remarked as they watched her retreating rump. 'Damn fine pair of knockers too. Come on boys, look alive. Morning Lola, or *bonjour* if you prefer.'

The others had joined them, except for Ginger, who could be seen hurrying across the field and look distinctly agitated, speaking to Henry as soon as he reached them where they stood together beneath the wing of Jazzy Jess.

'I was looking for you everywhere last night, Skipper. Do you know what, Pinks Pankhurst has been at it again, Sally and Georgina Hayes as well, one after the other ... for spankings, then side by side for six of the best! And when she was done, she sent them to look for you, to tell you, only you're weren't about.'

'I was busy,' Henry answered, glancing at his watch, 'but I've no time for Miss Pinks now, more's the pity.'

'We could fetch her?' Bunker suggested.

'What, and deal with her out here on the field, with the entire squadron looking on and her father to boot? Believe me, I'd love to do it, but I really can't see Sir Pomeroy putting up with having his precious daughter spanked in public, can you?'

'Well, no,' Bunker admitted, 'but we could get her in Jess, horsed up on Gorski's back, skirt up, knickers down and a good hard dose of what she deserves the most.'

'The cane,' Ginger suggested.

'A whip,' Bunker said. 'Nothing quite like a whip to tickle up a bad girl's arse.'

'Nah, nah, nah,' the Egg put in. 'What you want to do, right, is get one of them big garden squirters and put a couple of pints of water up her bum, then a piece of ginger root cut like a plug, all right? The ginger starts to burn, and what with that an' being spanked an' all, in the end she's gonna lose control of her ring, an' out it all comes, all over ...'

'We get the picture, thank you, Egg,' Henry cut him off. 'Now can it, you fellows, here comes the Yank.'

'Let's hope he's not like Jackson,' Ginger said quietly as the American approached, a tall, square-built man with two stars on each shoulder.

'I don't care if he is,' Henry answered. 'This time I plan to make my position clear from the off, and if he doesn't like it, he can bloody well walk.'

He stepped forward to greet the American, throwing a smart salute and speaking immediately.

'Good morning, sir, and welcome aboard. It should be a straightforward flight, but just one point. While we're in the air, I'm in charge.'

'Okay with me,' McLellan answered casually. 'You just do your job and you'll get no grievances from C.C. McLellan. Who's the doll?'

'Miss Lola Céret, a cabaret dancer,' Henry explained. 'Miss Céret, General McLellan. General McLellan, Miss Céret.'

Lola curtsied prettily. She was in uniform, presumably as the alternative would have been a cabaret outfit, but her exotic make-up and the large, red flower she had put in her hair looked anything but military.

'You were in the cabaret, weren't you?' McLellan asked.

'Cabaret, yes,' Lola replied.

'She's French,' Henry explained as the men started to climb aboard, with ground crew now approaching them along the line of Lancasters to prepare for take-off.

McLellan waited until the others were aboard, then spoke quietly to Henry.

'Say, you have a bit of a reputation in these parts, Truscott. Any chance of cutting me in?'

'Reputation?' Henry queried.

'Reputation,' McLellan confirmed, 'for knowing the right kind of girls, if you get my meaning. Your man Slick Delaney sells pictures, I think I'm right, of young Lola among others? If there's anything going, I want in.'

'Er ... yes, I don't see why not, sir,' Henry admitted, slightly taken aback by the American's boldness. 'Yes, why not, as long as Lola's game, and she generally is. After all, it's a long flight, and if there's entertainment to be had I can't see why you shouldn't have your share. No doubt she'd appreciate a small tip.'

'She'll get a tip all right.'

The general gave him a grin and thumbs-up, then climbed up the ladder and into Jazzy Jess, leaving Henry to follow. The crew had gone to their stations, except for the Egg, who was seated on the tail spar with Lola on his lap, one hand fumbling eagerly at the buttons of her uniform jacket.

'Put her down, damn you,' Henry ordered, laughing, 'or at least let me get this crate off the ground, first, you dirty bastard! I'm first, boys, then the General, but everybody stays put until we're in the air.'

The Egg threw Henry a casual salute and scrambled back to his position at the tail guns, leaving Lola flustered and smiling with a good deal of cleavage on show. Henry shook his head and continued forward to take the pilot's seat and start the routine for take-off. Already the next Lancaster in the rank was rolling out onto the concrete, and Henry soon followed, the familiar routine bringing back old fears as always, which died only when he was high in the air and had broken formation to turn west and north, across desert and the green of the delta. With Jazzy Jess in level flight and the blue of the Mediterranean visible far ahead, he engaged the automatic pilot and allowed himself to think.

So much had happened over the past twelve hours that several concerns were jostling for his attention. The situation with Captain Smith was less than satisfactory and might come to cause all sorts of problems, but he found himself equally concerned with Poppy's behaviour, and also puzzled. Ginger had not made clear why both Sally and Georgina had been punished, and in such a humiliating fashion, but it seemed to Henry that whatever the actual reasons given, Poppy's underlying intention had been to provoke him, and to do it in such a way that he quickly found out but had no opportunity for revenge.

It was all extremely unfair on Sally and Georgina, and sending the two spanked girls to find him a particularly cruel touch, ensuring their added humiliation, and was no doubt intended to make him set off on a futile search for revenge. While he searched the camp she would have either hidden herself away, or more likely, sought out the company of her father, allowing her to enjoy his fury and frustration to the full. That had failed, as he'd been involved in disposing of the Gorilla, but there was another annoyance, which he was sure she'd be fully aware of. Despite his very real sympathy for the two girls, it was impossible for him not to be aroused by the thought of their punishments, first made to take turns across Poppy's lap for bare-bottom spankings, then to kneel side by side for the cane. His cock was already hard, just to think of the two bare, pink bottoms thrust out, every intimate detail on display to the giggling audience of WAAFs and other girls, first spanked, then caned.

'Time for Lola,' he muttered, signalled to Gorski and moved back down the plane.

She was seated on the rear wing spar, her jacket still half undone but otherwise unmolested, and greeted him with a knowing smile. Henry took her hand, leading her further back, to where it was possible to obtain at least a little privacy. She was eager, laughing as he took her in his arms, and gave no resistance as he began to peel off her clothes, save to chide him for being so urgent when he managed to get her brassiere in a tangle. Soon she was nude, and still in his arms as she allowed his hands to move over her smooth, warm skin, feeling the curve of her waist and the full swell of her hips, the luxurious, fleshy weight of her bottom and the velvet softness of her cunt.

His cock had been hard from the start, and he wasted no time in seating himself and lifting her onto his lap, allowing his cock to slip in up her warm, inviting cunt. It felt good, as ever, but even as she rode in his lap he was having trouble keeping his thoughts from Poppy, wishing it was her his cock was inside, with her bottom warm and pink from spanking as he fucked her in front of the two girls she'd punished to get at him. The thought was too much and he came, before he'd even got his rhythm right, spunking deep in Lola's cunt and holding her down on his cock until he'd drained his balls inside her.

Feeling somewhat cross with himself, he gave her up to

General McLellan, who'd put her on her knees to suck his penis erect before Henry had even had a chance to tidy himself up. Back in the cockpit he changed places with Gorski, his mind still fixed firmly on Poppy and his determination to catch up with her and give her the spanking of a life time. It had to be done, both for the sake of honour and the desperate craving growing within him, which he knew that no amount of sex with other girls would satisfy.

Temporary relief was another matter entirely, and by the time Gorski had rejoined him in the cockpit, Henry was ready for more. Once again he went back down the plane, to find Lola bent over the tail spar, sucking eagerly on the Egg's big, crooked cock while Slick fucked her from behind. Henry watched, absentmindedly massaging his cock through his trousers as he waited his turn while admiring the sight of Lola being put through her paces. The Egg had soon come, pulling out at the last second and deliberately doing it in her face to leave her pretty, Latin features streaked and blobbed with spunk, while Slick soon followed, deep inside her, so that as he pulled free her cunt was left a sopping, juicy hole.

Henry took Slick's place, bringing his cock to full erection in his hand before slipping it up Lola's welcoming hole. Unfortunately she was sloppy with the other men's juices, making it impossible to get the friction he needed to his cock, while her upturned bottom tempted him with a tighter, and favourite, target. He pulled back, pressing his cock to the soft, tightly puckered mouth of her anus, already slippery from her repeated fucking. She gave a low moan at the realisation that she was to be buggered, but did her best to take it, pushing out on to Henry's cock and reaching back to rub his balls on her cunt once he was all the way in.

He let her play, buggering her with short, hard thrusts as she rubbed his balls in the wet mush of her sex and holding his cock deep as she came, after just a few moments, with her anus squeezing hard on his intruding shaft. Duty done, he begun to move inside her once more, fast and deep, enjoying the sensation of his cock in her rectum, the sight of her pretty bottom spread wide with her anus straining on his shaft, her gasping, grunting reaction to being sodomised. All of it was good, but even as he felt his orgasm start to rise once more his thoughts had slipped to Poppy, and how it ought to be her with his erection embedded balls deep up her well-spanked bottom as he squirted spunk into her bowels.

By the time Jazzy Jess put down in Toulouse Lola was barely able to walk, but managed to give each of the crew a lingering kiss and an affectionate hug before finally taking her leave. Henry had been in her three times, as had General McLellan, the others twice each, save for the Egg, who seemed to have an inexhaustible supply of spunk and stamina, managing to use her mouth twice as well as her cunt and anus, on the last occasion making her suck his cock after her buggering. Nevertheless, she gave him a farewell every bit as intimate as the others, before moving away towards the airfield gates with a final wave.

They took off again with dawn still a bright flush in the eastern sky, to fly north across the French countryside and then out over Biscay. Miles of sea passed beneath, a glittering, grey-green expanse visible through broken clouds, which at last gave way to a line of crumbling red cliffs backed by fields of lush green, the coast of England and, more importantly, Devon. Henry was forced to swallow a lump in his throat as he banked the Lancaster, to follow first the Teign Estuary and then the Great Western Railway, familiar landmarks, although he had never before seen either from the air.

A last hop across the shoulder of Dartmoor and he was able to see the airfield, a grey scar on the green downs he'd known since childhood. The runway was notably shorter than those he was used to, forcing him to pull up hard and bring Jazzy Jess down only a few miles per hour above her stalling speed, although he was pleased to note that neither Gorski nor Ginger showed the least trace of concern. With the engines now slow, he followed the directions of a signaller, adding the Lancaster to a line of smaller aircraft before finally allowing the power to die and following the others to the ground.

He stopped the moment his feet touched grass, to draw deep

on the Devon air, filling his lungs with the moist, sweet freshness, so different from the dry, sandy heat of Egypt. It was impossible not to grin, and he felt one more notch of tension slip away as he took another deep draught of air, then turned to the others.

'It's been a pleasure meeting you, General McLellan,' he said, offering his hand to the American, 'and so long as you're in these parts you'll always be a welcome guest at Stukely Hall. Everybody knows where it is, and who I am. Speaking of which, it would be ever so kind if I could borrow a staff car. I'll have it driven back later in the afternoon, of course.'

'My pleasure,' the general replied, taking Henry's hand in a powerful grip, 'and should you ever happen to be in Bedford, Indiana, look me up.'

'Much obliged. I'll be home in time for tea if I'm lucky, but I imagine the rest of you will be after something a trifle less sedate?'

'Like you say, Skipper,' Bunker answered, taking the hint.

'Any decent knocking shops in these parts, Skipper?' the Egg queried as the General moved away towards the car which had come to greet him.

'Try Plymouth,' Henry suggested. 'I imagine it's still a bit knocked about at the moment, but I dare say there are plenty of girls willing to oblige a flyboy, even you.'

'They're always up for me,' the Egg replied happily.

'Yes, I've noticed,' Henry answered, 'and I've often wondered … I mean to say, we were hardly in the air before you had Maria stripped down and willing, not to mention Lola, and, well, not meaning to be rude, but you're no Adonis … or even Gary Cooper. How do you do it?'

The Egg grinned and extended his tongue, a pointed, baby-pink article with which he licked first the top of his nose and then his chin.

'Good God!' Henry exclaimed.

'Gets 'em every time,' the Egg said happily, 'the experienced ones anyroad, 'cause they knows what they're in for. Virgins and that, they more usually run a mile, screaming, but sometimes they come back.'

'I see,' Henry said weakly. 'Anyway, Plymouth, yes … plenty of girls in Plymouth. Plenty of competition too, what with the Navy and the Yanks up here, but I'm sure you'll cope.'

He was being signalled towards the General's car and left the others, accepting a lift from the driver, first to a large house nearby which had been requisitioned as staff quarters, then out towards his own estate. His sense of nostalgia grew stronger by the minute as he was driven north along the flank of Dartmoor, past each familiar landmark, Pew Tor and Cox Tor, White Tor with Standon Hill beyond, Brat Tor with its stone cross on the summit and Doe Tor, where he had lost his virginity to the daughter of a local farmer one summer's day long before the war.

Stukely Hall was as ever, a grey-stone, Gothic pile set against the vast sweep of the moors, somewhat bleak in the tail end of winter, but with a welcoming yellow glow from the windows of the drawing room. His cousin Hermione had been keeping house while he was stationed away from home and greeted him with an affectionate kiss and a stream of questions, which continued as she put together a tea of scones, clotted cream and raspberry jam, along with cake and the obligatory brown bed and butter.

'Are you back for good?'

'Not yet,' Henry admitted, settling himself into his favourite chair. 'The crate's at Plasterdown and the crew are in Plymouth. We're off to Fairlop in a few days, but the next time it'll be for good.'

He took a piece of bread and butter first, a polite gesture, now instinctive, which made him smile for the memory of how long it had taken his mother to make him learn. Hermione continued to talk, her words barely registering in Henry's mind save to create a deep sense of wellbeing and safety, also a need for a piece of home comfort he had long done without.

'And how's Ginger Green?' Hermione was asking.

'In fine fettle,' Henry responded. 'You did him the world of good, you know. Er … speaking of which, would you mind, terribly? I mean to say, I've had quite a time of it, you know, and ...'

'Oh you poor lamb, of course!' she responded. 'Pop him out then, and I'll sit on the edge of the chair.'

'Thanks awfully, old thing!' Henry responded, already fiddling with his flies.

He pulled his cock free as she settled herself down beside him, to take it in her hand. Just her grip felt exquisite, firm but gentle, and as she began to tug up and down a sense of relief spread over him, stronger by far than sexual gratification alone, as if just to have his cock in her hand once again was soothing away all the stresses and horrors of the previous six years and more.

'That is true bliss,' he sighed. 'You always do it so well, even better than Stephanie.'

Hermione didn't answer, but continued to masturbate him, rolling her thumb back and forth across the underside of his foreskin as she tugged up and down. When he was erect she took hold of the base of his shaft to stretch his skin as taut as it would go and made a ring of her fingers to rub on his swollen knob and the glossy neck of his shaft, making him cry out in pleasure.

'You always liked it this way, didn't you?' she said. 'And having your balls squeezed.'

She'd changed her technique once more as she spoke, taking Henry's balls in one hand and squeezing gently as she once more began to toss at his shaft, faster now. His initial sense of relief had begun to give way to pure pleasure, and she made no objection when he reached out to cup the turn of her bottom, only wanking all the faster.

'Do you remember milkmaids and soldiers?' she asked.

'I do,' he answered, 'and yes, please.'

Hermione switched her left hand to his cock, still masturbating him as she reached out to scoop up a piece of clotted cream from the bowl. Stretching his foreskin tight down, she wiped the cream onto the head of his cock, smearing it all around until the first few inches were liberally coated with the thick, yellowish white paste. Henry pushed up with her hips, offered his cock to her mouth and quickly taken in, for

Hermione to suck and lick, swallowing down the cream until he was clean once more, only to paint his cock a second time for another go.

'I have to come,' he sighed, his fingers tightening on her bottom. 'Make me come, H.'

She ignored him, still teasing at his straining foreskin and the glossy flesh of his helmet, licking up the cream with the very tip of her tongue, until his teeth were gritted in ecstasy and he was begging for relief.

'Please, H, now ... or I'll do it in your face. I can't help it!'

At the last instant she bent low, to push her lips down on the head of his cock as he came, making him cry out in near unbearable pleasure, and again as she took him deep to swallow down his spunk as it came out. His helmet was well down in her throat, but that didn't stop her from swallowing all he had to give, and even when he'd drained himself into her mouth she continued to suck, cleaning him up until she'd eaten up ever last trace of cream and of spunk.

'Best not to risk making a mess,' she explained as she came off his cock.

'Absolutely,' Henry agreed. 'Thanks, H, you're a sport.'

'It was my pleasure,' she told him. 'I've missed giving you your little treats, Henry.'

She kissed him and once more began to ask questions about Egypt and his time away.

Henry spent a pleasant few days at Stukely Hall and in the vicinity, visiting his relatives, his old haunts and old flames, riding on Dartmoor and looking over the estate, which to his delight the war had barely touched. After the best part of a week a slightly pointed telegram from RAF Fairlop arrived, suggesting that it was about time he reported for duty. A quick trawl through the bars and brothels of Plymouth allowed him to retrieve his crew, all but Ginger Green, who had gone ahead, and the following morning he took Jazzy Jess aloft once more, arriving at Fairlop in time for lunch.

Leaving the Officers' Mess, the first person he saw was Sally Green, walking briskly towards the gate. In place of her usual WAAF blues she wore a smart fawn coat cut tight to her waist, and in each hand she held a suitcase. She was evidently on her way home and Henry lost no time in first offering her a lift, getting permission to leave camp, and then persuading the motor pool to give up a Hillman Minx for his use. An hour later and they were driving through the Hertfordshire lanes, between high chalk banks with the first green buds showing on towering beeches to either side.

Henry knew the way from previous visits to see Ginger, and was soon parked outside the rambling red brick and flint house almost in the shadow of Ivinghoe Beacon, with woods behind and the garden looking out across the Vale of Aylesbury. They had been talking constantly on the way, of how pleasant it was to be back in England, of the past few years and of their expectations for the future, but despite the warmth between them Henry had kept off the subject he most wanted to broach, Poppy's treatment of Sally's bottom before they had left Egypt.

She had already persuaded him to stay for tea, but it was still early afternoon and the house was empty, so they decided to climb the Beacon. As they set off up the chalky path their hands touched, then came together. Henry's cock responded on the instant, but he said nothing, knowing that when the time came there would be no resistance, simply enjoying being together in the bright spring sunshine. They were still holding hands when they reached the summit, to stop and look out across the countryside, and after a moment Henry took her in his arms, to kiss her gently, then with greater force. She responded eagerly, melting into him with her body already trembling to his touch, and when he reached down to give her bottom an experimental pat through her coat she clung closer still.

'You know what to do with me,' she whispered. 'You know so well. Take me back to the house and spank it. Spank my bottom, Henry.'

'With pleasure,' he told her, applying another smack through her coat, 'and talking of spanking, I know what Poppy did to you the night before I left Egypt, and to Georgina Hayes.'

They'd turned back down the hill, their arms now around each others waists. Sally didn't answer immediately, but when she did her voice was thick with excitement.

'Yes she did spank us,' she said. 'In front of everybody, and on the bare. First we were made to roll up our skirts and put our hands on our heads. Then she had Michelle Boudin take down our knickers for us, just to humiliate us even more. She had us standing to attention like that while she gave us a lecture, bare back and front with our knickers around our feet. Everyone was watching and laughing at us, until Pinks told them to shut up or they'd be joining the line. Next came our spankings ... oh that word, just to say it makes me want it, right now. Poppy did Georgina first, right in front of me so I could see what I was going to get ... how I was going to look, and all the time standing there with my bottom bare, and at the front, showing it all. How Georgina howled! She tried to be brave, but she couldn't help herself. Not me, I've always been a big baby about having my bottom smacked, always. I was crying before she even started, just for the shame, and she spanks so hard! She had one leg around mine too, and she took my knickers right off, so I was showing it all behind. Can you imagine?'

'Vividly,' Henry assured her.

'Then when I was done,' Sally went on, 'she had Georgina take her knickers off too and made us kneel down on one of the beds, side by side, with our bottoms right up. She gave us the cane, six of the best, right across our bottoms. It hurt so much. Some of the girls couldn't hold back their laughter, Henry, to see us like that, with our bare bottoms stuck up in the air and the red lines on our skin, and both of us crying so hard. Wasn't that cruel of them, Henry?'

'Yes,' Henry agreed, trying to sound stern and sympathetic, but confused and excited by her obvious arousal, 'but not as cruel as Poppy for doing it to you. You wait until I catch up with her, Sally, because I swear I'm going to give her the same treatment, and damn the consequences.'

She didn't answer, and was biting her lip in apparent uncertainty as they continued down the hill, only to start

144

talking again, in a rush of words.

'Don't punish her, Henry. Punish me. I'm the one who ought to be punished, don't you think? I'm the one who ought to be spanked, don't you think? You are going to spank me, aren't you?'

'You're going to be spanked,' he promised her, 'whether you ought to be or not.'

'Oh no, I ought to be spanked,' she told him. 'I ought to be spanked hard and long, on my bare bottom. Right here if you want to. I don't care who sees, because ... because if I've been naughty it shouldn't matter who sees, should it?'

She sounded near to desperation, and if her sheer urgency was somewhat disarming, he felt he ought to oblige, while his cock had reacted to what she was saying of its own accord, and was now painfully stiff. Henry found himself glancing around the downs, wondering if he dared take her across his knee then and there. A ploughman was at work in one of the pale fields, far below and a safe distance away, along with workmen in a chalk pit, further still, but there was nobody nearby, while a stile set in a fence just fifty yards away offered the ideal place for him to sit while he dealt with her.

'On second thoughts,' he said, 'you're right. You ought to be spanked, for what you do to me, for being such a flirt ... no, a tart, there's no other word for it, Sally. Now come here.'

He'd taken her by the ear as he spoke, drawing squeaks of pain and what might have been protests as she was dragged quickly down to the stile, but which sounded to him more like whimpers of pleasure. She was shaking badly, but absolutely compliant, allowing him to turn her across his knee even as he sat down. Her hat had fallen off and her long red hair had come loose, hanging around her face as she lay meekly across his legs, her breathing deep and ragged, but offering no resistance as he turned up her coat to reveal a pale blue dress beneath, along with her seamed stockings and smart black shoes.

'You're right that it doesn't matter who sees,' he went on as he took a firm grip on her waist. 'Because you're a little tart, Sally Green, and it doesn't matter in the slightest who sees a little tart get a spanking, does it?'

As he spoke he'd been adjusting her clothes, first hauling up her dress and then the petticoat beneath, to expose the tops of her stockings, her suspender straps and the bulging seat of a pair of full-cut, winter-weight knickers in regulation Air Force blue. Her shaking had grown more powerful than ever, her gasps and little whimpering noises louder and more urgent.

'No, it doesn't matter who sees you get spanked,' he went on, 'and it doesn't matter if they see your bare bottom either, does it, which is just as well, because there's a ploughman and about twenty quarrymen who're about to see exactly that! Down come your knickers, Sally.'

He'd done it as he spoke, peeling the big blue knickers slowly off her bottom to leave her pale cheeks bare to the cool spring sunlight and on display to the world. The men might have been a long way away, and they might not even happen to glance up to the hillside, but if they did there was going to be no mistaking what was going on. Henry found himself grinning, sure that if the men did see they'd merely assume that a girl was being punished, and no doubt for good reason, without ever suspecting that it aroused her, or what was now sure to happen when they got back to the house. It was a delightful prospect, and as he began to smack Sally's cheeks he pulled her tighter, pressing her body to the hard bulge in his trousers so that she would feel his cock and realise that he was erect.

'That's going inside you,' he told her, 'just as soon as we're indoors, and do you know exactly where inside you? Right up your sweet little bottom, Sally Green, maybe in your mouth too, but not just yet, not until you've been given a proper spanking!'

She'd began to kick and wriggle to the smacks as they got harder, tossing her hair and all the while gasping and moaning. Her reaction only served to encourage him to apply the slaps harder still, until she'd begun to make odd choking noises in her throat and he knew she was crying, although at the same time she was sticking her bottom up for more. The motion also showed off the tight, baby pink dimple of her anus and the sweetly pouted lips of her cunt in their nest of ginger fur. He could smell her excitement, tempting him to simply bend her over the stile and fuck her then and there, up her bottom or even in her virgin cunt, because with every smack her cheeks came apart, showing the dark red hymen that guarded her hole.

'I am so tempted to have you,' he grunted, still spanking, 'so tempted to push my cock in up that wet little cunt of yours, right up. How would that be to end your punishment, Sally, to have your virginity taken for playing the tart.'

Her body jerked, her thighs came wide to stretch her knickers as taut as they would go, and suddenly she was rubbing her open cunt on his leg in a display so shamelessly wanton that he stopped spanking her, but only for a moment. She was gasping out his name and begging him to spank her as hard as he could, so he obliged, his hand starting to rise and fall across her squirming cheeks to slap at the soft tuck of flesh where they turned down towards her anus. He'd knew she was going to come, but as her frantic wriggling gave way to an even, rhythmic bucking he realised that she wasn't the only one, because the way her body was rubbing against his cock was about to push him over the edge, and even as she screamed out her ecstasy to the open downs he had filled his underpants with spunk.

'What do you think?' Sally laughed. 'Do I look pretty?'

'Yes,' Henry agreed, 'very pretty, and very naughty. You really are a disgrace, Sally, although I wouldn't have it any other way.'

She smiled and curtsied, lifting the hem of the pinafore dress she'd put on to show off the puffy white towelling of the nappy that she wore beneath. She had been in a state of nervous excitement ever since her spanking, giggling over the thought of what the distant workmen might have seen and talking incessantly as they walked back to the house. Henry had been badly in need of a few minutes in the bathroom, and somewhat annoyed with himself for failing to hold back for the excitement of dishing out Sally's spanking and having her come while she lay over his lap.

Once in the house, she had insisted on helping, mopping up

the mess Henry had made in his pants with a damp flannel, using both a towel and talcum powder to make sure his cock and balls were properly dry, then fetching spare underwear from her brother's chest of drawers. By the time he was dressed once more Henry's cock had begun to stir, but she had eluded his attempts to get hold of her, insisting that he wait until she was in what she called proper clothes, and they had finished tea. Henry had complied, really quite grateful for a chance to recuperate and intrigued by her playful determination and by the thought of how she might dress.

He had waited in the comfortable, sunlit drawing room, idly reading Punch and giving his cock an occasional squeeze through his trousers, until at last she had come in once more, now carrying a tray laden with bread and butter, jam, honey, and two sorts of cake in addition to the actual tea he had been expecting. Yet he barely noticed the feast, his eyes immediately drawn to her, as she wore nothing but an abbreviated pinafore dress of such light material that the shape of her breasts and the outlines of her nipples showed clearly through the top, and so short that it barely concealed her sex at the front and showed off most of her bottom behind, or would have done had she not also been in a big, puffy nappy of plain white towelling and fastened at either hip with a large, pink enamelled pin.

'I know I'm a disgrace,' she told him as she gave a twirl to show off the seat of her nappy, 'and a tart, but only for you … and maybe Pinks, if you don't mind?'

'Not at all,' he assured her, thinking of how she'd looked being spanked across Poppy's knee and wondering if it might be possible to recreate the situation, perhaps after a similar punishment for Poppy herself.

'I'm glad,' she told him, 'and I'm also glad you like to punish me, because I do need to be punished, Henry.'

'You will be,' he assured her, 'frequently.'

She replied with a smile and sat down, wriggling her nappy clad bottom into the chair opposite Henry's, then began to serve tea as if nothing at all were out of the ordinary. With the edge already taken off his lust and somewhat bemused by her behaviour, Henry allowed things to go the way she wanted, accepting a cup of tea, a slice of bread and butter and another of cake. Sally ate even more than he did, and seemed to be exceptionally thirsty, finishing three cups of tea before Henry had got to the bottom of the first, then immediately returning to the kitchen for more.

He watched as she retreated, her neat little bottom wiggling in the bulky nappy, still unsure exactly what she wanted, save that it was sure to involve having her bottom spanked, but game for anything that made her happy. She was soon back, drinking yet more tea and talking of this and that, bright-eyed with excitement for all her casual manner. Only when she'd finished her eighth cup did she show any signs of distress, sitting back with one hand on her tummy and an expression of mild discomfort on her face.

'Oh dear,' she said, 'I think I might have been a little greedy, and I've definitely had too much tea.'

'You have rather been mopping it up,' he agreed.

'Come outside,' she said, still holding her tummy as she rose.

Henry followed her through the French windows and out into a tiny, enclosed garden, guarded from the wind and also from sight by a high wall of red brick and flint. There were several chairs, a table and a bench, all of cast iron, and Sally immediately sat down, indicating that Henry should go opposite her. She now had both hands on her tummy and her face was set in an expression at once stubborn and pained, while she had her thighs cocked wide, showing off the front of her nappy.

'Much too much tea,' she said. 'What a silly, greedy girl I've been.'

'You have rather,' Henry agreed, eager to play the game but still unsure of himself. 'Perhaps you should be smacked and sent up to bed?'

'No, not another spanking, please?' she answered him, with what seem like genuine need. 'If you were to spank me I don't think I could hold it … my pee. I think I might wet myself while you spanked me. I'm not sure I can hold it anyway, not

149

sure at all … oh, no, I'm going to do it, Henry, please don't be cross with me … please like me, Henry …'

She broke off with a sharp cry and her back had arched, pushing out her hips as her thighs came wider still, showing off the seat of her nappy as openly as she could as a low, bubbling hiss signalled that she was wetting herself. Henry could only stare, both in astonishment and fascination, as the piddle began to soak through Sally's nappy, appearing first as a wet spot directly over where the towelling was bunched over her cunt and then lower, spreading slowly downwards to wet her bottom cheeks and finally began to run out at the sides, splashing on the paving beneath her.

'Please … please like me, Henry,' she repeated.

'I do,' he assured her. 'I think you're the most fascinating, naughty, delightful little imp of a girl I've ever encountered. Go on, push harder.'

Sally had already shut her eyes, but at his words her mouth came open in ecstasy and her back arched tighter. Henry saw the muscles of her belly tense where they showed above the hem of her nappy, and for a moment the pee made a little fountain exactly over her cunt, before dying back as she relaxed. She had now thoroughly wet herself, the entire seat of her nappy soaking wet and dripping with piddle, while the stain at the front had crept up almost to her belly. Henry slipped a hand down to his cock, which had begun to swell once more, adjusting himself as Sally gave a long, contented sigh.

'Look at me, Henry,' she said softly. 'I've done peepee in my nappy and I'm all wet, and you like it, you really like it … oh Henry!'

She gave a gasp and her back arched once more as she pushed out, to make another little squirt of piddle fountain from her nappy, and as it died he saw that the damp bulge hanging beneath her bottom had grown fatter and heavier still. He swallowed hard, his cock now growing swiftly, as much for the thought of how utterly she had surrendered herself to him as for her body. As he watched she brought her legs up, to rest her heels on the bench, openly displaying the squashy bulk of her well soiled nappy where it hung below her bottom while her hand had gone to the front to massage her cunt through the soggy material.

'Now you're going to have to change me,' she sighed. 'You're going to have to change my nappy, and I suppose you're going to spank me too? Oh dear, what a naughty little girl I've been, to need spanking twice in one afternoon.'

'Come on then, you little disgrace,' he said, rising. 'I suppose we'd better get it over and done with. First a clean nappy, then a good spanking, and then, my girl, you're going to bed.'

Sally made no objection, but took Henry's offered hand, sticking her thumb in her mouth and sucking on it in a doleful manner as he led her back indoors and upstairs to the bathroom. She had clearly arranged things in advance, setting out a bowl of water on a table of bleached wood, along with flannels, a new towel and the same talc she'd used to dry his cock and balls, but Henry was beginning to get into the spirit of the things. When she began to climb onto the table he slapped her leg and ordered her to stand in the exact middle of the floor, her nappy now hanging heavy between her thighs.

'You do as you're told, young lady,' he instructed her as he began to look into the cupboards. 'Now then, some soap, a little cream, and ... ah yes, just the job.'

He had found a patent safety razor and a packet of blades, which he showed her before adding them to the equipment on the table. Now humming cheerfully, he began to unbutton his jacket as he spoke to her once more.

'Yes, I am going to shave your cunt. It would be appropriate, don't you think, for a grown up girl who wets her nappy? Now, I don't want to spoil my uniform, so you can stand in the corner while I undress. Yes, that's right, at attention, but with your hands on your head. Oh, and you can pull up your dress while you're at it, right up to show your breasts, to help remind you that you're in disgrace.'

Sally obeyed, turning her face to the big mirror that decorated most of one wall, lifting her pinafore dress and tucking it up to leave her breasts exposed, then placing her hands on her head. Her nappy had begun to sag, heavy with the pee that was still dripping slowly from the seat, and had pulled down a little, so that the top inch or so of her bottom slit and the first swell of her cheeks was on show as well as her breasts.

Henry took his time, removing his clothing article by article and piling each neatly to one side. Only when he was fully naked did he turn his attention back to Sally, scooping her up in his arms and putting her down on the table, laid on her back with her legs up in the right position to have her nappy changed. She'd given a little squeak of surprise as she was lifted, but as he set to work her thumb had gone back into her mouth. He was still humming to himself, behaving in a deliberately matter-of-fact style as he unfastened the big pins at her hips and peeled the sodden towelling away to expose her cunt, as if her nudity were utterly inconsequential.

She reacted with equal lack of embarrassment, sucking contentedly on her thumb as she was lifted by her feet to have the wet nappy pulled out from under her bottom, for all that it left her in nothing but her pinafore dress, which was still tucked up over her breasts, while with her legs rolled high it was blatantly obvious what she'd done. Only as Henry began to clean her did she start to react, making little mewling noises deep in her throat, and when he wiped her anus the little hole begun to squeeze and open to a slow, gentle rhythm.

By then Henry's cock felt as if it was about to burst, but he forced himself to carry on as if nothing was out of the ordinary, making sure she was fully clean before working up a lather with the soap and rubbing it well in to the gingery bush on her sex. Taking a fresh blade and holding her by one ankle to spread her as wide as she would go, he began to scrape away the hair, working slowly and carefully and trying to ignore the pale juice now squeezing from the tiny hole where her hymen failed to fully block her vagina.

The urge to pull out his cock and force it up the tiny hole, splitting her hymen and taking her virginity where she lay was strong and grew rapidly stronger as he shaved away her hair, bit by bit, applying the razor and then washing away the soap to reveal freshly denuded flesh. With her mound bare and pink and wet, he set to work on her cunt lips, stretching the sensitive flesh out between his fingers to get at every little bulge and crevice, before finishing with the few, tiny hairs that grew around her anus. With the last of the soap washed away her cunt was left as bald as an egg, also puffy with excitement and wet with juice.

She was groaning softly as she sucked on her thumb, her eyes lightly closed, her breathing deep and even, clearly completely available to him, in any way he wished. Still he held back, knowing that she needed a spanking before she could be fucked, whether up her bottom or the increasingly tempting hole of her vagina, and while he was shaving her cunt he had thought of a cruel and amusing twist to her punishment.

'Open wide,' he told her as he picked the bar of now rather soggy soap from the dish, 'and I'll show you what happens to little girls who wet their nappies.'

Sally's eyes came wide, to stare disconsolately at the bar of soap he was offering to her mouth.

'That's not fair!' she protested. 'That's for bad language, having my mouth washed out with soap! I wet myself!'

'You used the word tart earlier,' he told her, 'which is hardly the sort of language I'd expect from a young lady.'

'It's not fair,' she insisted and her face set into a sulky pout.

'Open wide, Sally,' Henry insisted.

Sally's mouth came open, slowly, reluctantly, but wide enough to allow Henry to push the bar of soap well in, whereupon her sulky expression changed to disgust and what he would have sworn was genuine resentment.

'And keep it there,' he told her, 'until your spanking's finished.'

He took hold of her ankles once more, rolling her legs up to give himself access to the cheeks of her bottom and incidentally spreading out her cunt and anus, a position utterly lacking in dignity, even more so than being over his knee.

'A little powder to dry you first,' he said, reaching for the talc.

He upended the shaker over her cunt, sprinkling the bare pink flesh with flecks of white, then more, between her thighs on her bottom cheeks, lastly in the slit between to powder her

153

anus, leaving the little puckered ring dry but for a tiny pink star at the very centre. The wetness of her cunt also showed, a slippery pink slit between her lips, to create a view at once intimate and rude, which brought a fresh smile to his lips as he began to pat the powder in.

'There we are, clean and dry,' he said cheerfully. 'So, a little cream perhaps, then let's get you spanked and into a nice fresh nappy, shall we?'

Sally didn't even try to answer, now sucking disconsolately on the bar of soap with bubbles squeezing out from around the sides and between her lips, but as he continued to pat the powder into her cunt and buttocks her face was working with emotion, one instant full of resentment and consternation, the next in rapture. With her bottom properly powdered, Henry took up a tub of hand cream, making sure she could see as he dipped a finger in to scoop up a good-sized blob, which he then wiped on her anus.

'Yes,' he said, 'a little cream so your bottom hole doesn't get sore, why not? And of course, you might find it useful if I want to use that little bottom hole once we're in bed, don't you think?'

He'd pushed his finger a little way in up her bottom as he spoke, past her anus to feel the warm, wet cavity beyond. Sally's back arched in pleasure at the treatment and she began to wriggle her bottom on his finger until he pulled it free.

'Be patient,' he told her. 'You haven't even had your spanking yet.'

Wiping his finger on her belly, he turned his attention to her punishment, rolling her higher still to allow himself full access to her bottom cheeks and starting to slap them, turn and turn about as she sucked on the bar of soap in her mouth, now with bubbles running down both cheeks and creating a froth that almost hid her lips.

'Naughty Sally,' he chided as she made the smacks harder, 'naughty, naughty Sally, spanked twice in one day, outdoors too, but I bet it's not the first time, is it? Oh no, I bet this little pink bum has had many an airing on the downs, and I bet you've had it spanked just as often as was necessary, haven't you, and always bare.'

A sob escaped Sally's throat and her fingers began to clutch at the pale wood of the table, while her expression was now set in ecstasy, for all that she was sucking hard on the soap bar, only the end of which now protruded from her mouth, while bubbles had begun to come out of her nose. Henry changed his tactic, spanking her cheeks directly across her distended anus to make the little hole twitch and her cunt squeeze, pushing out thick white juice that filled the air with the scent of excited girl.

'Many a time, I'm sure,' he went on, 'bare bottom on the downs or in the drawing room. Skirts up and knickers down, eh Sally? Skirts up and knickers down in front of anybody who happens to be watching, maybe your brother, maybe house guests, because a naughty girl has to be spanked and it doesn't matter who sees her bare bottom, does it, Sally?'

Her body gave a little jerk, not an orgasm, but something close to it, and Henry realised that if he didn't take advantage of her immediately he was going to have another accident in his pants. As he freed his cock he had slipped a finger back up her bottom, to push it deep several times before pulling it out, only to immediately press the head of his cock to the slippery little hole.

'And this,' he told her, 'is what happens to bad girls who show off their bottoms to men, especially me.'

He pushed, watching in delight as her bottom hole spread to engulf the head of his cock, and again, to leave her anus a tight, pink ring around the neck of his erection. Sally had taken hold of her legs as he began to interfere with her anus, holding them up and open to spread herself to his cock, while she seemed to be trying to eat the bar of soap in her mouth, chewing on the now half dissolved mass and blowing glistening whites bubbles from her nose and around the sides of her mouth.

Again Henry pushed, his eyes fixed on the junction between her straining anal ring and his erection as it went slowly up, inch by inch, until his balls were nestled between her well spread cheeks. She was hot and wet inside, and deliciously slippery, encouraging him to bugger her deep and hard, but the focus of his eyes had changed, to her well spread cunt and the little red bulge of her maidenhead. It was tempting to pull out his cock and take her, popping the little red cherry with one hard push, to make her his completely, but he struggled to hold back, mumbling to himself as he buggered her.

'That's the way ... that's the way to treat a bad girl, spank her naughty bottom and then bugger her ... oh Sally, you are such a treat, so sweet, my little spanked tart.'

He'd taken hold of her under her knees to keep her rolled up and she let go, her hands moving to her breasts and her cunt, rubbing between the freshly shaved lips, then spreading them to show off her virgin hole. Henry shook his head, but he'd already partially withdrawn his cock and was easing it in and out of her bottom hole as he fought to resist the temptation of her virgin cunt.

'If you want to go to town,' he muttered to himself as his eyes flickered between Sally's twin holes, one already well plugged with cock, the other virgin but available, 'first Lady Pink then Mrs Brown, but never ever ... oh sod the pair of them! I'm going to fuck you, Sally Green ... I'm going to fuck you now!'

His cock pulled free of her anus, to stand proud above her cunt for one moment before he grabbed it and pushed it down, pressing his helmet to her virgin cunt hole. Sally cried out through her mouthful of soap, her fingers locking on one pert breast and the mound of her cunt. Henry pushed again, her hymen taut against his cock for one last instant before it burst, tearing wide to let him slide himself deep in up her slippery, willing cunt hole, no longer virgin.

Sally had cried out in pain as her hymen tore, and she was whimpering and clutching at herself as he fucked her, his cock shaft smeared with her virgin blood as he pushed it in and out. Her mouth was still caked with soap, her face a mess of bubbles and snot, her skin sweaty and glistening, her buggered anus oozing juice over Henry's balls as he fucked her, deeper and deeper, faster and faster, until at last he could no longer hold back and came, deep up her cunt, filling her with spunk as he cried out, first in ecstasy and then in a promise to make her his for life.

Chapter Nine

HENRY SPENT THE NIGHT with Sally, not wanting to leave her. He had excused himself from returning to Fairlop by pretending the car had broken down, and without a trace of guilt. With the war over and his duty well and truly done, it seemed absurd to worry over petty niceties, especially when the alternative was to spend the night in bed with his fiancée.

Five times in the course of the night they made love, and a sixth when Henry awoke to find Sally's hand clasped firmly around his morning erection. Each time he had come inside her, which made a short engagement seem the wisest choice to avoid the risk of her having to walk up the aisle with a conspicuous bulge beneath her dress. When the papers had arrived Henry had taken only a brief glance at the headlines before turning to the section listing births, deaths and marriages.

'I'll send something in straight away,' he said, 'unless you think I ought to ask the Pater?'

'Daddy will be delighted,' she assured him. 'He approves of you?'

'He does?' Henry asked in surprise.

'Yes, for your war record, and because he says you helped to make a man of Ginger.'

'He should thank my cousin for that, really,' Henry responded, 'and the Mater?'

'Mummy's a bit old-fashioned,' Sally admitted, 'but she'll come around, and she does know who you are.'

'Exactly the problem, I'd have thought.'

'I meant being from such an old family.'

'So did I, but then I dare say she hasn't researched my family history, or not in detail anyway. One of my ancestors was known as Devil John, and with good reason. Then there was the first Henry, who ... Hang on, what's this?'

An advertisement in the paper had caught his eye, a picture of a smiling, rubicund male face surrounded by smaller pictures of girls in gaudy costumes and several lines of text, all within an ornate border that appeared to be designed from items of discarded female underwear. Henry had recognised the face, but had to read the text three times before the full implications of what he was seeing sank in. Only then did he speak to Sally once more.

'Good God! Listen to this - "Pettigrew Presents: Poppy's Pin-Ups, the new theatrical burlesque, fresh from entertaining our boys abroad, a veritable extravaganza of the exotic and the daring ..." Why, the little brat ... the two-faced, scheming little brat! Did you know anything about this, Sally?'

'No, I ...,' Sally answered hastily, but the look of alarm in her eyes told a different story and she had quickly broken off before hanging her head as she went on. 'Well, yes, I suppose so. Poppy did ask if I'd like to be in the troop, but I said no, and ... and I didn't know you'd be cross.'

'Cross?' Henry demanded. 'That's my cabaret troop!'

'She did do most of the work,' Sally said gently.

'Michelle did most of the work,' Henry retorted. 'All Poppy did was push herself forward, that and take advantage of her father's influence. I swear she's as bad as the Yanks, turning up at the last minute and then pinching all the credit! And you might have told me!'

'I'm sorry,' Sally answered, her voice barely audible. 'Spank me if you want, but please let's not row.'

Henry hesitated, tempted to put her across his knee and take out his anger on her bottom, but he knew it wouldn't be just.

'No,' he told her, 'let's not row, because it's not your fault, and it wouldn't be fair to spank you for Poppy's bad behaviour. You don't deserve it. Poppy, on the other hand, does deserve it, and she's going to get it!'

*   *   *

Henry's fury had barely cooled by the time he left Sally, headed not for Fairlop, but for London. As he drove he was conscious of a nagging voice at the back of his mind, arguing that he should have paid more attention to what was going on with the cabaret and less to indulging himself with the performers, but it only served to highlight what he saw as Poppy's treachery. He was also determined to spank her, regardless of the consequences, and having told Sally and promised himself he would go through with it, there was no question of backing down.

'Thirty-seven West Grove, Highgate,' he said, repeating aloud the address given to him by Sally. 'Thirty-seven West Grove, Highgate. Some grand suburban mansion, no doubt. What if there's a maid?'

He had reached the local village and was forced to slow down a trifle, resuming his solitary conversation the moment he had left the houses behind.

'What if there's a maid? She gets to watch her mistress spanked, that's what, and the same goes for the cook, the butler and the boy who blacks the boots, if they have one. By God yes, that would do the little brat some good, a world of good, to be spanked in front of the servants, even better than doing it in front of her subordinates in the WAAF! Oh yes, Miss Pinks, I do hope you have plenty of servants, because every single one of the buggers is there to watch you get your fat little tail warmed!'

He went quiet, his teeth gritted as he savoured the image of the Pankhurst family servants, lined up as if to receive their Christmas gifts, watching in open shock but also secret delight as their mistress had her bottom first exposed and then smacked. It was an immensely satisfying image, too much so for him to bother about the likely reaction of any servants there might be to his attempts to dish out physical chastisement to the daughter of the house, but other possible obstacles did manage to break into his fantasy.

'What if she's out? I'll wait, damn it, if it takes all day. What if Sir Pomeroy's there? Now that might take a bit of doing, to spank her in front of her father, but by God I will if I have to. No Truscott ever backed down to some walrus-faced old buffer of a father, damn it, and I won't be the first!'

He put his foot down, accelerating on to the Aylesbury road, which was almost entirely empty, allowing him to keep his speed up until he reached the suburbs of London. He had visited Highgate before, and found West Grove to be much as he had imagined it, a broad, tree-lined street of substantial houses, among which thirty-seven proved to be one of the last, looking out over the tops of other houses towards the Heath. Getting out of the car, he paused for a moment, imagining Poppy in the atmosphere of reserved suburban wealth the street represented, perhaps as a child, being scolded for getting mud on her pinafore dress, or as a young woman, laughing with a group of friends.

'Sure to breed brats, I suppose,' he remarked to himself, 'and I'll bet she was spoiled.'

Climbing the short flight of well-scrubbed steps to the door, he prodded on the bell, which evoked a bass chime from somewhere deep within the house. There was no immediate response, and he was about to ring again when the door was opened, by Sir Pomeroy himself, leaving Henry with the sudden realisation that, however strong his determination, he could hardly gain entry by announcing his intention of dishing out a spanking to the householder's daughter. Henry decided to make a tactful remark on the photographs of Georgina in bondage but Sir Pomeroy spoke first, his tone friendly if a trifle nervous.

'Ah, Truscott, just the man I was hoping to see. I want to have a word with you.'

'Your photographs will be ready in a few days, sir,' Henry assured him. 'We weren't able to do anything about them while we were in the West Country.'

'I await them with anticipation,' Sir Pomeroy answered, 'but that wasn't what I wanted to talk to you about, not immediately. Do come in, anyway. Is it too early for sherry, d'you think?'

'I'm awake,' Henry responded as he stepped over the threshold to find himself in a tastefully decorated hall with a floor of black-and-white check mosaic.

Sir Pomeroy looked puzzled for an instant, then gave a low chuckle.

'Quite, yes. I see what you mean. Do come through.'

He ushered Henry into a drawing room as neat and understated as the hall, although the sideboard was well supplied with decanters, from one of which he poured out two glasses of pale amber liquid before he carried on talking.

'It's Poppy, you see. She seems determined to be involved with this cabaret business, and I mean to say, what, I didn't mind while it was for the troops, but this is commercial. It's tantamount to being on the stage!'

'I couldn't agree with you more, sir,' Henry said with feeling. 'It's hardly the sort of behaviour you'd expect of a young lady.'

'Absolutely,' Sir Pomeroy agreed, 'there must be limits, after all, and she won't listen to me any more. Mark you, she never did, unless I absolutely put my foot down, if you see what I mean, and now that she's a grown woman that's not really practical. So I was wondering if you might be able to talk some sense into her?'

'Me?' Henry asked, puzzled.

'Who better?' Sir Pomeroy answered him.

'Well, yes, perhaps,' Henry said cautiously, wondering exactly what Poppy had, and had not, told her father.

'After all,' Sir Pomeroy went on, 'yours is an old family, and in the circumstances it would hardly do. I imagine your mother would be scandalised?'

'Quite possibly,' Henry said, now thoroughly confused but keen to capitalise on his excuse to seek Poppy out. 'I'll have a word, of course. Is she about?'

'Not at present. She's down at the Hackney Palace, with that awful man Pettigrew and the girls.'

I'll go there then,' Henry replied and swallowed his sherry at a gulp.

The Hackney Palace proved to be a huge cube of dirty red brick with an ornate front. Henry had parked nearby, and paused in front of the high doors of polished wood, glass and gilt. As he drove across from Highgate he had been mulling over what Sir Pomeroy had said, which was certainly licence to scold Poppy, if not to actually spank her. Nevertheless, it strengthened his hand, especially if there were any repercussions for what he now felt he had to do. Steeling himself to the task in hand, he marched in at the doors, ignoring a man in a suit of what appeared to be cherry-coloured velvet and striding on into the great crimson and gilt auditorium, from which he'd heard voices.

Sure enough, the girls were on the stage, rehearsing, Jamila, Ainikki, Jacinta, Zokie and another half-dozen he'd never met, all dressed in costumes of a pale leaf-green with laces at the front to allow a teasing glimpse of cleavage and tattered skirts designed to allow a rather more than teasing glimpse of shapely bottoms encased in bright green tights. They also wore little green hats, each with a pheasant feather sticking up at a jaunty angle, knee-length suede boots of a darker green, a miniature bow and a quiver of arrows. Michelle stood at the front of the stage, instructing them in some complicated piece of dance, while Pettigrew sat in the front row, as round and as pink as ever. There was no sign of Poppy, but Ginger Green was seated a few rows in, to Henry's surprise.

'Ginger?' he asked quietly, sliding into the seat beside his friend. 'What are you doing here?'

'Just keeping an eye on things,' Ginger answered, with more than hint of guilt in his voice.

'How do you mean?' Henry demanded. 'What's going on, and why does nobody tell me anything?'

'Terribly sorry, old chap,' Ginger answered, 'but I didn't want to tell anybody until I was sure. I have asked Michelle if she'll marry me, and she's agreed.'

'Michelle?' Henry responded, taken aback for a moment. 'Well, why not? Nice girl, Michelle … suits you … um, yes, congratulations, old chap. I'm sure you'll be very happy. In fact, I know you will be. Congratulations! But what about this cabaret business? It's bit rich, isn't it, Poppy just taking over without so much as a by-your-leave?'

'Ah, well, that's Pinks for you,' Ginger answered him. 'A very determined young lady, Miss Pankhurst.'

'A bossy little madam, more like,' Henry responded. 'Where is she anyway?'

'She went home. About half-an-hour minutes ago.'

'She went home? Damn! Oh, and speaking of getting married and all that sort of thing, I'm engaged to your sister.'

'Sally?'

'Yes, Sally. You don't have any other sisters, do you?'

'Well, no … congratulations, only I thought, you and Poppy?'

'Me and Poppy!? Whatever gave you that idea?'

'She did.'

'She did? Well, I suppose that explains what her old man was wittering on about, but it's news to me. How did this come about?'

'We were talking,' Ginger explained, 'after she happened to walk in to Michelle's changing room when … when Michelle …'

'Was giving you a good seeing to?' Henry filled in, guessing the details from the colour of his friend's face.

'Something like that,' Ginger admitted, 'and well, you know how Michelle is, and well, she … she asked Poppy if she'd like to watch, to, err …'

'To add to your embarrassment,' Henry supplied. 'Sounds fun.'

'Rather!' Ginger agreed. 'And when they'd finished … I mean to say, Poppy took a turn, they were talking about how men needed to be tamed, as it were, and Pinks was saying that you'd make a jolly good husband once you'd been tamed, and …'

'Tamed?' Henry echoed. 'Me, tamed!?'

'Well, yes. She said you were made of the right stuff, but a little wild, and so needed to be tamed before she could marry you.'

'Tamed!?' Henry repeated. 'Right, that does it. I'm going back to her house and I'm going to give the little brat the spanking of a lifetime, of ten lifetimes. If her father's there to

163

watch, all the better. If I catch her in the street and her neighbours get to see, all the better. If they call the police, well, by the time they drag me away she's going to have a bottom the colour of a ripe cherry, that's all, and a few weeks in Pentonville will be well worth it, believe me. Must dash.'

He left Ginger gaping after him as he once more made for the car, now running. As he drove he was muttering to himself once again, and repeating the same word over and over – "tamed". Far from calming down, his indignation grew stronger still, and by the time he got back to Highgate it had reached boiling point. He jabbed hard at the bell, once and then again, his fingers clenching and unclenching in fury as he thought of how if it was Poppy who answered the door he would take hold of her by the scruff of her neck, drag her outside, strip her bottom and spank her in the street.

When the door was finally opened it was by a maid and Henry was forced to announce himself, but when the girl went to see if Poppy would receive him he followed her into the house, ignoring her squeak of protest as he passed her and mounted the stairs, also Sir Pomeroy's questioning voice from somewhere at the back of the house.

'Poppy!' he demanded as he reached the first floor landing. 'Poppy! I want a word with you, girl, now!'

There was no answer, but one of the doors was slightly open and a faint noise caught his attention. He pushed through, to find himself in a room devoted to games and trophies, with a billiard table in the middle and display cabinets around the walls to show off an astonishing array of cups, shields and rosettes, all of which Henry dismissed with a single glance as he focussed on Poppy. She was on the far side of the billiard table, wearing a plain blue frock that set off her golden hair and gave her a vulnerable, even girlish, look made stronger by the pallor of her face. Her eyes were wide and frightened, her lower lip was trembling and she was struggling to control her voice as she spoke.

'If you come near me, Henry Truscott,' she began, but he cut her off.

'Ginger called ahead, did he?' Henry remanded. 'Well, you

and little Michelle may have got him tamed, but you'll find I'm not so easy. In fact, it's not me who's going to be tamed, Miss Pinks, but you. I am going to spank you, and I am going to spank you well, over my knee, the way it ought to be done. Now come here!'

'No,' Poppy answered in sulky defiance. 'You wouldn't dare!'

'Oh yes I would,' Henry assured her, moving along the edge of the billiard table, only for her to begin to edge the other way. 'You can count on it, and you can count on getting it bare-bottom.'

'You pig!' Poppy spat. 'You dirty pig!'

'That makes us a fine pair then,' Henry retorted, 'given the way you like to strip girls down when you do them, but this time you're the little piggy who's going to get her bare bottom smacked.'

'It's hardly the same, between women!'

'So you say, and I say you're overdue a spanking, Poppy Pankhurst, from a man, just the same way you like to dish it out to women, and that's what you're going to get, and not just for your cheek, either, because there are one or two other matters I want to discuss with you, such as pinching my cabaret act for one, and the spankings you gave Sally Green and Georgina Hayes for another. I warned you what was going to happen if you touched Georgina, didn't I? And what did you do, you immediately spank and cane her, and Sally too. Why, anybody would think ...'

He broke off as realisation dawned, an explanation that accounted not only for her treatment of the other girls but every aspect of her behaviour towards him, even what she'd said to Ginger and Michelle. It was all designed to taunt him, to make him so angry that he finally took her to task and spanked her in raw anger, to give her the real discipline it seemed she craved.

'You want it, don't you?' he demanded. 'You want your little tail warmed, don't you?'

'No!' Poppy answered hotly. 'Certainly not!'

'Oh yes you do,' he told her. 'You've been angling for it ever since I dealt with you after the poker game, haven't you,

165

maybe longer.'

'No!' she repeated. 'What an idea! Now stop it, or I'll call for my father!'

'Please do,' Henry offered, 'with any luck, by the time he gets up here I'll have you bare and nicely pink, and he can watch his little brat of a daughter getting what she deserves.'

'You really wouldn't dare!' Poppy retorted, but she was still edging back and forth along the far side of the billiard table, while the expression on her face registered something close to panic.

'Wouldn't I?' Henry asked, moving back to prevent her making a dash for the door. 'Perhaps you'd care to place a small bet on that? In fact, it might interest you to know that he's asked me to have a word with you about being involved with the cabaret. He doesn't approve, now that you're in civvy street, and it's not that big a step from scolding you to spanking you. In fact, I've a good mind to call him upstairs myself, explain what's happened and ask his permission to punish you.'

'You wouldn't!' she gasped, and her face had gone paler still.

Henry had made the threat purely in order to add to her embarrassment and indignation, but at her reaction he realised that he'd touched a nerve.

'So Daddy might not be all that disapproving after all, eh?' he said, making no effort to keep the gloating tone from his voice. 'He's an old-fashioned sort of chap, I suppose, so perhaps he approves of the idea of a young fellow like me taking his daughter in hand, especially as seems to think we're engaged. And what's all that about, while we're at it, eh?'

'I ... I ...,' Poppy stammered, now blushing, 'I thought, because you ... you had me, that you'd want to, and then ... all those other girls, but I'd already said ... implied anyway, and ...'

She burst into tears, great wrenching sobs that shook her entire body, and when Henry made a dash around the table to reach her she made no effort to escape. Now less sure of himself, he put an arm around her shoulder and for an instant she yielded, only to spin around and land a slap full across his face.

'I thought I meant something to you!' she stormed, 'And all the time you just wanted to stick your dirty great thing up my bottom, you pig, you filthy, dirty, lecherous pig!'

Henry barely heard, his feelings finally tipped over the edge by the sting of the slap. Grabbing one wrist, he pulled her away from the table to where a set of high-backed chairs stood in the window bay. Poppy realised his intention on the instant and tried to slap him again with her free hand, but he caught it and used his hold to drag her down as he settled himself onto a chair, across his knee and into spanking position with both her wrists twisted up behind her back. Having her wrists pinned didn't stop her fighting, or talking, her legs kicking frantically up and down and her body writhing against his in a furious attempt to escape as she babbled out a mixture of threats and pleas, insults and reason, saying anything that might even conceivably make him think twice about spanking her.

'Stop it, you great pig! Get off me! Henry, you can't do this, you really can't! Please no, please! It's not proper, it's ... it's not fair! Please, no! I'll get you back, I swear I will! I'll have Michelle and the girls give you the same treatment, you dirty pig! They'll do it, they will, and then you'll learn how this feels, you pig, you beast, you utter bastard!'

He had lifted her dress as she spoke, followed by her slip, to reveal her long legs, tightly sheaved in expensive stockings with a neat seam running from her ankles all the way to where the top met the smooth white bulge of her thighs, with four straining straps holding them up to her girdle, each passing beneath the pair of big, white, winter-weight knickers that encased her bottom. She was still struggling, although he was sure she could have tried a lot harder if she'd been really determined and as he tucked her dress and petticoats securely up into the small of her back he spoke to her, as calmly as he could manage.

'We both know that this is what you need, Poppy Pankhurst, and what you want. Not that it matters. You're going to be spanked and that's that, so your best bet would be to try and accept your punishment with good grace. Come along, show me how a young lady takes it, with a little dignity.'

For a moment she continued to writhe and kick, only to suddenly go limp.

'Good girl,' he told her, and applied a gentle pat to the seat of her knickers, making the firm but distinctly plump flesh packed within quiver and shake. 'How does that old rhyme go? Wibble wobble, wibble wobble, jelly on a plate? I always think of that when I see the way a girl's bottom jiggles while she's spanked.'

'You would, you dirty pig! Go on then, spank me, if you have to.'

'Oh I do,' he assured her, 'but you're not quite ready yet. Bare bottom, didn't I say?'

'No, please,' she replied 'Leave me some modesty.'

'I can't imagine why I should,' he responded, shifting his grip on her wrists to allow him to take hold of the waistband of her knickers. 'As I recall, you always take down your girls' knickers for their spankings, so why should you be any different?'

'Just not this time, please,' she said, now with rising panic in her voice as he begun to pull at the thick white material, revealing the first couple of inches of her bottom slit. 'Please, Henry? I'll be good, I promise, just do it on my knickers, please?'

'Spankings should always be given bare,' he said as he cocked one knee up to make a better display of her bottom and show off between her thighs. 'As you know perfectly well.'

'Yes, but … not this time!' she begged. 'Henry!'

'Bare bottom,' he repeated and began to peel down her knickers.

'Not my knickers!' she wailed. 'Please, Henry, at least leave me that, please!?'

'Bare bottom,' he said once more.

She gave a frantic jerk, freeing one arm from his grip, to snatch back at her now half lowered knickers, locking her fingers into the thick white cotton in a desperate effort to stop them being pulled down. To Henry's amusement her action only succeeded in pulling the material up between her cheeks, spilling out a good handful of girlish bottom flesh from either leg hole and leaving the lips of her cunt encased in tight white cotton.

'What a pretty cunt you have,' he remarked, 'but prettier still naked. Come on, Miss Pinks, no nonsense now!'

He gave the exposed half of one cheek a hard slap as he spoke and immediately snatched her wrist, pulling it up and using her dress to trap her arms behind her back.

'Please!' she begged as her legs began to scissor in a desperate and pointless effort to stop her knickers being pulled down properly.

She succeeded only in striking a variety of increasingly ridiculous poses, making Henry chuckle as her took hold of her knickers once more and peeled them down with a single, firm motion to finally leave her with her bottom fully bare.

'What a fuss!' he laughed. 'And all because you have to go bare bottom. Oh, I see …'

Poppy was now stripped behind, and her struggles had tipped her forward so that she was hanging head down over Henry's lap with her legs up in the air. She was still kicking, her thighs pumping in her knickers as he held them, and also spread far enough to show off the mound of her cunt, revealing to Henry why she had been so desperate not to be exposed. The thick blonde down that covered her sex was no longer uniform, but had been shaved into a pair of neat corporal's stripes.

'Stop it, you pig!' she snapped, her voice now furiously sulky in response to Henry's open laughter.

'I'm sorry,' he told her, 'but what a sight! You must admit it's funny. Who shaved you?'

'Lift me up,' she demanded. 'The blood's going to my head.'

Henry had been holding her upside down to inspect her cunt and obliged, returning her to the normal over-the-knee position, now with her knickers around her knees and her bottom fully bare. With the exposure of her shameful secret all the fight had gone out of her and she lay still, no longer trying to escape, with her thighs still a little apart to let her cunt lips and anus show behind.

'Who shaved you?' he repeated. 'Did you lose a bet or something? I bet that's it. You lost a bet and had to let some lucky fellow shave your corporal's stripes into your fanny hair. I wish I'd been there to watch, or better still, to do the shaving.'

'It was nothing like that,' she retorted. 'I thought you were going to spank me, not touch me up?'

He'd been gently fondling her bottom as he spoke, but gave her another slap, then a third, now delighting in her surrender.

'Tell me then,' he asked. 'What? Did you do it for Georgina, maybe?'

'Michelle, if you must know,' Poppy answered sulkily. 'She has one stripe.'

'How sweet,' Henry answered, now spanking her to a slow, gentle rhythm. 'I'd love to see the two of you side by side, bottoms in the air to show it all off, the same way you made Sally and Georgina pose for the cane.'

'I bet you would, you pervert,' she answered.

'Pervert, is it?' Henry queried. 'Right then, just for that you get your dress turned up all the way, right up, over the titties, and let's have this silly brassiere out of the way too, shall we?'

'Pig!' she spat, but there was no resistance as he levered her dress up around her armpits and tugged her bra away to spill out her breasts.

Henry treated himself to a quick squeeze of each dangling tit and turned his attention back to her bottom. Her pale skin had already begun to take on a rosy flush, while his cock was stiff in his pants and pressing to her side, but he reminded himself that she needed to be punished before he could indulge himself with her. As he began to spank her once more he was also talking to her, determined that she should be fully aware of why she had ended up in such a humiliating position and what her bottom was being smacked for.

'Right, Miss Pinks,' he told her, 'this spanking is being administered for a number of crimes. First, there is the matter of the punishment you gave Georgina Hayes.'

'She likes it!'

'So do you, and as we both know very well, Miss Poppy, it

is entirely possible for a girl to like it and hate it at the same time, isn't it?'

'Yes,' she answered miserably, with her bottom now bouncing to hard, regular smacks.

'Second,' he went on, 'there is the matter of punishing Sally Green. I suspect one hundred smacks will answer each charge, as long as you're properly contrite when I'm finished with you. Third, there is the matter of pinching my girls and taking over the cabaret act.'

'What are you talking about!' she protested. 'It was ... ow! Not on my thighs, you beast!'

Henry merely chuckled and gave her two more firm smacks on the back of her thighs before he went back to work on her bottom.

'If you talk back, you get your thighs smacked,' he told her, 'or if you call me names. Yes, I know I left the cabaret in your hands, and no doubt much of the fault lies with that fellow Pettigrew, but you should have at least consulted me, and that's going to earn you another hundred smacks. Your father also disapproves, as you no doubt know, but he doesn't feel it would be proper to deal with you himself, so on your father's behalf, another hundred.'

'You ... you unutterable ... ow!'

'What did I say? Nasty names earn smacked legs. So, that's four hundred smacks, and I think another hundred just for being such an impudent little brat!'

As he spoke the last words he'd laid in properly, applying his hand to the upturned cheeks of her bottom with all his force. She let out a squeal like a stuck pig, her legs kicking wide in her half-dropped knickers, much to his satisfaction. It felt good to punish her, and her reaction made it all the better as he took his feelings out on her bouncing, wriggling bottom as she yelped and kicked, squealed and bucked, hair flying and titties jiggling, all dignity lost in the pain of her spanking.

He was counting as he spanked, determined that she should know exactly how many she'd had and how many were coming, so that her punishment was official and when it was done she would know that she'd been given, and accepted, formal chastisement. Only then, when it was done and done well, would he relieve his aching cock in her mouth or up her bottom, although with every smack showing off the taut red hymen that blocked her cunt it was growing increasingly tempting to take full advantage of her, stealing her virginity, not to complete her punishment, but because as he spanked her he was growing increasingly sure that was exactly what she wanted.

A hundred spanks had passed and she was jerking and gasping to the smacks, both her shoes lost from her earlier, more frantic kicking, her thighs cocked wide in her well lowered knickers and her feet waggling pathetically in her surrender. Two hundred and she'd started to cry, but her struggles had died to a meek squirming motion punctuated by little jerks of her torso and legs in response to the more painful smacks. Three hundred and she was blubbering her heart out over his lap, but she had begun to lift her bottom of her own accord. Four hundred and she had given in completely, snivelling weakly over his lap with her bright red bottom thrust high, her cheeks parted to show off the twitching dimple of her anus and the wet, ready mouth of her cunt, convincing him her virginity was on offer.

Henry tried to focus on his promise to Sally, telling himself that Poppy was merely getting what she deserved and that a helping of spunk to swallow down or left dribbling from her bottom hole would be the ideal climax to her punishment, but his cock knew exactly where it wanted to be, in the soft, warm wetness of her cunt. She was keeping her bottom well up too, lifted to him no matter how hard he spanked, while the palm of his hand was sore and smarting, making it hard to deliver her punishment with full force. After four hundred and fifty spanks he slowed down and began to break off to fondle her, exploring her bottom and teasing her anus in the hope of sparking her resentment once more and turning his rising need back to a desire for vengeance.

She was still sobbing bitterly, with the tears running hard down her nose to drip on the carpet beneath, but as his fingers touched her anus she merely sighed and lifted her bottom higher still. Henry bit his lip, determined not to give in, and let his groping fingers move down further still, to open the mouth of her cunt and probe at the tiny opening where her hymen held her vagina sacred from the intrusion of a cock. Again she sighed, a low, soft moan, and spoke for the first time since he had begun to spank her properly.

'No ... not like this. Properly, Henry, please not like this ... not with your fingers.'

He went back to spanking her, his teeth gritted, once more counting the smacks. With twenty to go he began to count down, smack after slow, hard smack with his arm locked tight around her waist and her helpless bottom thrust high. She began to count with him, which seemed to him acceptance of her need to be punished and his right to punish her, making it all the harder to resist the prize on offer.

' ...five, four, three, two, one,' he counted, finishing with a hard slap to the very seat of her bottom. 'There, you're done, and I hope that will teach you a lesson?'

'Yes, Henry,' she answered, meek and breathless with need. 'I'm sorry.'

'Yes, well,' he answered, 'I should hope so too, and now ...'

'Perhaps you should cane me?' she broke in, to his surprise. 'It's best to cane me, for a proper punishment. And then ...'

'Well, yes,' he said after a moment, struggling to ignore the implication of her final, unfinished comment. 'Yes, I think, a few strokes of the cane would do you good. Six-of-the-best, in fact, which I believe is the traditional punishment for naughty girls?'

He was fighting to keep his voice even as she rose unsteadily from his lap, not bothering to pull her knickers up, or adjust her dress, but merely squeezing her hot bottom as she stood with her mouth slightly open, her eyes wide and wet in her tear-stained face. Her small, high breasts were keeping her dress and bra up, with her upturned nipples looking more like a pair of ripe raspberries than ever, while her cunt showed puffy with arousal beneath the smart double V of the corporal's stripes shaved into her pubic hair.

'Yes, Henry,' she repeated. 'I'll fetch a cane.'

She went to a stand by the door, drawing out a long, viciously thin whalebone switch from among the umbrellas and walking canes. Henry couldn't remember when he had seen a more painful-looking implement, but there were at least two ordinary rattans and a malacca, all clearly suitable for application to her bottom, which she'd ignored.

'This is my naughty cane,' she said, her voice barely audible as she offered it to him.

'Then it's just what you need,' he told her. 'Bend over the billiard table.'

Poppy got into position without the slightest hesitation, bending down and lifting herself on to her tiptoes with her back pulled in to make the best possible presentation of her naked red bottom, and of her cunt. Henry came behind her, admiring the view as he adjusted his throbbing erection in her pants. She saw and gave a single, trembling nod, then spread her arms to clutch the sides of the table, bracing herself for the cane.

Henry came close, to tap the wicked implement across her soft, faintly quivering cheeks, lift it and bring it down in a hard, well aimed cut. Poppy screamed as the cane bit into her flesh, and she was dancing up and down on her feet in her pain as the welt he'd laid across her bottom turned from white to a double line of livid scarlet, but she held her position. Again Henry measured up his stroke, to lay a second fiery line a little below the first, and again she screamed and stamped her feet, but held still.

The juice from her cunt had begun to run down her thighs and the air was thick with the smell of her arousal, making the temptation to fuck her stronger than ever, although the twitching pink star of her anus was also tempting and as he lined up the third stroke Henry told himself that his cock would be going up her bottom just as soon as her beating was over. When the cane struck again she responded with her usual cry of pain and little, stamping dance, and as she resumed her position she gave her bottom an encouraging wiggle, a sight that only served to make his cock stiffer.

'By God you're asking for it,' he grunted, 'and you are

going to get it, Poppy Pankhurst, right up that sweet little bottom.'

'You can do as you like,' she breathed, 'but ... but not up my bottom, please? Why ...'

Her words broke to a fresh scream as Henry lashed the fourth stroke down across her cheeks, adding one more neat red welt to the collection. Again Poppy spent a moment with her feet thumping on the floor and her teeth gritted against the pain, and again she'd quickly stuck out her bottom once more.

'Why ... why do you have to be so dirty with me?' she asked, panting. 'You know I'm yours, so ...'

'Shut up,' Henry told her as he put in the fifth stroke, harder still, deliberately making her scream to choke off the offer of her cunt, but as soon as she'd stopped jiggling about and got her breath back she spoke again.

'Look what you've done to me, Henry, just look, look how I am for you.'

'Damn tempting,' he admitted, 'especially that little rosebud of an arsehole.'

He brought the cane down for the sixth time on the last word, laying it full across her cheeks to leave the welt running directly across the little hole he'd threatened to penetrate, broken only in the deepest part of her slit. Her answering scream had rung out louder than before and she danced for a little longer, but soon came back into position, on tiptoes, back well in and bottom thrust high, for all that the caning was over.

'Now to finished your lesson,' Henry told her. 'Let's have you stripped.'

He pulled her dress up and off, taking her already dishevelled brassiere with it to leave her in nothing but her girdle, stockings and the pair of big white knickers stretched between her ankles. Her knickers followed and he pulled them on over her head like a ridiculous hat before treating himself to a quick rub against her bottom and a few more slaps. She didn't speak at all, snivelling faintly over deep, even breaths as she was stripped and as he returned the cane to the stand. There was a display of rosettes on the wall nearby, and he selected a large, blue one, which he stuck to one of her suspender straps, marking her bottom as Best in Show, Hertford, 1936.

'And I'll bet it was,' he remarked as he opened his fly, 'because by God they don't come much better, if at all. Now then, let's get that little rosebud buggered, shall we?'

'Not up my bottom, please?' she answered, but she stayed put, unresisting as he laid his erection between her well spread cheeks.

He began to rub in her slit, still fighting the urge to fuck her, and filled with guilt both for her obvious need and his promise to Sally, but the state of his cock allowed no going back. Taking a firm grip on his shaft, he pushed it down, to rub his helmet between the lips of her cunt in order to gather some juice for her buggering. Poppy gave a low moan and pushed her bottom out, inviting penetration, then a whimper of disappointment as her pulled up his cock and began to paint her anus with her own slime.

'I'm truly sorry, Poppy, darling,' he gasped as her ring opened to the first push of his helmet. 'You know I'd love to pop your little cunt hole, but I can't.'

'You are such a pig,' she told him, but she was breathless with pleasure and was making no effort to stop him penetrating her anus. 'All right, if you have to be dirty, do it up my bottom.'

She broke off with a long sigh as her anal ring came open to accept the head of Henry's cock.

'Pig,' she breathed as another couple of inches of cock were eased in past her now gaping bottom hole. 'Why not then? Right up my poor smacked bottom ... right up, until I can feel your balls on my ... my cunt. Oh that's such a dirty word. Don't you like my cunt, Henry? Don't you want to put your big, hard thingy in my cunt?'

'Shut up!' he gasped, now all the way in, with his thumbs spreading her welted bottoms cheeks apart to show off the junction between his cock shaft and her straining anus.

'At least tell me you like my cunt?' she moaned, her fingers now clutching at the baize of the billiard table in reaction to her buggering. 'Tell me what you want to do to me, Henry, like you did just now, how you want to ... to pop my little cunt hole.'

'Shut up!' he repeated. 'Shut up, or I swear I'll finish in your mouth, Poppy, straight from your bottom hole and into your mouth!'

'If you have to,' she groaned. 'If you really want to be that filthy with me, but while I suck tell me you'd like to pop my little cunt hole.'

'That does it, damn you!' Henry swore, and he'd begun to pull his cock from her anus.

Poppy's bottom hole closed with a long, soft fart as he came free, but before he could grab her by the hair and force his erection into her mouth she had twisted around to accept him, deliberately taking him as deep as he could go, his helmet jammed well down her throat. Her arms went around his middle and she was clinging to him, her body shaking furiously hard as she sucked on his penis, deliberately fucking her own throat to squeeze bubbles from her nose and around her lips.

Henry relaxed, closing his eyes in bliss as he thought of how good it had felt to spank and cane her, and what a gloriously depraved state the punishment had got her into, begging to have her virginity taken and willingly sucking on his cock when a moment before he had it deep up her bottom. He was going to come, his orgasm rising as his knob squashed deeper still down Poppy's throat, only for her to suddenly pull back, jump up and spread herself out on the billiard table, her thighs cocked wide.

'Just fuck it, you bastard!' she screamed. 'Pop my cunt!'

She'd grabbed his cock, pulling on his slippery foreskin and rubbing his helmet between her lips, her muscles already in contraction. Faintly, Henry realised that she'd been playing with herself as she sucked his cock, but he too was on the edge of orgasm, his will to resist completely gone in the face of ecstasy and lust as he snatched his erection from Poppy's hand and thrust at her hole, deflowering her in one push as he sunk himself to the balls in her virgin cunt.

Poppy screamed as her hymen tore, and again as Henry gave a second, hard push to make her virgin blood squash out and spatter hot on his balls. He'd started to come even as he

177

entered her, spunking up deep in her newly fucked cunt. So had she, the muscles of her vagina in powerful contraction as she milked his cock into her body, all the while screaming and gasping and telling him over and over again that she loved him. Henry was barely aware of what was going on as he drained his balls into her hole, save for her violent reaction to sex and the kisses she showered on to his face as she pulled herself up into his arms. He responded, the only possible reaction, but as his ecstasy slowly faded he became aware that he and Poppy were not alone.

Slowly, Henry turned around, with Poppy still clinging to his neck, her cunt impaled on his cock and her virgin blood dripping from his balls and trickling down the cheeks of her well-whipped bottom. Air Commodore Sir Pomeroy Pankhurst stood in the doorway, his face stern, one eyebrow raised in disapproval, and while his voice was remarkably calm when he finally chose to speak, it had lost all trace of its earlier mildness.

'I trust an appropriate announcement will be appearing in tomorrow's paper?'

Chapter Ten

'AND THAT,' HENRY EXPLAINED, 'is the long and the short of it.'

None of the crew answered immediately, each pondering what Henry had told them until the Egg at last broke the silence.

'So, you're engaged to both of them?'

'Yes, and there's no way of pretending otherwise,' Henry replied, pushing the two papers he had bought that morning forward.

Both contained an announcement of his forthcoming marriage, one to Miss Sarah Green, the other to Miss Poppaea Isabelle Chastity Pankhurst. Both gave his name correctly, which he'd rather been hoping they wouldn't, as Mr John Henry Truscott of Stukely Hall, near Lydford in Devon. Both were sure to have been seen by a wide circle of friends and acquaintances, so that it could only be a matter of time before the girls found out.

'Look on the bright side, Skipper,' Slick chirped up. 'When they find out, both of 'em are going to hand you your hat, and that's that. I had two birds on the go at the same time once. Joan and Mavis. When they found out about each other ... well, they were not happy, that's all.'

'I would actually like to marry Sally,' Henry pointed out, '... or perhaps Poppy.'

'That happened to me once,' the Egg remarked. 'They held me down an' took turns to sit on my face, boot blacked my cock and balls, stuck a parsnip up my arse and went off together, arm in arm, cool as you please.'

'You get a lot of that in the Bunk,' Bunker put in. 'Usually the two girls fight it out, in the street sometimes, which is always good for a laugh.'

'That's the way to do it,' the Egg said. 'What you want is a good, big pigsty, like the one my uncle Harold's got down near Woolston, full of straw, an' mud, an' shit and that. You put the two girls in it, dressed up to the nines – wedding dresses is best – an' you let 'em fight it out. They have to strip each other, see, an' the first one to get the other one in the nuddy with her knickers up her cunt, she's the winner, see?'

'Thank you for that, Egg,' Henry replied, 'but somehow I don't see either Sally or Poppy accepting the conditions, to say nothing of Sir Pomeroy and Lady Pankhurst or Mr and Mrs Green.'

'Become a Mohammedan,' Bunker suggested. 'That way you can marry both of 'em, an' Hills, an' Georgina maybe, an' maybe that Jamila, she likes you, an' maybe ...'

'They are only allowed four,' Gorski put in.

'Not under British law,' Henry said, 'and besides, I don't see them agreeing to that either, let alone their parents.'

'No?' the Egg queried. 'They're always in each other's knickers, them two.'

'True,' Henry admitted thoughtfully, then shook his head. 'There's still their parents, not to mention my family. My aunts are probably having the vapours this minute, or they will be soon enough. We only take *The Times*.'

'Who would you rather marry?' Gorski asked.

'I'm not sure,' Henry admitted. 'Probably Sally, as I did ask her first, and Poppy rather tricked me into it, possibly with her father's connivance.'

'Tricked you into it? Bunker queried. 'I thought you said you beat her an' then shagged her over the billiard table.'

'Up her bottom,' Henry explained, 'but she was desperate for me to take her virginity, and Sir Pomeroy turned up nicely on time, even though he must have heard us long before, what with the fuss she was making over her spanking, a real tantrum at first, and she wasn't exactly quiet about taking the cane either. He was pretty cool about it too, considering what he saw.'

'You reckon she fixed it all up with her old man?' Slick asked doubtfully.

'I don't know,' Henry answered. 'Probably not. When I told her she was due for a spanking she threatened to call him upstairs, but I called her bluff, telling her I'd call him myself if she wanted. She was not at all happy about that, and if she was faking then she's a good actress, and by God you should have seen the colour of her blush when he caught us at it, positively beetroot!'

'He could've fixed it himself,' Bunker suggested. 'He's got the guts. An ace during the last lot, he was. Twelve kills.'

'He certainly had some idea what was going on,' Henry agreed, 'and he doesn't want her involved with Pettigrew and the cabaret. But then Poppy's no innocent, and she's hard to read, that one. After all, she'd been angling for a spanking ever since I did her at Babu's, but she had to have it for real, you know, as a punishment, instead of telling me what she wanted. I ask you, women!'

Another long silence followed, this time broken by Slick.

'Talking of women, we ought to go and see the girls at the Hackney Palace.'

Henry drew the car to a halt in Campbell Road, where he had agreed to drop Bunker with his family before going on to Hackney. As they had driven in through north and east London there had been no shortage of reminders of the recent war, with raw scars where buildings had been hit, mainly by rockets. Campbell Road seemed to have suffered worse than most, with windows and roofs gone and several of the apparently respectably built houses in a state of collapse.

'You caught it rather,' he remarked to Bunker as they got out of the car.

Bunker gave him a hurt look.

'We ain't had no bombs, not one. It's just kids an' that. Mind you, the old place 'as gone down a bit.'

'I see,' Henry replied, looking around at the decaying slum, which was far worse than he had imagined. 'Look, don't take

181

this the wrong way, old chap, but if you and your family ever want to move to Devon I have quite a bit of property. You could set up as a photographer.'

'The missus would kill me, sort of pictures we've been taking,' Bunker joked as he slung his kit bag over his shoulder. 'Besides, this is my patch, but I'll think about it. Ta, Skipper.'

He moved away, towards one of the few intact houses, holding his free arm wide in an attempt to embrace all the half dozen children running towards him at once. Henry took another glance around, then got back into the car.

'How about the rest of you?' he asked as they set off again. 'Determined to stick it out as a flyboy, Gorski?'

The big Pole simply nodded.

'I reckon there's a fortune to be made with these pictures,' Slick put in. 'Maybe I'll start my own magazine. Like Men Only[9], but dirtier.'

'I'm back to the farm, me,' the Egg said happily. 'You ought to come down, get some pictures maybe, you know, girls forking hay or mucking out the stables in the altogether, that sort of thing, or fighting in mud, like I was saying Pinks and Sally ought to do, or playing cunt tease. I like a good game of cunt tease, me. The girls get down on all fours, see, and turn up their skirts to see who can get mounted ...'

The Egg carried on as they drove through the streets of Islington, with Henry, Slick and Gorski listening in ever-increasing disbelief tempered only by the absolutely casual way in which the Egg was describing the perverted game. He was still going strong when they drew up near the Hackney Palace, finishing a description of a particularly messy game known as Maid's Covers.

'... and the amount of spunk you wouldn't believe. Must have been a pint, I swear!'

'I advise against including his suggestions for pictures in your magazine, Slick,' Henry remarked. 'You'd get locked up, probably in an asylum. Here we are then.'

They had arrived early, and having paid their entrance fees found themselves in a nearly empty auditorium, with the curtains firmly closed and only a handful of the seats occupied.

Ginger was among the few present and Henry steeled himself for the first of what seemed likely to be a long string of awkward conversations.

'Ah, Ginger, old man,' he greeted his friend, 'you've seen the morning papers, I imagine?'

'No I haven't,' Ginger snapped back. 'Look at these.'

He had thrust a sheaf of documents towards Henry, who took them, reading Michelle's name on the top sheet.

'Ten shillings a week and accommodation, he agreed with Poppy,' Ginger went on, 'but he's making deductions for meals, and linen, and wear and tear on their costumes, and goodness knows what besides.'

Henry was studying the documents, each of which showed the girl's pay in one column and deductions in another, with a final figure at the bottom. Michelle was shown as having earned one shilling and eight pence. Jamila's showed a total of three pence ha'penny, the others negative sums down to minus six shillings and tuppence for Zokie.

'This won't do at all,' he remarked. 'In fact it's outrageous. The man's a bloody swindler!'

'It's a common game,' Slick told him. 'You offer money, less expenses, and make sure the expenses always add up to more than the pay. That way you've got 'em where you want 'em and you're not paying a penny for the work.'

'So I see,' Henry replied. 'I think we'd better have a word with Mr Pettigrew, don't you?'

'I have had a word,' Ginger responded. 'He won't budge an inch. Says it's all there in black and white, he does, and there's nothing we can do about it.'

'What about Poppy?' Henry asked. 'And speaking of Poppy ...'

'She's on a percentage of the booking fee,' Ginger interrupted him, 'but I'll bet the slimy bastard will find some way to wriggle out of his obligations.'

Henry drew in his breath, determined to explain how things stood with Poppy and Sally, only to realise that Gorski, Slick and the Egg were no longer behind him. Somewhere to the side of the stage a door banged shut.

'Damn!' he swore. 'They've gone after Pettigrew. We'd better catch up before they do anything stupid.'

He started for the door, with Ginger following close behind, only to discover a passage leading in two directions with a flight of stairs directly opposite him. A sign pointing up the stairs indicated the direction of the manager's office and Henry started up, only to halt at the sound of raised voices from a different direction. He doubled back, rushing to the back of the stage and into a large, open store-room where Gorski, Slick and the Egg stood counting through a wad of notes. To one side were several tea chests full of props, and in one case also of Mr Pettigrew, who had been inserted upside down, so that only the seat of a pair of ample and rather loud check trousers and two waggling legs showed above the edge. He was doing his best to escape, but the tea chest had been jammed in among others, preventing him from tipping it over. Henry watched for a moment before speaking up.

'Come on, boys, you can't just rob the fellow.'

'He owes the girls,' Slick pointed out.

'Very true,' Henry agreed, 'but we must make it legal.'

He sauntered over to the tea chests as he spoke.

'Mr Pettigrew, I presume?'

The legs began to kick a little harder, accompanied by the muffled sound of Pettigrew's voice demanding to be let out.

'Not just yet,' Henry replied. 'I wish to conduct certain business negotiations and I find your current position to my advantage. Firstly, please allow me to apologise for the behaviour of my crew, who have a tendency to express themselves physically rather than to negotiate. Secondly, there is the matter of the girls' remuneration, which as I'm sure you are aware is the reason you have been placed in the tea chest. Thirdly, I'm sure that you'll be pleased to hear that Miss Pankhurst is willing to sell her share of the concern, including the name, for say … how much do you have there, Slick?'

'Two-hundred and eighty-one pounds and ten shillings,' Slick answered with a touch of awe in his voice. 'More than I earn in a year.[10]'

'Let's see then,' Henry continued. 'We're on fifteen percent each, give or take, so let's say … thirty pounds each, including Bunker and Poppy of course, which makes two-hundred and ten pounds. That seems a reasonable sum, don't you think?'

'That's bloody robbery!' Pettigrew yelled from within the tea chest.

'If you say so,' Henry replied. 'After all, you should know. Anyway, that leaves us with seventy-one pounds and ten shillings, so I suggest ten pounds each for the girls and the remainder to cover our expenses. How about it?'

'Seems fair,' Slick agreed.

'You'll not get a penny, damn you!' Pettigrew cursed.

'We already have,' Henry pointed out. 'Two-hundred and eighty-one pounds and ten shillings to be precise, but we do require your signature. Otherwise … well, we're flying to Bremen tomorrow night, which means crossing the North Sea. We could drop you off, if you like, about halfway.'

'You were only bluffing, weren't you?' Ginger asked Henry as he took a pint of beer from the row on the bar. 'You wouldn't really have given him the long drop?'

'Of course not,' Henry answered. 'After all, we'd never have got away with it, and we're not going to Bremen anyway.'

Henry lifted his own pint and took a long draught. With the necessary documents safely signed, they had collected the five girls and made their way to a local pub, where they'd hired an upstairs room. The girls had been only too glad to leave Pettigrew's employment, and each had gravitated to one of the men as the group walked up Mare Street. Michelle and Ginger had been holding hands from the start, Jamila had come straight to Henry, clinging to him with embarrassing affection. Zokie held on to Gorski's arm in much the same manner, attention he accepted with his usual calm certainty, while Jacinta had gone to Slick, and they seemed a natural couple with their Mediterranean good looks. The same could not be said for Ainikki and the Egg, she tall and blonde and elegant, he shorter by a head and looking like nothing so much as a lecherous goblin as he showed off his remarkable tongue.

As they made themselves comfortable in the room above the Nag's Head the same couples stayed together, Jamila settling herself comfortably on Henry's lap the moment he had sat down. He let his hand stray to the warm softness of her bottom and she responded with a pleased wiggle, which drew a grin from Ginger, who had Michelle in a similar embrace. Henry smiled back, feeling more than a trifle awkward to have the beautiful Egyptian girl cuddling up to him when he was engaged to Ginger's sister, and deciding not to mention Poppy for the time being.

'Here's to Poppy's Pin-ups,' he said, raising his glass, 'and to Percival Pettigrew, of course. After all, he's paying.'

The others returned the toast and they relaxed, enjoying their beer and laughing with the girls. A young and obviously very junior barman had been sent up to keep an eye on them and seemed fascinated to see five such varied girls, but otherwise they were entirely on their own. Ginger and Michelle were soon kissing, while Zokie, oblivious to British morals, had began to tease Gorski's cock through his trousers.

'She's foreign,' Henry explained to the now pink-faced barman.

Zokie smiled and said something to Gorski in her thick pidgin French. He shrugged and indicated the barman, then applied a firm pat to her bottom. She got up, grinning, and walked slowly across to the bar, her hips swinging beneath the somewhat tawdry dress Pettigrew had provided as day clothes. The barman watched, astonished and not a little alarmed, his eyes flickering between Zokie's chest and Gorski, who sat with his massive arms folded across his chest, grinning.

'Take what's on offer, that's my advice,' Henry suggested.

The boy returned a nervous nod as Zokie reached out to take a firm grip on his tie. He was wide-eyed as she pulled him out from the behind the bar, and stood as he was, apparently unable to react as she dropped to her knees and unfastened his fly to extract a long, pale cock. She spent a moment stroking his shaft and rolling his foreskin back and forth before popping him into her mouth, sucking with her thick, deep red lips. His mouth had fallen open and he was staring down at her as she sucked his penis, his hands still hanging limp at his sides, even when she unfastened the front of her dress to show off her full, black breasts.

Henry watched in amusement, enjoying the view and also the barman's mixture of bliss and discomfort. Jamila was giggling and her fingers were fiddling with Henry's fly, but when he threw a guilty glance towards Ginger it was to find his friend tugging up Michelle's skirt to get her bare on his lap, as she didn't appear to have any knickers on. He gave in, allowing Jamila to free his cock and masturbate him as they watched Zokie sucking the barman off.

He was erect in her mouth, his cock a long, thin pole of pale flesh between her dark lips, his balls bulging out beneath as she squeezed and stroked at them. To judge from his excitement it wasn't going to take long at all, as he was moaning and pushing into her mouth as she sucked him. Sure enough, he gave a little cry and a jerk, Zokie gulped as she swallowed what he'd done in her mouth and it was over, at least for him. She went straight to Gorski, crawling across the floor to first nuzzle her face into his lap and then pull out his cock, straight into her mouth.

Jamila had also gone down, to suck on Henry's penis and lick at his balls, her eyes bright with pleasure and happiness as she worked. Ginger had gone down on Michelle rather than the other way around, with her skirt bunched up to show off her cunt with the single V of her lance-corporal's stripe shaved into her hair as he kissed her boots. Slick was more conventional, holding Jacinta by the hair to work her head up and down on his already stiff penis.

The barman watched in awe as the three men were sucked off, also casting the occasional slightly worried glance to where Ginger was kneeling for Michelle, and to the Egg, who was licking Ainikki's breasts as she pulled at his big, crooked cock. The barman's own cock was still out, dangling limp from his fly, the skin still wet from Zokie's mouth. Henry raised his glass in friendly salute and took another swallow of beer, then twisted his hand into Jamila's luxurious black hair and began to masturbate into her mouth. He already needed to come, and didn't intend to hold back, knowing he'd be ready again soon enough, while Jamila had always seemed to take more pleasure in satisfying him than in her own needs.

Not that she was content merely to suck, with her skirts up and one hand between her thighs, but as she pulled off his cock he realised it was to get herself ready as much as for pleasure. He let go of her hair, allowing her to sit herself back in his lap, only now directly on his cock, spearing herself on his erection with the cheeks of her bottom pressed to his front. She began to bounce in his lap and he took hold of her, spreading her cheeks to show off the tight brown star of her anus and the junction of cock and cunt. An instant later he gave in to his pleasure, coming deep up her hole without thought for the consequences.

The Egg had also come, all over Ainikki's hand as he licked at her tits, while Slick was plainly on the edge as he fed his erection in and out of Jacinta's mouth. Ginger was little better, masturbating furiously as he licked at Michelle's cunt, while to judge by the expression on her face she wasn't far from orgasm herself. Only Gorski remained cool, sipping beer as Zokie worked on his erection with one hand while she licked his balls and played her breasts, only for his cock to suddenly erupt, the spunk spurting high to splash in her face and hair, to her open delight.

Jamila had stayed on Henry's lap, his cock still inside her, wriggling her bottom to pleasure herself, with one round, golden brown breast in each hand. He let her get on with it, already growing keen for more as he took a swallow of beer to refresh himself. Next to him, Ginger had come on Michelle's boots and was busy bringing her to orgasm with his tongue and fingers, while Slick had done it in Jacinta's mouth and was holding her head down to make her swallow. Henry waited politely until both Slick and Michelle had finished before giving Jamila a slap on the bottom to make her dismount and speaking up.

'Later, yes, darling? That's the way to do it, eh, boys? One each and still some to spare for the help.'

'Or three for you, Skipper,' the Egg put in.

'Yes, quite,' Henry answered him and gave an

uncomfortable glance to where Ginger was tidying himself up, 'and er … speaking of which, Ginger, I …'

'Don't worry,' Ginger cut him off. 'After what we've been through together, that sort of thing doesn't seem so important any more. And besides, you know how it is with the girls, between Poppy and Sally, and Poppy and Michelle.'

'Very true,' Henry admitted, reflecting that Poppy had been through almost as many women as he had over the previous few weeks, or quite possibly more, 'but it's jolly white of you anyway.'

'And you're being decent about not mentioning Michelle's previous profession,' Ginger pointed out. 'The Pater and the Mater would make a frightful fuss.'

'Yes,' Henry agreed, 'but speaking of Poppy …'

'Where is Pinks anyway?' the Egg interrupted. 'I thought she'd be at the Palace?'

'Oh no,' Ginger told him. 'She's gone to visit Sally.'

'Visit Sally?' Henry echoed. 'Hell!'

Henry slowed the car as he came out from the woods and on to the flank of Ivinghoe Beacon, only then wondering why he had driven so fast. It was inevitable that Poppy had already reached the Greens' house, and equally inevitable that he had been among the first topics of conversation between the two girls. The only uncertainty was whether anybody else would be there, such as Mr and Mrs Green or even Sir Pomeroy and Lady Pankhurst. What seemed absolutely certain was their reaction to the news, and as he climbed from the car he gave a rueful shake of his head.

Ever since leaving Hackney he had been rehearsing possible conversational gambits for when he joined the two presumably furious and tearful girls, but nothing he could think of really did justice to the situation. They, on the other hand, were sure to have plenty to say, much of it relating to his personal morals, but there at least he felt on secure ground. To his certain knowledge no Truscott for many generations had had any personal morals at all, at least when it came to sex, and he was no exception.

As he stood by the car he made a few careful adjustments to the fall of his uniform, set his jaw and started for the house. The downs were bathed in sunshine and silent but for birdsong, the occasional bleat of a sheep and faint noises from the distance chalk quarry, but as he drew closer to the Greens' house he began to pick out another sound, as distinctive as it was familiar, feminine squeals punctuated by fleshy smacks. It was the sound of a girl being spanked.

He slowed his pace, listening carefully for voices. As Sally had no sisters it was almost certainly her bottom which was being attended to, possibly by Poppy, possibly by her mother or father. Whatever the case, he felt it would be wise to find out exactly why she was being punished before interrupting the proceedings, and so he approached with great caution, ignoring the front door in favour of the gate to the little walled garden where Sally had wet herself for him, and peering in at the drawing room window through a gap between the curtains and the frame. It provided an excellent view.

Poppy was seated in the exact centre of the sofa, perched on the edge in order to make a lap for Sally, who lay in classic spanking position, face down, her feet and hands braced on the carpet, her bottom raised and spread to show off two pink little cheeks, with the lips of her cunt peeping out from between her thighs and her anus on plain show save for what appeared to be an ornate china decanter stopper had been stuck up the hole. She was in the nude, her clothes scattered on the floor near her head, while Poppy was fully dressed in smart tweeds. Evidently Sally had agreed to accept a spanking and stripped in preparation, but the sullen expression on her face suggested that she was far from happy about it, as did their conversation, which Henry could now hear.

'You're a silly goose!' Poppy was saying. 'What are you?'

Sally remained obstinately silent, her lips set in a sulky pout, only to spring wide as another smack was applied to her bottom.

'What are you?' Poppy repeated, her hand poised above Sally's bottom. 'You are a silly goose, that's what you are, not to mention a wanton little tart who should learn to do as she's told. I'm the one who is going to marry Henry. You are the one who is going to come to live nearby so that we can be together. Didn't we agree from the start?'

'I don't see why it shouldn't be the other way around,' Sally said, her voice both sulky and defiant.

'It should not be the other way around,' Poppy responded as she began to spank once more, 'because ... because my way makes more sense, and ... and you are the one with your bare bottom in the air and a bung up the hole!'

'You can be a real beast sometimes, Poppy!' Sally managed, although she was making no effort to escape the firm swats being applied to her naked bottom cheeks.

'And you,' said Poppy, 'can be a silly little trollop. It's going to be much more difficult to arrange now, after you've broken the engagement. People will talk, and ...'

'I'm not sure that will be strictly necessary,' Henry remarked as he stepped in through the open French windows.

Poppy jumped back in shock, tumbling Sally from her lap to land with a yelp as her already well smacked bottom struck the floor.

'Henry!' both girls chorused.

'Yes, Henry,' he replied, 'your fiancé. No, not a word from either of you. Am I to understand, from what just been said, that you two little inverts had decided that one of you, evidently you, Poppy, would marry me and the other move close by so that you could carry on your clandestine love affair without creating a scandal?'

Poppy had hung her head and was fiddling with her fingers, which was answer enough, but Sally spoke up.

'Yes, but please don't be cross, Henry. We ...'

'I'm not cross,' he interrupted. 'Not in the least, as long as your feelings for me are genuine?'

'They are,' Sally assured him, but Poppy remained silent.

'Poppy?' Henry insisted.

'In ... in a manner of speaking,' Poppy answered, her voice little more than a whisper.

'In a manner of speaking?' Henry queried. 'Come on, Miss Pinks, out with it, unless you fancy another dose of what you got the other night?'

'You're such a beast,' Poppy answered him, 'but, yes, I suppose so. Anyway, I like it when you punish me … I need it. I wasn't lying the other night, I just didn't tell you the whole truth, because I'm in love with Sally, and with you, in a manner of speaking. I need you to … to give me my punishments.'

'I'm not even going to try and understand,' Henry responded, 'but I don't see why you had to be so secretive about it all? You know I like you both.'

'I … I wanted you to myself,' Poppy admitted, 'as the man to punish me, and the father of my children.'

'And Sally too?' Henry queried. 'That's a bit greedy, isn't it?'

Poppy was still studying her fingernails and merely shrugged.

'Very greedy,' Sally agreed, with something close to spite in her voice, 'and we know what happens to greedy girls, don't we?'

'Not in front of you it doesn't,' Poppy replied.

'Says who?' Sally demanded. 'Go on, Henry, spank her, then make her go in the corner with her bottom showing and I'll pleasure you.'

'That's an appealing suggestion,' Henry admitted, 'but hang on a moment. Look, I can't marry you both, and it wouldn't be fair to marry one of you. So why don't you both come down and live with me at Stukely Hall? This isn't the Victorian age, you know.'

'My parents seem to think it is,' Sally told him, with Poppy nodding agreement.

'You're old enough to make your own choices,' Henry pointed out, 'and you'll find I can support us in moderate comfort. I'll tell your parents too, face to face.'

'We'd be living in sin,' Poppy pointed out.

'Living in sin?' Henry responded. 'What do you think you've been doing these last few months? The church doesn't approve of inverts, you know, girls or boys, and do you know what? I don't give a damn. I don't believe there even is a God anyway, not after what I've seen, but if there is he seems to have gone on an extended holiday, and he clearly doesn't give a tinker's cuss for mankind. As for the church, damn the lot of them. Over the last few years I've been bombed and shot at by the Krauts, harassed by snowdrops and brass hats, frozen stiff and burnt to a crisp, not to mention being threatened with castration by a human gorilla, so I'm damned if I'm going to toe the line to please a bunch of mealy-mouthed bible thumpers. There's only one thing worth having in this life, and that's pleasure ... happiness if you like, so come on, what do you say?'

Sally nodded, then Poppy. Henry found himself grinning in triumph, and equal to a dozen aggrieved parents, also ready for sex.

'That's that settled then,' he said, 'and now, Sally, what exactly is it that happens to greedy girls? You imply that it's rather more than a straightforward spanking?'

'Don't you know the rhyme?' Sally answered and began to recite. 'Greedy little Poppy, her face full of cake; off come her knickers for her own silly sake; pop them up her bum for her and spank her rosy red; feed her supper to the dog and send her up to bed.'

'It's not Poppy. It's Lucy,' Poppy responded, her face crimson with blushes. 'Greedy little Lucy. That's the name of the poem, and it's not "pop them up her bum for her" either, you dirty little tart, it's "pop them in her mouth for her and spank her rosy red".'

'That's what you did to me,' Sally retorted, 'and I hadn't even been greedy!'

'Oh you had ...,' Poppy began, but Henry cut her off.

'I've never heard either version,' he admitted, 'but I'm intrigued. How do you manage to get a girl's knickers up her bottom, for instance?'

'With butter, and lots of it, if Poppy's doing it,' Sally answered, 'but that's not how it's supposed to be done. First you have to take your knickers off in front of everybody, and then they go in your mouth. It's awful, because they're dry, and you can't say anything during your spanking, just make silly noises, and everybody laughs at you. Then you're sent to bed without any supper.'

'Thank you,' Henry answered her, 'and yes, I think a certain young lady ought to be given a greedy punishment. Poppy?'

'Not in front of Sally,' Poppy answered.

'Oh no, not in front of Sally,' Henry told her. 'By Sally.'

'Oh no,' Poppy answered. 'She's not allowed to spank me. Only you're allowed to spank me, Henry. If you want to punish me, take me upstairs ...'

'Uh, uh,' Henry cut her off, 'since when did any girl get to choose how she's punished? Come on, stand up and take off your knickers, now!'

Poppy flinched, then looked away, her face beetroot red and sullen.

'Stand up and take off your knickers,' Henry repeated.

Poppy's lower lip had begun to stick out in a resentful moue, but she got up, very slowly, to stand with her hands in lap, pouting badly as her eyes flickered between Henry and Sally, who was now sitting cross-legged on the carpet. Henry sat down in one of the armchairs, his hands folded in his lap.

'Your knickers, Poppy,' he ordered.

She threw him a dirty look, but reached up under her skirt to lever her knickers down and off. They were pale blue and lightweight cotton with a lace trim.

'Very pretty,' Henry remarked. 'In your mouth they go ... no, first, let's hear that little poem again.'

Poppy hesitated, her held knickers dangling between finger and thumb, her eyes shooting daggers at him, and when she did finally start to speak it was in a barely audible mumble.

'Greedy little Lucy ...'

'Poppy,' Sally corrected her. 'It's about you today.'

'I agree,' Henry put in. 'Come on, do it, then in go your knickers, and if you don't start showing a little more spirit I'll send Sally for the butter.'

Poppy grimaced, drew in her breath, then began to recite.

'Greedy little Poppy, her face full of cake; off come her knickers for her own silly sake; pop them in mouth for her and spank her rosy red; feed her supper to the dog and send her up to bed. All right, satisfied?'

'Barely,' Henry responded, 'but it will have to do. Right, Sally, I think it might be more dignified if you were wearing at least your own knickers, so put them on, then pop Poppy's in her mouth.'

'I'll do it,' Poppy said quickly.

'Uh, uh,' Henry chided. 'We're going to do this properly. Sally?'

'May I take the bung out of my bottom hole first, please?' Sally asked.

'Yes, of course,' Henry agreed. 'I quite forgot about that. Why had she plugged you anyway?'

'Just to humiliate me. She loves sticking things up my bottom.'

'Fair enough, so do I. Out it comes then, and seeing as she's so keen on humiliation, you can pop it up her bottom in a minute.'

'No!' Poppy protested. 'That's not fair!'

'Why not?' Henry asked. 'You stuck it up her bottom, so she can stick it up yours.'

'This is for being greedy,' Poppy retorted. 'I spanked her for being such a little idiot.'

'So that's the punishment for being a stupid girl, is it?' Henry laughed. 'A spanking with her bottom hole plugged? Anyway, it's not a very sensible thing to call a girl when you're about to go over her knee, is it, so you certainly deserve the treatment. And frankly, I think you should count yourself lucky it's not your knickers going up your bottom and the plug in your mouth.'

Sally had got up as Henry spoke, looking thoughtful as she extracted the decanter bung from her anus, then thoroughly smug as she retrieved her discarded knickers and pulled them on, wriggling her distinctly pink bottom into the seat in such a way as to ensure Henry got a good view. Poppy had stayed as she was, the sulky expression on her face stronger than ever, but she passed Sally her knickers and opened her mouth without having to be told.

'Wider,' Sally instructed, as she'd balled Poppy's knickers

in one hand.

Poppy obeyed, and Henry watched with deep satisfaction as the little blue knickers were crammed into their owner's mouth, all the way, so that only a wisp of coloured cotton and lace showed between her lips.

'Skirt up,' Henry ordered.

He was obeyed with only a trace of reluctance, Poppy quickly rucking her close-fitting tweed skirt up around her waist to show off her stockings and the straps of her girdle framing soft pink thighs and the golden puff of her pubic hair with her neatly shaved corporal's stripes. Henry made a gesture with his finger and Poppy turned around, showing off the sweetly turned cheeks of her bottom, still decorated by the six cane marks he had administered, before returning to her original position.

'Quite perfect,' Henry remarked, 'and quite perfectly smackable. Now your breasts.'

Poppy didn't question his command, but shrugged off her jacket and unbuttoned her blouse before lifting her brassiere to bare her firm, high breasts. For a moment she seemed to want to cover them, then her hands had gone to her sides, leaving herself fully exposed. Henry gave a nod of approval.

'You're learning, that's good, and I do love the way your nipples point up and a little apart, ever so sweet. Now then, sit down where she was, Sally, put her over your knee and give her a good spanking.'

Sally responded eagerly, seating herself in the middle of the sofa with her knees extended to make a lap, exactly as Poppy had sat to administer the earlier spanking. Poppy's response was far less eager, in fact extremely hesitant, as if she were about to surrender something important which she knew she'd never be able to retrieve.

'Why so much fuss?' Henry asked. 'It's not as if you haven't been spanked before, many a time, I suspect.'

Poppy responded with a hurt look, not even bothering to try and speak through her mouthful of knickers. Henry took a guess as to her feelings.

'But not by Sally?' he asked. 'And presumably not by any

of your other girlfriends? No, when it comes to girls you're always the one in charge, aren't you? Well, it's about time we put a stop to that, don't you think? No? Well I say it is. Come on, over Sally's knee you go, and get that pretty bottom well up.'

The tears were beginning to well up in Poppy's eyes, but she obeyed, laying herself slowly across Sally's knees and lifting her bottom to show off the lips of her cunt and the base of the bung in her taut pink anus. Henry sat back, to open his fly and free his cock and balls to the air as the spanking began, gentle pats that barely made Poppy's bottom quiver. Sally saw what he'd done and giggled, then began to spank ever so slightly harder.

'She's not made of china, you know,' Henry remarked as he began to masturbate, 'she won't break. Or would you prefer something to spank her with, a kitchen spoon, perhaps, or a hairbrush?'

'Yes, please,' Sally answered, ignoring Poppy's instant but muffled protest. 'Look in the cupboard under the stairs and you'll find what Miss Pinks here calls my naughty paddle. It's got my name on it.'

Henry went to the cupboard, to find a row of three slender wooden paddles hanging on pegs behind the door. To his amusement one was marked "Thomas", Ginger's real name, and another "Arabella", which meant it was for Sally's mother. The third had the word "Sarah" picked out in pokerwork, also a double row of little bottoms done in ink, much like the rows of bombs besides the picture of Jazzy Jess on his Lancaster. Each seemed to denote a spanking given. He tested it on his hand, and was grinning as he returned to the drawing room, where Poppy's bottom cheeks had begun to flush pink as the spanking continued.

'She was spanking you before Egypt then?' Henry asked as he handed Sally the paddle.

'Oh yes,' Sally told him, 'almost from the day I joined up. She's a beast, but I do love her. Oh, and I've always wanted to get her back!'

As she spoke she had applied the paddle to Poppy's bottom.

Her earlier smacks had been getting little reaction, but the paddle plainly stung, making Poppy buck and wriggle, a delightful sight that sent the blood pumping to Henry's cock.

'Go on then,' he urged, 'spank her well, and then you can add another little bottom to the score on your paddle.'

'Oh no, those are just for me,' Sally answered. 'We'll make a new paddle for Poppy, won't we? And we'll hang it in the kitchen, where everyone can see, with her name on it, just like mine, and a little round bottom for every time she's spanked.'

Sally was laughing as she spoke, and applying the paddle to Poppy's bouncing bottom cheeks with ever greater force. Henry watched in fascination and delight as Poppy's bottom grew quickly redder, his cock erect in his hand. She was now crying openly, and making muffled noises through her mouthful of underwear, with her legs kicking and her thighs open to show off her cunt. Her hole was open, and Henry began to tug harder on his cock as he remembered how he'd taken her virginity.

'Hold her,' he told Sally. 'I'm going to fuck her.'

As he got up Sally had curled a leg into place to spread Poppy's thighs and taken a firm grip with her hands, but it wasn't necessary. Poppy made no effort to resist at all, just the opposite, pushing up her bottom to meet Henry's cock as he slid it deep into her hole. She was already wet and he went in easily and all the way, allowing him to fuck her with long, slow strokes while he stayed upright, leaving her bottom exposed to the paddle. Sally began to spank once more, laughing as she watched Henry's cock slide in and out of her friend's sopping cunt.

'Now in your mouth,' Henry instructed, pulling free to let his erection spring up, glistening with Poppy's juices.

Sally took him in her mouth, sucking eagerly until he pulled back, not wanting to risk coming before he'd taken his full pleasure with both girls.

'We really ought to send her up to bed without any supper,' he told Sally, 'but it's not even teatime, and I don't think she's had a proper spanking yet either.'

'No, she hasn't,' Sally agreed, and brought down the paddle

across Poppy's bottom with a meaty smack, 'not nearly enough. Would you pass the decanter bung, please?'

Poppy gave another muffled squeak, but they ignored her. Henry retrieved the bung and gave it to Sally, then spread Poppy's bottom cheeks to show off her anus. Sally leant forward and spat on the little pink hole, making it twitch, then abruptly leant forward to bury her face between Poppy's hot bottom cheeks, licking at her anus. Henry nearly came just to see one girl lick another's bottom, but managed to control himself, gently nursing his erection as Sally readied Poppy's anus and pushed the plug up.

'I think I'm going to have to put my cock up there,' he said. 'Where's the butter?'

'Not butter!' Sally protested. 'It's on the ration. Use her juice, like you did with me, or there might be an egg if you go out to the chicken coop, if you want to stick her knickers up her bottom like she did to me.'

Poppy gave a sudden jerked and a muffled complaint that turned to a squeak as the paddle smacked down once more, but was once again ignored.

'Egg?' Henry queried.

'It works very well,' Sally assured him, 'but get a tea towel so we don't make a mess.'

'We can only try,' Henry answered. 'Just carry on with her spanking.'

He made for the kitchen, nursing his erection as he opened the back door and peered carefully outside. The chicken coop was visible, at the far end of the garden beneath the trees but in view of the road, and he was forced to put his cock away in order to reach it safely. There were several eggs, which he took indoors, placing the majority in the larder and two in a small bowl before picking up a tea towel. Back in the drawing room Sally was still at work, happily spanking away at Poppy's now very red bottom.

'Eggs and a tea towel,' Henry announced 'Pull out her knickers and we'll soon have them up her behind.'

'You utter beasts!' Poppy spat the instant her knickers had been pulled from her mouth. 'Both of you!'

'Shut up and suck on this while Sally deals with your bottom,' Henry told her, offering his now half-stiff penis to her mouth. 'What a fuss over a little spanking, eh Sally?'

'A little spanking? I ...' Poppy began and ended with a gulp as Henry fed her his cock.

She began to suck, reluctantly at first but with greater enthusiasm as Henry's cock started to grow back towards full erection. Sally had set to work, slipping the tea towel under Poppy's belly and extracting the decanter bung, which she passed to Henry. Poppy had kept her bottom up without having to be told, allowing Sally to break first one egg and then the other between the trim pink cheeks, rubbing the mess of yolk and white well in and up the little hole between. With two fingers in up her bottom, Poppy had begun to moan on her mouthful of cock, and to suck in earnest, forcing Henry to pull back before he came.

'I'm pretty close,' he told Sally. 'Let's get her finished. Uh, uh, you're not quite finished sucking things yet, Miss Pinks.'

He had offered the decanter bung to her mouth as she spoke.

'Pig!' she said, but her mouth came open to take the bung in and she immediately began to suck on it, for all that her face was screwed up in disgust.

'I think I'm just beginning to understand the way she works,' he told Sally as he came round behind Poppy. 'Let me do that.'

Sally had been about to poke the edge of Poppy's soggy knickers in up the slippery hole of her anus, but Henry put them on his cock instead. Straddling Poppy's thighs, he put his erection to her anus, pushing in the first little bit of knicker material, withdrawing to collect more, and again. Poppy began to sob and pant as her knickers were stuffed slowly up her bottom on Henry's cock, while Sally was giggling to watch it being done and applying the occasional swat with the paddle when she could get at a cheek.

Henry was fighting not to come with every push of his erection into Poppy's slimy, gaping bottom hole, and very glad he'd had Jamila before. Yet there was only so much he could take, and as he pushed the last scrap of cotton in to leave

Poppy's anus so wide that a little piece of blue showed in the hole his will snapped. Spunk erupted from his cock, all over her bottom, then into the wet, open hole of her anus as he finished himself off, jerking hard on his shaft and at the last moment shoving it up her bottom to squash against her knickers.

'Damn!' he swore. 'I didn't mean to do that, but it was good. Anyway, I think we can fairly say she's been punished, eh Sally? Over to you two then.'

The girls immediately came together, kissing passionately the instant Poppy had spat out the decanter bung and rolling off the sofa to land on the rug. Henry watched, thoroughly pleased with himself as they broke their kiss to go head to tail, each licking at each other's cunt with desperate urgency. Poppy was on top, her smacked bottom spread in Sally's face, her cunt glistening wet with her own juices and with egg, while the blue of her knickers still showed in her open bottom hole.

Sally came first, crying out in ecstasy as her slender thighs locked tight around Poppy's head, but she had gone back to licking before she was even done, her face buried in her lover's cunt. Poppy sat up, wriggling her bottom into Sally face. A moment more and her mouth was wide in ecstasy and her muscles had started to contract, squeezing her little blue panties slowly from her bottom hole, to flop into Sally's face before both girls collapsed giggling onto the rug.

'I think I could live with this arrangement,' Henry remarked to nobody in particular. 'Yes, it's very acceptable. In fact, it's perfect.'

Epilogue

HENRY TRUSCOTT SAT AT ease in the back garden of Stukely Hall, a private space sheltered from the wind and inquisitive eyes by tall, dense hedges of clipped beech. His trousers and underpants were around his ankles, his legs were braced well apart, allowing both Poppy and Sally space to kneel as they licked and kissed at his cock and balls. Both girls were nude, and both sported a pair of pink-flushed cheeks behind her, the result of spankings dished out for no better reason than that it amused Henry to give them regular punishments.

Beside Henry's chair stood Jamila, wearing nothing but a truncated maid's uniform that left her bare brown bottom peeping out from beneath the hem and her naked breasts supported in a froth of lace. She too had her bottom smacked on a regular basis, and not always by Henry, but she was now watching the two English girls suck cock with a faint and slightly smug smile on her pretty face. In her hands she held a silver tray, on which stood a bottle of well-chilled white wine and glasses, ready for when the girls were done.

Two months had passed since the day he became engaged to both girls, during which he had faced down scandal and accusation from almost every quarter. At first he had attempted to put his case, but it had plainly been a hopeless task and before long he'd been forced to retire to the seclusion of rural Devon, where he had finally achieved something approximating to peace, with the added bonus that his five aunts were no longer talking to him. His father had accepted the news with an amused grunt, precisely as Henry had anticipated, while his cousin had been every bit as accommodating as he'd hoped.

202

Smiling happily, he reached out to fondle Jamila's bottom, which made her giggle and stick it out to invite his fingers between his cheeks. With his free hand he began to stroke Poppy's hair, then Sally's, admiring their mingled tresses, blonde and copper, as much as their faces as they worked earnestly on his genitals. Poppy was licking at the underside of his erection while Sally sucked his balls, but suddenly pulled back to look up at him.

'Oh, I forgot to say. General McLellan telephoned ...'

'I'm sure he did,' Henry responded, pulling her head down onto his cock to make her take it deep into her mouth, 'but you can tell me what he had to say later, but yes, if he's coming round I might well send one of you upstairs to suck him off before bed. It seems only polite. For now, I think I'm about ready to come.'

He had pushed his cock well into Poppy's gullet and she responded with a gulping noise, possibly trying to speak, or to stop herself from being sick. Henry ignored her, maintaining a firm grip in her hair as he began to fuck in her throat. She started to gag, while Sally now had both of his balls in his mouth and was tickling his anus with one long fingernail, a combination of sensations he knew full well he could only endure for a few seconds before he came.

'That's the way,' he sighed. 'Oh you little angels ... and little tarts too! Now swallow it like a good girl. Yes ...'

His words broke to a sigh as he came in Poppy's mouth, holding her deep until he was finished. She did her best, gulping down the spunk as she gagged on his cock, although when he finally let go she had a froth of sticky white bubbles hanging from below her nose. Henry passed her his handkerchief to wipe up, then relaxed contentedly into his chair as Jamila began to serve the wine.

'You're getting very good at that, Pinks,' he remarked to Poppy as she blew the spunk from her nose. 'A little more practice and you'll be able to do it without making any mess at all. Now what were you going to say about Mac?'

'What I was going to say,' Poppy replied, 'before you forced your dirty big thingy down my throat, was that he rang to say that another American had been asking for you, an Air Force Colonel.'

'An Air Force Colonel?' Henry queried. 'Damn, it must be that fellow Jackson. I hope Mac didn't tell him where I live.'

'There was another call for you as well,' Sally put in. 'A very rude man who put the receiver down on me when I said you weren't in, without so much as a thank you. He wasn't American though, not a trace of accent.'

'How strange, I ...' Henry began, and then broke off.

Two men had appeared in one of the arches cut into the beech hedge. One was large, with a bristle of greying hair showing around his USAF cap and colonel's insignia on his shoulder tabs. The other was larger still, a true giant, with massive shoulders and beetling brows over which hung a tangle of jet black hair.

'Ah,' said Henry, 'Colonel Jackson, Captain Smith. What an unexpected surprise.'

Both men spoke in unison.

'Truscott!'

Notes

1 – The fez smuggling operation is drawn from real events in 1946 and took place more or less as described. It was one of many such more or less illegal or officially disapproved of scams, although the great majority involved the selling of cigarettes or drink rather than hats. The episode in which Henry buzzes a herd of a thousand camels in a Lancaster is also drawn from history, although not the wholesale smuggling of girls across the width of North Africa.

2 – The Berkha was Cairo's red light district for the first half of the twentieth century. Centred on the Wagh el Birkhet, the area was frequented by British and Commonwealth soldiers during both the first and second World Wars, during which it achieved a reputation not only for rampant prostitution but also for drunkenness and trouble, often between soldiers of rival regiments.

3 – During World War Two an RAF bomber crew would typically fly thirty missions before being dispersed to training and other less dangerous tasks. The chances of returning from all thirty missions were between twenty and forty per cent, depending on circumstances, so about one in three.

4 – An alternative to the Berkha for those seeking less than respectable entertainment during World War Two were the Nile house-boats. Moored along the banks of the river, these provided drink, floorshows, girls and more, and seem to have been only marginally less insalubrious than the land-bound brothels.

5 – The Campbell Bunk was the popular name for Campbell Road in Islington, near Finsbury Park Station, a notorious slum with a reputation as the most lawless street in London between the wars. So bad was its reputation that many employers would refuse to take on residents for any form of work whatsoever, while it provided a known haven for criminals of every sort, hence the expression "done a bunk", meaning to make a run for it and take refuge in Campbell Road. The street was demolished in 1956, and all that remains is a short dead-end, now named Whadcoat Street.

6 – *La Pucelle* (The Flea) was a classic striptease of the French music hall era and involved a girl stripping in order to catch a flea which had managed to get under her clothes. Many, if not most, acts featured a reason for the *artiste* to undress, such as getting ready for bed or the bath, but *La Pucelle* gave an added opportunity for comedy and a touch of embarrassment.

7 – Plasterdown Camp was one of many military camps set up in preparation for D-Day. In 1945 it housed several thousand troops and included an airfield and a hospital, but nothing now remains save a few broken pieces of concrete under the turf, the outlines of huts and a gap in the trees of a nearby wood, still just discernible, where an aircraft misjudged its approach to the runway.

8 – *The Girls of St Cyprian's* by Angela Brazil was published in 1914. It was one of the most popular girls' school stories of the early twentieth century and would have been almost compulsory reading for girls. Although mild and wholesome by today's standards, or even those of St. Trinian's, Angela Brazil's school stories were considered sufficiently subversive to earn them bans in many British girls' schools.

9 – *Men Only* magazine was founded in 1935 and is still running, showing the evolution of the British glamour magazine across nearly three-quarters of a century.

10 – There was a great deal of variation in RAF pay during the Second World War, according to both rank, specific skills and time spent in the air, but a sergeant acting as radio operator in a Lancaster would have been earning between £3 and £4 per week.

Also by Aishling Morgan

Waking up from death, Melody J finds her personality has been copied and recreated as a computer game character to satisfy teenage boys. Just like Tomb Raider Lara Croft, Melody J finds herself under the game player's control, but that's where the similarities end as she is caught up in games where she must express her sexuality in ways she never could when she was alive.

Drawing on imagery from Japanese hentai adult cartoons, Slave To The Machine is fantasy for grown-ups who still like to play games.

ISBN 9781906373689 £7.99

Aishling Morgan's how-to book is about pleasure; joyful, liberated, sexual pleasure. User-friendly – it's designed for the curious amateur. It's about pleasures that go beyond what most people are used to, and beyond what is generally accepted as mainstream, not just sex, but naughty sex, the kind of sex that involves more leather than lace, more kink than kissing, that involves bound wrists and smacked bottoms and perhaps even the occasional jugful of custard!

Topics covered include -
Domination/Submission
Fetishism and Erotic Display
Bondage
Spanking
Role Play including puppy and pony games
Messy Fun

ISBN 9781906373863 £9.99

Maid to Order
Penny Birch

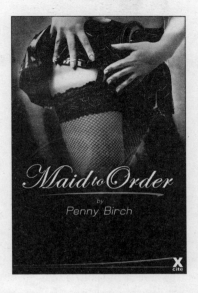

Penny's niece, Jemima, is in disgrace and has been sent away to work in a hotel for the summer by her scheming step-mother – a woman who delights in dishing out bare-bottom spankings. This is no coincidence. Not only is the hotel owner the notorious Morris Rathwell, organiser of the kinkiest parties in the country, but Jemima also met the hotel manager, Mr Hegedus, at one of Rathwell's debauched parties. Then there are the hotel guests, her fellow staff and the truly appalling Mrs Hegedus to contend with. So that by the time Jemima is dressed up in her severely abbreviated maid's uniform, she knows she's already in serious trouble.

Maids, secret worlds behind closed doors, and good old-fashioned punishment for bad girls – Penny Birch hits the spot again with the preoccupations her readers love.

ISBN 9781907016356   £7.99

Saddled Up
Penny Birch

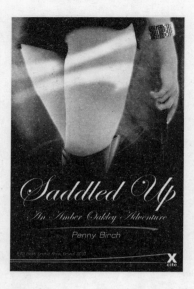

Amber Oakley is back! Determined as ever to avoid getting her bottom smacked but her own deep needs and the awkward circumstances she finds herself in trying to solve her financial difficulties mean otherwise.

Offering riding tuition to girls from wealthy families seems like a good idea, but Portia and Ophelia Crowthorne-Jones prove to have a few ideas of their own, and are soon indulging both their lesbian desires and their cruel sense of humour at Amber's expense. Will she end up as their plaything, or can she turn the tables and teach the little brats the lesson they so clearly deserve?

ISBN 9781907761843 £7.99

The Education of Victoria
Angela Meadows

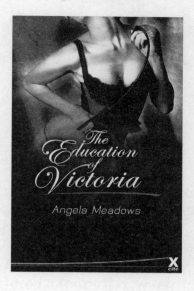

A saucy romp set in a Victorian finishing school for young ladies...

Sweet English rose Victoria is packed off to the Venus School for Young Ladies to learn how to be a dutiful wife. But she discovers that she has a lot to learn in the arts of pleasure when she encounters the strictness of Principal Madame Thackeray and her assistant, the domineering Madame Hulot.
Returning home to England, she turns her newfound education to good use to save the family estate.

ISBN 9781906373696, £7.99